JEFFREY ROUND

SHADOW PUPPET

A DAN SHARP MYSTERY

DUND

TORON

Cover image: © istock.com/CribbVisuals
Printer: Webcom

Library and Archives Canada Cataloguing in Publication

Round, Jeffrey, author
    Shadow puppet / Jeffrey Round.

(A Dan Sharp mystery)
Issued in print and electronic formats.
ISBN 978-1-4597-4060-0 (softcover).--ISBN 978-1-4597-4061-7
(PDF).--ISBN 978-1-4597-4062-4 (EPUB)

    I. Title. II. Series: Round, Jeffrey. Dan Sharp mystery

PS8585.O84929S53 2019   C813'.54   C2018-903160-3
    C2018-903161-1

1 2 3 4 5   23 22 21 20 19

 Conseil des Arts du Canada Canada Council for the Arts   Canadä 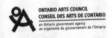 ONTARIO ARTS COUNCIL CONSEIL DES ARTS DE L'ONTARIO an Ontario government agency un organisme du gouvernement de l'Ontario

We acknowledge the support of the Canada Council for the Arts, which last year invested $153 million to bring the arts to Canadians throughout the country, and the Ontario Arts Council for our publishing program. We also acknowledge the financial support of the Government of Ontario, through the Ontario Book Publishing Tax Credit and the Ontario Media Development Corporation, and the Government of Canada.

Nous remercions le Conseil des arts du Canada de son soutien. L'an dernier, le Conseil a investi 153 millions de dollars pour mettre de l'art dans la vie des Canadiennes et des Canadiens de tout le pays.

Care has been taken to trace the ownership of copyright material used in this book. The author and the publisher welcome any information enabling them to rectify any references or credits in subsequent editions.

— *J. Kirk Howard, President*

The publisher is not responsible for websites or their content unless they are owned by the publisher.

Printed and bound in Canada.

VISIT US AT

👥 dundurn.com | 🐦 @dundurnpress |  dundurnpress | 📷 dundurnpress

Dundurn
3 Church Street, Suite 500
Toronto, Ontario, Canada
M5E 1M2

SHADOW PUPPET

DAN SHARP MYSTERIES

In memory of

Dr. Mark Ernsting
(September 9, 1976–December 15, 2015)

Mark Round
(May 18, 1961–July 21, 2017)

A good puppet master disappears into the shadows above while sustaining the illusion of life below.

Dr. Sardonicus

AUTHOR'S NOTE

ALTHOUGH THIS VOLUME IS THE sixth title to appear in the Dan Sharp mystery series, it comes fourth chronologically between *The Jade Butterfly* and *After the Horses*. And while it was inspired — if that is the correct word for it — by a series of disappearances in Toronto's gay community between 2010 and 2017 that seemed obviously the work of a serial killer, at least to many in the community if not to the Toronto police force, my book was in fact finished and submitted for publication before an arrest was made and revelations ensued. Apart from the most obvious facts, any similarities between factual events or people and the fictional events or characters in this book are, as they say, coincidental.

PROLOGUE

2010: The Master

HE FELT LIKE THE WORLD'S greatest puppet master. No matter who they were or where they came from, he could make them sing and dance. All it took was a little reassurance. With a gentle smile, he let them know he understood their suffering. The shame and fear, the condemnation and humiliation. Oh yes, all of that and more.

Best of all, he could make them weep.

That was when he felt most powerful, an avenging angel, as though he could scoop up their tears and wash away their sorrow. It was also when he felt closest to the lost lambs who followed him home and undressed for him, shedding their innocence along with their clothes. Giving up the purity that would take them to paradise. He stripped them of all of that.

†

The man over in the corner had been eyeing him across the bar for the past ten minutes. Light-skinned, a hint of facial hair. Muscular, but not too big. Just the right hesitation in his glance: *Are you interested in me, brother?*

Music pounded as video screens threw shadows across the room. He glanced back, gave a gentle nod: *Yes, I am interested.* Then he turned away, not to let the other get too cocky. The time would come to spark his confidence, to let him think he was in control. But not yet. Not right from the beginning, when his hands had deftly begun to pull the strings, bringing the puppet to life with each twitch and flutter.

The song ended and a new beat edged in. The two headed for the bar at the same moment, random atoms propelled by chance. The bartender, in black leather, looked up at the shaved-headed man.

"Dude?"

"A Molson Dry, please."

He turned to the other. "For you?"

"Same, please."

"Two Molson Dry coming up."

As the bartender moved off, the larger man let his arm brush against the young man's arm. The crowd was packed in so close there was no room to step aside, just the subtle warmth of skin touching skin.

"Habibi." They were facing each other now. "You like this place?"

The younger man nodded shyly. The bartender returned, deftly clipped the caps off the bottles and pushed them forward where they gleamed under the lights.

"I've got it." The larger man passed a bill across the counter and waved away the change.

The new acquaintances picked up their beers and made their way through the crowd to a pair of stools against the far wall.

"Chokron." The younger man lifted his glass and swallowed long and hard.

"You like beer?"

"Yes. I like it."

"That's good. It relaxes you." The shaved-headed man laughed and clasped him around the back of his neck, feeling the smooth skin and warm flesh.

"Tell me, where are you from?"

"I am from Iran," he said. His eyes skittered nervously, knowing what it meant to discuss such things openly.

"A great country."

Talk ensued. The older man had lived in Toronto for almost a decade; the younger had been there less than a year, he said. *Do you get lonely? Yes, I miss my family all the time.* All good men missed their families. They agreed and clinked bottles. Of course, the families did not know they frequented bars and drank alcohol and invited the devil into their beds.

"I am Joe. What's your name?"

"Sam."

"Good to meet you, Sam."

"And you."

"Back home I was a dentist," the shaved-headed man said. But his certificate was useless in Canada. In a year or two, he said, he would go back to school and upgrade his papers. But everyone said that, the dream easier spoken of than accomplished.

They talked of being immigrants, of the ridiculousness of all things Western and the treacherous stranglehold the

West had on world affairs. Their bottles were empty now. The younger man bought another round. He was already on his third, stumbling when he stood to use the bathroom.

"Let me help you."

The older man took him by the arm and led him to the urinals. They stood side by side looking down, the older man's hands lingering, stretching and letting go with a snap before the stream of piss came with an impressive splash.

He looked over. "We are friends, yes? Same-same? You and I?" He rubbed two fingers together in case the other hadn't already got the message.

The younger man nodded, a lamb drawn to the slaughter. "Yes, brother. I like you."

"Come, habibi. We've had enough drink. It is time for us to go and make ourselves better friends together, away from this place."

Their walk took them through quiet streets. Despite the hour, people lingered here and there. Two men together in that neighbourhood would not be noticed.

The moon was full, its light obscured by an oncoming storm. High-rises towered above. A slate of new condos being erected showed how fast the city was growing. Rain began to fall, lightly at first then more heavily. The pavement glistened, the lights of passing cars picking up their silhouettes then sliding softly away.

Beware, they seemed to say.

The younger man stopped to lean against a street lamp, the silvery glare from above outlining his features. The older man put a hand on his shoulder, gently turning him till they faced one another. He leaned in. Their lips met. The younger man shivered and turned away.

"Please, I cannot!"

"It's okay. I know what you want. No one will ever know."

The wind was picking up, the leaves thrashing and turning overhead like startled birds trying to escape the storm that was nearly on them.

"Yes, it is true. No one will ever know."

The younger man nodded, conquering his fears as the pair moved along.

The game was on again.

"Is it far?"

"Not far. Just another block."

As they walked, the younger man spoke more openly about his family, how he'd grown up with goats, a backyard that opened onto the desert, relatives who lived in tents. More than anything, he talked of his father, who did not understand his desire to remain in the land of Satan. But a good father nonetheless, he conceded.

"I will be your father here," the other claimed.

"You? But you are not old enough."

"I am almost old enough. Or maybe just a big brother then. I will show you the sure way among the treacherous paths of the city. Would you like that?"

"Yes, I would."

They all wanted something: fathers, brothers, sons, loyal friends to love them forever. He wanted to be all those things.

A walkway led to a three-storey affair recessed from the

street. The light over the vestibule was burned out, all the windows facing the street darkened except for a dim glow in an upper right-hand frame. They could barely make out the building's name: The Viking.

"Is this it?"

"Yes."

"I've been here before."

"Really?"

"Yes. Just a job I did once. It was nothing."

Fingers manipulated the lock. The door snapped open onto a hallway that reeked of something gone off, like sour milk. The walls were rough, but recently painted. The floor tiled black-and-white harlequin.

A sign identified the superintendent's apartment. A handwritten note had been pinned to the door — AWAY FOR THE WEEKEND — with an emergency number scribbled beneath. No one to see, no one to hear.

On the right, at the end of the hallway, a heavy industrial door was padlocked and secured. The smaller man's footsteps scuffed drunkenly as they made their way to the apartment on the left.

A black filigree key slid easily into the lock. It was the sort of key that had secured thousands of doors like this until the middle of the previous century, but was now more likely to be a curio consigned to a dusty antique shop.

The door opened into a fresh-smelling apartment where they hung their jackets side by side in the hallway. Lights glowed softly as they passed into a living room. Heavy curtains shrouded the space. The furniture was hand-carved, intricately upholstered.

Against the far wall a row of faces leered at the new-comers, an army of puppets hanging limply from metal frames. The tiny audience silently watched the men enter, as though waiting for the cue to spring to life.

"You have friends."

Fingers reached up to caress the wooden figures. Like the lock and key, they, too were old-fashioned, the sort of puppets only a master craftsman could make.

"Very nice. You made these?"

"Yes. I am a puppet maker."

"Beautiful. Back home we had puppet makers, but I never met one here."

"Please. Be at home."

The younger man stumbled as the other pushed the drunken boy onto the couch, removing his shoes and socks for him. The boy giggled at the touch, but did not pull away from the hands caressing him.

The older man sat back on his heels and unbuckled his belt, pulling until it slithered free of the loops. "That bar we were in tonight — it's a leather bar. Do you know what that means?"

Concern lit up the young man's face. He eyed the belt. "No, I do not. What does this mean?"

"It means that men dress up in leather — like this." He gripped his T-shirt by the bottom and pulled it smoothly over his head, revealing a muscular chest and a harness fastened behind his shoulders and under his armpits. The studs gleamed. "Habibi. You are lovely," he said, rubbing the younger man's thighs. "Do you like this?"

"Yes, I like it."

"Have you done this with other men before?"

"Once or twice."

"And did you enjoy it? Even though you know it's wrong for our kind?"

"Yes, yes." The younger man leaned forward and buried his face in the older man's shoulder. "I want …"

"What do you want?" he asked, lifting the boy's shirt over his head. "Tell me. I am going to be a good father to you."

"I want you to do it to me."

"You want us to be together? Same-same?"

The look on the younger man's face was pure intoxication, though fear still danced in his eyes. "Please. Shall we have another drink first?"

The older man ran a hand over his shaved head. "Of course."

They had come so far; it was just a matter of time. Puppet masters were patient.

Drinks were poured and sipped, the glasses set aside. The older man unbuckled the younger man's pants, ignoring his feeble protests as he tossed them on the floor. He slipped a condom from his pocket.

The younger man shook his head. "No. This is for gays." His eyes pleaded with his companion. *Only gay men get AIDS,* they said. *We are not gay. We are real men.*

So be it.

The older man rose up, some force in him coming alive. The boy squirmed beneath his touch, his legs parting with a brief protest as the older man entered him all at once.

"Habibi!"

He thrust forward and placed his fingers around the younger man's neck, gripping and squeezing. There was no resistance. "Do you like this?"

"Yes," the boy cried. "I like it!"

Their actions were quick, the excitement palpable. Then suddenly it was over. After all that effort.

With a groan, the older man lay back and closed his eyes. He reached out for his drink but his arm fell back, knocking the glass onto the carpet. When he opened his eyes the puppets were gazing down in mute wonder.

Without warning, the boy straddled him again.

"Brother, are you ready for paradise?" the puppet master asked, securing the hood over the other's head, deftly tying the knots and pressing against the older man's eyelids.

He glanced up at his puppets. How contented they looked. He carried a chair over to the couch and sat watching as each inhalation pulled the bag tighter and tighter.

ONE

Burial

THE CHURCH WAS PACKED, THE pews full to overflowing. Half an hour before the service it was already clear that not everyone would be accommodated if the crowds kept coming. And come they did, braving the chill and the rain. Extra chairs were hastily set up and new arrivals directed to the basement where loudspeakers broadcast the proceedings one floor above. These were the lucky ones. Others had to be content to stand outside on the sidewalk, armed only with their umbrellas and overcoats, to say goodbye to a much-loved friend.

The minister spoke in soft, confident tones about the cancer researcher they were mourning that day, addressing the gathering at length. Then, his commemoration over, he introduced a large man with a bewildered expression.

The man leaned forward to speak into the microphone. "Thank you all for —"

His words boomed in their ears. He looked up, amazed by the sound of his voice, then stepped back and tried again.

"Thank you all for coming today. My brother would have been honoured to see so many people here. Anyone who knew Randy knew he was a philosophical guy. He often wondered what kind of impact his life would have. I think it's what drove him so hard in his work, to make life better for others. This gathering would have told him he was pretty important to a lot of people, not just his patients and other researchers. As I stand here, it strikes me that I know so few of you. I wish I had been a bigger part of Randy's life in Toronto. Even though I don't know you all, I know he cared for all of you because he talked about his friends constantly. I just didn't realize how many he had." His voice cracked with emotion. "My brother had the biggest heart of anyone I've ever known. He was an extraordinarily gifted man, both in life and in his work. It's with a very heavy heart of my own that I take leave of him here today."

A sister came forward next and addressed the crowd. She was followed by the dead man's husband, Nathan, who spoke about their relationship of ten years.

"If there is one thing I could wish for you right now, Randy, it is not that we will find the person or persons responsible for this, for we will. But rather, I wish that you are at peace despite the terrible fate you have endured."

The minister returned, inviting people to queue on either side of the transept and share their thoughts. Friends, colleagues, and patients stepped up, some openly expressing their grief, others masking it with humour and reminiscences. All told the same story: they felt a considerable loss for the man they were honouring that day.

After the last person had spoken, the minister nodded to the choir. Voices rose gently, hovering in the air. The mourners waited until the final notes faded, as though they, too were waiting for a cue. Then slowly they rose and began to exit.

In the front row, private investigator Dan Sharp sat with his best friend Donny, Donny's partner Prabin, and their longtime friend Domingo. Prabin slumped forward, face hidden in his hands. His shoulders shook.

"I should have been there for him."

Donny reached over to his boyfriend's arm. "You would have helped him if you'd been there."

The doors of the church opened onto a grey afternoon. A crowd of reporters waited at the foot of the stairs as the crowd spilled into the street. Randy's husband glanced worriedly at the TV cameras, then stepped forward. No, the police had no further leads, he told them. They were looking on it as a random attack, not as one motivated by hatred or homophobia. On the face of things, it seemed to have been a simple robbery gone wrong. As hard as it was to believe, his partner's death was likely the regrettable consequence of a botched holdup.

Dan watched from a distance then turned to Prabin. "Where did they find him?"

"Behind a rooming house on George Street. The police think he was killed nearby and dragged there to hide his body."

"I know the area. It gets pretty seedy at night."

"It's outside the ghetto, but it doesn't look as though he was attacked because he was gay."

"I heard the attack was savage. It was angry."

"Very savage. He was stabbed repeatedly."

Dan took this in. "It could have been personal then. Especially with a knife. People think guns are dangerous, but I'd rather take my chances with a shooter whose hands might shake. Knives are far deadlier."

Domingo nudged Dan. "I don't think Prabin needs to hear that just now."

"Sorry, just speculating," he said, turning to face her. "What do you make of it?"

"I think it will turn out to be two people," she said softly. "Drugs will fit in the scenario somewhere."

Prabin shook his head. "Randy never did drugs."

"Then possibly they were robbing him for money for a drug habit," Dan said. "Drugs are expensive."

Prabin glanced at the journalists, who had surrounded Randy's brother. His expression hardened. "You'd think they could leave the family alone. They're always looking for the sordid angle. S&M, torture, prostitution. This guy was a cancer researcher. He sang in a church choir. They'd never believe you can be gay and get murdered for no reason."

Donny put an arm around Prabin's shoulders. "Thanks for coming," he told Dan and Domingo. "Prabin and I are going back to the apartment, if you want to join us."

"Do you want us to come?" Domingo asked.

"Please." Prabin nodded. "I could use the company."

The four friends sat talking in low voices around a coffee table. Soft jazz played in the background, an impromptu requiem for the dead man. Outside the windows, a grey haze obscured the horizon.

"Randy and I met at Queen's while we were both under-grads," Prabin said. "We were a weird match. I was the immigrant and he was the blue-eyed WASP. I was in the business program and he was in neurosciences. The only thing we had in common was the pool. We were both competitive swimmers. Then later we both joined the choir. Randy always loved to sing his heart out."

Donny patted his lover's arm and went out to the balcony. He lit a cigarette and stood looking in at the others.

"I wanted to go up and speak today, but I couldn't," Prabin continued. "I wanted to say that he was my first real lover. But I didn't want to draw attention away from his family, particularly his husband."

"I wouldn't have been able to say a word," Domingo said. "I always find it hard to speak at funerals, especially when the death is sudden."

Prabin grabbed a tissue and blew his nose. "After graduation, we went in separate directions. I didn't know we'd both ended up in Toronto till a few months ago when I ran into him at the Y. It was more than ten years since we'd last seen each other, but he just grabbed me in a big hug. His career was well underway and he was very successful. It sounded like his life was perfect. He said he'd even found the ideal husband." He looked over at Donny and gave a smile. "I didn't think there was such a thing, but I found out different. Well, almost ideal except for his smoking."

"Just remember — it keeps me calm," Donny called back to him.

"When did you last see him?" Domingo asked.

"Just that one time. We exchanged cell numbers and spoke a few times by phone. He kept saying we should get together for coffee, but I put him off." He shrugged. "You know how it is. You always think there'll be time next week or the week after. The last time he called was last Wednesday."

"The day he died."

Prabin nodded and rubbed his forehead. "I put him off again. It's weird to think that if I'd said yes, and maybe altered his schedule, he might not have been doing whatever he was doing when he was killed."

"They said his walk schedule was pretty regular," Donny reminded him, flicking ash in a potted plant. "He always went out at eight o'clock in the evening."

"Still, it might have changed things," Prabin answered gloomily.

Domingo gave him a sad smile. "I like to think that we go when our time is up and we've served our purpose here on Earth. It's the rest of us — the ones who stay — who still have things to learn and accomplish."

"I'm not ready to go yet," Donny said, butting out his cigarette and coming back to the couch. He rested a hand on Prabin's arm. "I just met this guy. I'm not ready to let go."

Domingo shook her head. "I'm not afraid of death. I'd miss Adele, and you guys, too, of course. But not much else."

"I'd miss Ked and all of you," Dan added. "I doubt anyone would miss me outside this group."

A storm of protest rose.

"Randy just proved we're missed by a lot more people than we might expect," Domingo pointed out. "We just don't know it till we're dead."

"That's the sad part," Prabin said. "He was a great guy, always wanting the best for everyone. Just what his brother said about him. Why anyone would kill him is beyond me. He was researching a new way of treating cancer. And he was brilliant enough to find it. It seems pointless that such a good life could be snuffed out while there are so many people out there who don't care whether they live or die."

Donny shrugged. "By the time I was thirty-five, I'd already known three gay men who were murdered. Not one of their killers has ever been convicted."

"How were they killed?" Domingo asked.

"One was strangled by his lover when he tried to leave him. The other two were knifed to death. One by a hustler, the other by a drug dealer. They all got off."

"And now there's Randy," Prabin added.

Domingo gave him a sympathetic look. "Randy's killers will be caught and convicted."

"I hope so," he said, turning to look out over the horizon that was now completely wrapped in grey clouds. "I'd do anything to make sure this doesn't happen to anyone else ever again."

TWO

Serial

DOMINGO WAS WATCHING DAN thoughtfully, the mood between them solemn as they rode down side by side in an elevator the size of a small bedroom. The doors opened and they made their way out to the street in silence. The rain had turned to a sloppy, wet snow covering the ground and cars. It declared fall was now permanently out of reach and spring would be a long time coming.

"Do you think someone is preying on gay men in the community?" Domingo asked at last.

"I always think someone is preying on gay men in the community. Usually it's other gay men," Dan said.

Domingo slipped a pair of gloves from her coat pocket. "You must have seen the notices of missing men pasted on street lights and mailboxes lately. There've been a couple."

"I hadn't noticed, but then I'm not a downtown boy so maybe I just don't spend enough time walking around the neighbourhood."

She gave him a skeptical look. "Well, get your ass down here more often. I keep telling you you're never going to find a boyfriend if you don't get out and circulate."

"The presumption being that I'm looking for one?"

"I know you, Dan. You're not the type to go through life alone."

"Sadly, I don't find the type of men I appeal to have much appeal for me in return. And vice versa, I'm sure."

"You want someone sensitive."

He smiled. "That's one word for it."

"Adele and I have been putting our heads together to see if we can come up with someone," she ventured.

"That dating friends of friends thing never works. Thank you for the thought, though."

Domingo waved her hands. "Not just friends. Neighbours and colleagues. We're throwing a wide net. So even if it all goes bust, you'll never be embarrassed to find yourself at a cocktail party stuffed to the gills with people you dated once and never wanted to see again."

Dan laughed. "Not much chance of that, given my dating history."

"I know you don't like it but I've been doing my 'thing,' as you call it."

Dan stiffened. By her "thing" he knew she meant "other-worldly" skills. While he tolerated her belief in such abilities, he wasn't entirely comfortable having them turned on him.

"You've been alone for a while. I think it's time for you to start looking in earnest."

"Oh, you do, do you?"

"Yes, I do." She was stern. "And both Donny and Prabin

agree it's time for you to circulate again. We thought you could use a helping hand."

"Ah, it's a committee."

Having Donny as a best friend meant Dan was expected to put up with a lot, but sometimes he simply held a hand up and said, "No more." Since becoming a fixed item with Prabin, however, Donny had become more of an unknown quantity, a slightly off-kilter version of the reliable nag he'd once been. Dan didn't resent the change, and some days he actually liked it. Domingo, on the other hand, had come into his life when they were both neighbours raising young sons. Only Domingo's boy disappeared following an episode of adolescent-onset schizophrenia, while Dan's son Ked was maturing into a responsible adult who would soon leave the nest for university and find his place in the greater world.

Dan was fond of Domingo for many reasons, not the least of which was her big, open heart. They both came from the wrong side of the tracks, she from a small town in Trinidad and he from Sudbury, a stunted mining town in northern Ontario. Both had been emotionally and physically abused as children, Dan by his alcoholic father and Domingo by a domineering, cold-hearted mother whose only legacy to her daughter was a belief in her so-called other-worldly abilities. For the most part, she and Dan spoke the same language. Where their swords had crossed in the past, however, was when it came to Domingo's "thing." She would look off into the distance and speak certain spooky truths that sometimes unnerved him. She had, in fact, accurately dissected the mind of a killer Dan encountered when even the police couldn't catch him. It had been helpful, he later begrudgingly acknowledged, but he didn't like it when she turned her X-ray vision on him.

"Well, it's nice to know you've been scheming behind my back again."

"Trust me — it's for your own good. Don't worry, we'll weed out the self-absorbed assholes — there's always loads of those — and see what happens if we narrow down the potentials. There is someone out there for you, I just feel it."

"You know what they say. No one laughs at a clown after midnight and no one loves a gay man after forty. Not even other over-forty gay men."

"Which is a very sad reflection of our ageist, looks-conscious society. But the thing is, Daniel, you are a commodity. I just wish I could make you see it."

"Funny, Ked says the same thing. Only he doesn't meet many middle-aged gay men to introduce me to."

"What is your ideal man, by the way?"

"Well under forty and extremely good-looking."

She *tsk*ed. "You need to take me seriously if I'm going to narrow down the potential candidates."

"Okay, on my wish list would be such sterling qualities as sincerity, loyalty, reliability, generosity —"

"You're describing yourself, but go on."

"And, of course, the ability to tolerate my temper as well as understand my strange and potentially alarming career choice. You will remember that's why Trevor left me."

"So I recall."

"He couldn't stand worrying about me every day, always dreading what might have happened if I was late getting home for supper or if I called to say I was going to be out at night investigating something unusual."

"You need someone with a strong emotional base. I think you may be surprised to find that not everyone is bothered by such things. What about physical attributes? Do you have a preferred type?"

"Impossible to pin down," Dan said, getting into the swing of things. "Donny claims I'm attracted to everything I'm not, so I guess it's true that opposites attract."

"Well, that leaves it pretty wide open. Age?"

"Emotionally mature. Preferably within a decade of my age. Just no kiddies or daddies-in-waiting."

"What about dating techniques?"

Dan let out a whoop. "I have none. I'm absolutely defenceless on that count."

Domingo shook her head. "What I'm asking is whether you like to date casually or formally. Serially or singly. Do you like to see a variety of men or are you —"

"A serial monogamist? The latter, I suspect. I get a little proprietary about my partners and I don't care who minds if I do. I'm very old-fashioned that way. You can call me a one-man dog, if you like. I won't take offence."

"Well, then it should be easy. I know a lot of guys out there who are looking for a nice, uncomplicated guy like you."

They came to a crosswalk and waited.

"Next you'll be calling me respectable," Dan said.

Domingo gave him a wry look. "I would never do that. You don't have the right wardrobe, for one thing." The light turned green and they walked on. "Anyway, it's a start. Let me get back to you."

"What makes you so confident you can find me some-one?"

"You remember Kent? That sweet man who lived upstairs from Adele before she moved in with me? You met him at my birthday party."

Dan nodded. "Sort of. He wasn't my type."

She swatted his arm. "Let me speak. What I wanted to say is, he once put a personal ad in the paper. This was back in the days before email and cellphones. Anyway, one afternoon he showed up at my door with a grocery bag full of letters. He wanted my help sorting them. It would have taken hours to read and reply to them all, people were so desperate back then. This was when AIDS was still killing everyone who got infected, don't forget."

"Not that I could."

"Anyway, I made him dump the whole lot on the carpet," she said, indicating the ground with her gloved fingers spread wide. "I let my eyes roam over all those envelopes. One stood out from all the others. It was as if it had a glow. I picked it up and said, 'Answer that one first.' He did, and fell in love with the most marvellous man in the world. They're still together sixteen years later."

Dan considered this. "And what about all the other poor guys left lying on the floor? What if there were thirteen other equally deserving Prince Charmings in the batch?"

She shrugged. "He couldn't very well date them all, could he?"

"I guess not. Anyway, if you can find the right man for me you've probably got a good chance at a career in profiling."

"It's not that far from what I do now."

"Event management?"

She scowled. "You're determined not to take me seriously today, aren't you? No, I mean the *other*. My 'thing,' as you call it."

He was silent for a moment. "I just wish I understood it better."

"It's okay. Most people don't. But since that case you asked me to look into, the one with that sexually abused young man —"

"Gaetan Belanger."

"Yes, that poor boy. Since then I've been looking into how serial killers think. It fascinates me, I don't know why."

Dan stopped. They were standing outside a pizza store. "Tell me again what you felt about Randy's murder."

"Two people, one to distract and the other to attack. I don't think he was targeted for personal reasons. Wrong time and place is all."

"Could it have been prevented? If Prabin had gone to coffee with him, for instance?"

"Can you outrun fate? I doubt it. As we say in Trinidad, if the bullet has your name on it you can't outrun it forever."

"Never?"

She gave him an odd look. "If you do then someone else has to take your place. Just to even out the scales." She shrugged. "At least that's what they say back home."

They continued walking.

"Do you think whoever killed Randy is behind the disappearances you mentioned?"

Domingo shrugged. "I'm not sure, but it struck me there might be a serial killer out there who is being overlooked because he's abducting and killing gay men rather than young girls. When it's girls, you immediately think sex. When it's men, it might seem more random. There've been at least two in the past year."

"Spot on, I'd say. Though technically there needs to be four victims to get you a title of serial killer."

"The count may eventually turn out to be higher than that if someone looks into it carefully."

"Then the problem will be figuring out what the victims have in common. You need to find a connection. Meanwhile, the victim's families live in hope and fear. Though sometimes, but not often enough, a missing person returns home without warning years later. There could be a million reasons why. You just never know."

She glanced over at him. "How do you decide when it's time to declare someone dead so the living can get on with their lives?"

"I don't. I never do. I'm not God. Without proof, hope lives on forever."

"Like a virus that never dies."

"You know that as well as anyone."

She smiled grimly. "Yes. Sometimes I wish I could forget him and go on, but I never will. Not till I know for sure. Even though …"

Dan looked over. "Even though you don't believe he's alive?"

"No, even though I don't feel him here." She pointed to her head. "But he is still alive for me here." Her hand trailed down to her heart. "That will never change. There is not one single day that goes by when I don't think about him."

"I'd feel the same about Ked if he disappeared," Dan said. "I couldn't imagine ever forgetting. Alive or dead, they'll always be a part of us."

"But hope?" Domingo shook her head. "Not anymore. I know when he died. It was when I stopped feeling him thinking of me. One day it just ended and never came back."

She linked her arm in his and they walked on, past the bars and store windows along Church Street. An adolescent boy clad in a corduroy jacket, loose-fitting jeans, and a newsboy cap came toward them, walking a dog wearing red boots and a bright yellow sweater.

"Dom!"

Domingo stopped. "Edie — hi!"

They embraced while the dog danced nervously to avoid having its paws stepped on.

Domingo turned to Dan. "My neighbour — Edie Foxe."

Not a boy then.

"Hey, there. Nice to meet you," Edie said, her voice deep and resonant.

Dan caught a slight accent. Eastern European.

"A pleasure. I'm Dan."

"Cool." She turned back to Domingo. "Coming to my next gig? I've got a show at Lola's this Saturday. Come check it out."

"I'll see if Adele's feeling sociable."

"You tell her I expect to see her."

"Will do."

"Good to met you, Dan."

"Likewise."

She turned and walked on with the dog at her heels. Domingo caught Dan watching her go.

"Edie's a boi," she said.

"She kind of looks like a boy."

"No, I mean she's a b-o-i boi. She's a star of the local BDSM scene. Sexual contortionist and all that exhausting stuff. Addie and I caught a late-night show where she performed a piece about being wrapped in tape. It was fascinating, though it scared the crap out of me. Addie was bored, as usual. She prefers Scrabble. I'm not into the live demos, but even hearing about it was an eye-opener for a naive island girl like me."

They came to a stop.

"Here I am," Domingo said, reaching up to kiss Dan's cheek. "Thanks for walking me home."

"Any time. Say hello to Adele for me."

"Will do." She turned to the front door then looked back. "Think about my offer. I plan to see you married off one way or another."

"I hope you're patient."

"I am."

On his way back down the street, Dan stopped in at Cumbrae's and picked up a couple of steaks for himself and Ked. A growing boy could never have too much protein, he reasoned. He thought again of Domingo's son. Lonnie had shown signs of a mental disorder before disappearing just after his sixteenth birthday. Two years later Domingo had had a brief phone call from him, sparking hope once again, but nothing since. She'd held out hope till then, but after that she no longer believed he was alive. She'd grown resigned to it, she said, but that didn't make the acceptance any easier.

The snow was flying when Dan walked out of the store with his groceries. Outside a bar, a poster caught his eye. Tattered and faded, it looked as though it had been there for some time. Dan found himself staring at the face of a good-looking man around his own age dressed in black leather. A shaved head and smiling eyes with plenty of laugh lines. He looked familiar. Beneath the photo were the words MISSING — HAVE YOU SEEN JOE?

THREE

Missing

THE FACE OF THE MISSING man haunted Dan all the way back down Church Street. *Do you think someone is preying on gay men in the community?* Domingo had asked. Preying was one thing. Kidnapping was another. In the transient downtown community, faces came and went from one day to the next. Someone you thought of as a neighbourhood fixture might vanish suddenly, only to turn up on a street in Vancouver or Halifax the next time you visited there. The city had grown far too big to keep track of everyone who came and went. What had once seemed a tight-knit inner-city of individuals banding together for identity as much as safety was now a vast sea whose restless swell never stopped.

Dan recalled a popular bar he'd frequented in his twenties — before becoming a father — and all the friends he made there. One by one they'd disappeared, leaving him to surmise who had succumbed to AIDS, who had taken a job abroad, and who had simply hooked up with a partner and settled elsewhere. The bar had lived out its allotted lifespan before closing and being transformed into a Starbucks.

One day while walking on Church Street, he saw a notice for a reunion on the tenth anniversary of the bar's closing. Feeling nostalgic, he called up Donny and they went together. That night, he was happily surprised to see dozens of faces he hadn't seen in a decade. Some had grown fat, while others stayed sleek and youthful. Some had lost their hair and others had grown beards. Not all had died or moved away, he realized. They'd just gone out of circulation, like old postage stamps.

The lights were off when he arrived home. The snow had picked up, great swirls drifting from the sky. The house appeared diminutive, just one more indistinct outline along the street, as though someday it might disappear forever. Tracks showed on the walkway, boot prints surrounded by paw marks. Ked and Ralph had gone for a pre-dinner walk.

Dan headed up to his office. There was still time for a bit of sleuthing before supper. He turned on his computer and searched for murdered or missing men in Toronto. The list was far too lengthy. He narrowed the search to within the past two years, but still found it daunting. The only thing distinguishing the current year from any other was the number of teens who'd been killed. Barely out of childhood, they'd been picked off before their prime. Some of the deaths were gang-related; others appeared to be innocent victims of drive-by shootings. It did nothing to reassure him as the parent of a quickly growing teenager.

Typing the name *Joe* failed to bring up anything current. Nor did adding the words *gay* or *homosexual*, though a number of past cases were revealed in depths as far back as 1967. What struck him, however, was how few disappearances or murders were tagged as pertaining to gay men, all the victims apparently having been lumped in together.

One link yielded an interview with a convicted murderer who claimed to have killed more than a dozen times, picking on the socially and physically vulnerable, gay men in particular. He boasted how he'd become skilled at baiting and killing them. His preference for using a knife might have made him a shoo-in for the murder of Randy Melchior, except that he was currently in prison serving a life sentence.

He described several locations where he'd killed, hinting at where his victims' remains might be found. The eerie nonchalance of his claims and his apparent enjoyment of the memories were unsettling. The article warned that he would kill again. Indeed, a follow-up link a month later reported his latest victim had in fact been his cellmate. Not too difficult to find that body, Dan mused, wondering what improbable universe prison officials lived in that convinced them serial killers should have cellmates.

Randy Melchior's name brought up surprisingly few hits. The *Toronto Star* ran the longest article. It was scant on details except to say police were investigating what appeared to be a straightforward street robbery.

The memorial service was played up. No doubt it would make a brief ripple on the nightly news for the next few days then disappear, just one more instance of the increasing violence in the city's downtown core. Hardly a weekend went by now without a shooting or stabbing. Torontonians had been lucky till then, but the tide was turning and there were plenty of armed youngsters ready to murder their way into history.

It occurred to him that a disappearance from the gay neighbourhood might be listed on a community billboard. The 519 Community Centre had a link. He clicked and found himself staring at the face from the poster. He knew now why it was familiar. Joe had been a contender in a leather competition several years earlier. Dan had been there that night. Despite Joe's intimidating gear, Dan's first impression was that he was a friendly, likeable fellow. And he'd be the first to say not to judge a book by its cover or a Mr. Leatherman contestant by his attire.

A second photo caught his eye. Adam Carnivale, a dancer at a local strip club, had been reported missing at the beginning of summer. Also good-looking, he was younger and more muscular, with broad cheekbones and full, sensuous lips. Dan thought he caught a hopeless look in his eyes, as though he'd had a hard ride in life.

Downstairs, the front door opened and closed. Dan closed his computer. Ked had returned with Ralph, the ginger retriever who had been his sidekick since he was four. Ralph was verging on his golden years in more ways than one. At seventeen, Ked had just begun morphing into man-hood. His eyes were dark, unlike his father's glacial grey. He wore his hair in a long, shaggy cut that fell around his ears.

"Hi, Dad!"

"Welcome back."

Ked hung Ralph's leash on the door handle and headed for the kitchen. He grabbed a chocolate bar, tore it open, and wolfed it down.

"Don't ruin your supper."

"Why do parents always say that?"

"It's our job."

"Don't you want me to be full and happy?"

"Happy, yes. Full, no." Dan pointed to the table, where a cutting board was laid out with a knife alongside carrots, onions, and potatoes. "Supper will be ready in half an hour."

"Need help?"

"Sure. Make yourself useful."

Ked sat and chopped, tossing Ralph a carrot top now and again. Dan eyed the dog, who spent a long time fussily chewing the rinds before spitting them onto the floor. Ked saw his father eying the mess.

"Don't worry, I'll clean it up."

"I thought the saying was dogs have masters and cats have servants. Ralph seems to have turned the equation around on you."

Ked reached down and hugged Ralph, who gave him a sloppy lick. "It's okay. He's worth it."

Dan laid the steaks in the pan. The raw flesh sizzled on contact. He looked over to where his son sat chopping an onion. Whatever Ked did, he seemed to do happily, mostly to Dan's relief but also to his consternation. He'd always thought a boy's teen years were supposed to be his most troubled. Had he gone wrong as a parent? When did angst come in to fill the void and make Ked more normal and miserable?

Once, Dan had spared Ked the more upsetting details of his cases. At some point not long after the drive-by shooting of one of Ked's school friends, however, he realized it was pointless to whitewash the world for him. Ked would encounter it in all its broken glory soon enough, and if a little forewarning would help then Dan wanted his son to have that. Other parents moved to the suburbs thinking they were shielding their children, only to discover different kinds of threats waiting there. Moving to a pleasant-looking neighbourhood did not make them better kids. It merely left them bored and more inclined to personal deviousness.

"When you're out walking around the streets at night, do you stay alert to who and what is around you?"

Ked let his eyes search the room as though this might be a trick question he was being trapped into answering before invisible witnesses.

"I guess."

"The city's not as safe as it used to be."

"I try to be aware."

"I'm not trying to make you paranoid, but it strikes me there are a lot more shootings and knifings in the news now that we didn't hear about even ten years ago."

"Yeah, some kids bring knives to school. Or so I've heard."

The aroma of frying steak filled the air. Dan swept Ked's pile of onions into the pan and pushed them around with a wooden spatula.

"Would you report it if you saw one?"

Ked put down the knife and looked at his father. "I guess it depends on who had it."

"Meaning?"

"Meaning, if I thought it was someone who was just doing it to show off I might not say anything, but if it was someone like Wayne Dumfries, who has a history of violence, I might tell one of the teachers."

"I hope you *would* tell them, not just *might* tell them. You wouldn't want to think later that you could have saved someone's life if you had only alerted the right person." Dan waited and watched as Ked went back to his cutting. "Does that make sense?"

"Yes."

"So, please. Make sure you do alert someone, even if it's just a prank. School is no place for weapons."

They worked in silence for another minute.

"You might be wondering why I'm telling you this," Dan said. "I was at a memorial service today with Uncle Donny and Prabin and Domingo. A friend of Prabin's was murdered last week. It was a knife attack."

"I saw it on the news," Ked said. "That doctor, right?"

"Yes, that's the one."

"Who did it? Did they catch him?"

"Not yet. And no one knows if it was a him or a her or a them. You can't make assumptions like that anymore."

"Statistics say that eighty-eight percent of violent crimes, including murder, are committed by men. Also, I read that seventy percent of murders are committed by family members and acquaintances rather than strangers."

"Well, I'm glad you know your statistics, but don't make assumptions about real life. It's often far more complicated than statistics."

Dan transferred the steaks to a platter, scooped the onions on top, then set the platter on the table.

"Now, before I make your young life any more serious than it needs to be, why not tell me what you're up to?"

"Elizabeth and I are going to see Lester's band on Friday. It's her birthday."

"Right. Always keep the girlfriend happy. What's the band called again?"

"M-Power. It's Lester on horn and another guy on bass and one on keyboard. They're pretty cool. Hip hop and some rap. Lester's really stoked about this gig. It's at a warehouse in the east end."

"A likely place for weapons," Dan said without thinking.

Ked looked askance. "I never thought about it. They'll probably have a bouncer at the door frisking people."

"If they don't, then don't go in."

Ked looked at his father for a second then nodded: easier to agree than to argue, Dan suspected. He speared a steak and pulled it onto his plate before passing the platter to his father.

"Is Lester still in touch with his birth parents? Does he talk to you about that?"

"He talks to his mother on the phone now and then. He said his stepdad doesn't want to talk to him."

After rescuing Lester from the streets, Dan had asked Donny to take him on as a temporary charge. The charge had now lasted more than three years. Once he'd reached the age of majority, Lester had opted to stay with Donny rather than return to his drama-laden family and their condemnatory, narrow-minded beliefs.

"Is it hard on him or is he okay with that?"

"He's okay with it. I guess she tries to pressure him to come home, but Lester knows he's better off with Donny and Prabin than going back to Oshawa."

"Keep your eye on him. If he ever starts to talk about going back, let us know. It was a disaster the last time he did that, but I wouldn't put it past his mother to try more emotional blackmail on him."

"Nah. Lester's too smart for that now. It won't happen again."

"Good." He paused and watched Ked eat. "How's the food?"

"Great, Dad. Thanks. You're the best."

"So are you. Now finish everything on your plate and make me happy."

FOUR

Cupid's Bow

TRUE TO HER WORD, DOMINGO set Dan's inbox ringing with queries from eligible suitors. Out of consideration for her efforts, Dan replied to them all but begged off the first round of senders. Just looking at the subject-headers demanding his attention made him feel tired. Then curiosity got the better of him and he started examining the queries in detail.

Most had photos attached. Several of the men were extremely attractive. Some were chatty, outlining their hopes in print; others offered to send private photos, as though their physical attributes would make him take their requests more seriously. But personality was what mattered, Dan believed. An enthusiastic note ringing with exclamation marks did nothing to convince him he wanted to meet the sender, though a nicely worded greeting might.

He found himself intrigued by one note in particular: *I'm serious about dating*, it said. *Domingo and Adele tell me that you are a serious contender as well. Would you be interested in meeting for coffee to see where our compatibility lies?*

Dan contemplated the picture at the bottom: a professional-looking portrait of an attractive man with red hair, blue eyes, and a quixotic expression. The writer assured him he was genuinely looking for a commitment, not just a tumble in bed. He did not end by offering to send nude photographs on request. The note was indeed nicely worded. Top score on looks, too.

I'm available for coffee any afternoon after three, Dan replied. He considered attaching a photograph of himself then thought better of it. If the letter writer was serious then he could take his chances on meeting an unknown quantity.

The reply showed up a minute later. *It's 2:58 and I'm free now. I live in your neighbourhood. I can be at the Tango Palace for coffee in twenty minutes*. It was signed, *Terence Hardy*.

An eager beaver, Dan thought. Was that a good sign or an indication the sender lived for instant gratification? Then again, why kick eagerness in the teeth? If he, Dan, didn't feel much enthusiasm these days, there was no need to denigrate it in others.

He glanced in the mirror, noting the ridge running down his temple where he'd been thrown against a door jamb by his father when he was ten. Some men found his appearance a little too hard-core, while others seemed turned on by it. There was no accounting for taste. Luck of the draw then. Mr. Hardy would just have to take his chances on this "serious contender."

†

Dan clocked him on entering: an alert-looking man wearing a turquoise shirt and sporting a pricey haircut, seated at a table just inside the door. He didn't mind that Terence had gone all out to impress him, but with such short notice it was clear Dan hadn't done the same. Casual was fine for neighbourhood coffee shops, as far as he was concerned. If he was being judged for his clothes then all bets were off.

The Palace was in full swing, with boho trendies and film-industry workers out for a late-afternoon break. A life-size plaster angel hanging on the wall opposite the bar trumpeted the news of Dan's arrival with the full force of her silent notes. Terence heard them, apparently, and turned to lock eyes with him. At first glance, he was stunning.

The small talk was no more awkward than Dan would have expected. Thankfully, his potential suitor had a sense of humour and a penchant for chattiness, no doubt fuelled by the nervousness of a first encounter. If nothing else, it made it easier to stare at such an attractive man when he was trying so hard to be entertaining.

Terence expressed no surprise when Dan declared his profession. "Is it interesting?" he asked, without the look of wide-eyed surprise some men gave Dan, as though he might have come straight from the morgue or digging up corpses in shallow graves.

"Interesting, yes. But not always exciting. That's the television version. Usually it entails a lot of fact checking. Sometimes I find the people I'm looking for and sometimes I don't. The day-to-day reality is that it's a job."

Dan had a similar reaction on learning Terence was an actor. "I wouldn't be surprised to hear you say it's not all it's cracked up to be either."

"It's not. The glamour wore off a long time ago. As you said of your profession, it's a job."

Dan was glad when Terence didn't launch into a recitation of recent roles he'd played or series he'd been in. To his mind, there was little as boring as listening to artists discuss their careers. Except maybe politicians extolling their own virtues.

A pause ensued. Dan checked his watch and gave a polite smile. "We've managed to cover professions in the first five minutes. What else should we talk about?"

"I haven't got a clue." Terence shrugged. "The whole dating thing is weird to me. I didn't date in high school. I wasn't into faking it with girls and none of the guys showed up on my gaydar. I suspect it might've been faulty."

"I felt much the same. I'm sure they were there, if we'd only known where to look." Dan paused. "How about family? Are you close to yours?"

Terence gave a shrug. "Not particularly. I have a sister in Australia and my parents are in the Maritimes. It's far, but I make sure to visit them a little more often as they get older."

"I have a teenage son, Kedrick, who lives with me. We're very close."

Terence looked wistful. "That's so nice. So you were married before?"

Dan shook his head. "No, never, though I'm close to Ked's biological mother. I had a live-in partner until a couple of years ago. But my profession scared him off. He was always worried for me. He wanted more of the stay-at-home type."

"I get told that stay-at-home thing, too," Terence confided. "To tell the truth, I'm a little surprised to find myself looking for a partner in my forties. I thought I'd be settled down by now — kids and cars and a dog in the suburbs kind of thing."

"It's not easy finding the right person," Dan agreed.

"Or in my case, it's easy to find him but not to hang on to him. I've met three Mr. Rights over the past few years. But here I am alone and single."

"Three? That sounds surprisingly high."

"Maybe I'm easier to please than I look." Terence gave a winsome smile.

"Fair enough. What happened?"

"Fate happened. The first guy got a job doing IT work in Dubai and left a month after we met. Beautiful man. I was sorry to lose him. The second had a change of heart and went back to his wife and kids. Probably for the best. If you don't know what you want by forty, chances are you never will."

"Amen to that."

"The third time, I began to think I was cursed. Then again, I should have known better than to date another closet case."

"Another one with a wife and kids on the side?"

Terence shook his head. "No, this one was unattached. We'd been seeing each other off and on for a few months. Just casually. I suspected he wasn't ready for anything serious, but I liked him. Then one day he disappeared. I never heard from him again."

"And you have no idea why?"

"Not really. Though I know he was having trouble getting his visa extended, so maybe he got sent back home. But it was strange how he just disappeared. The last time we spoke we had talked about going away for the weekend. I booked a hotel and sent him a text. Then I waited, but he never got in touch. When I tried calling his cellphone the mailbox was full. A week later the number was disconnected."

"Did you go to his place to see if he was all right?"

"Three times. There was never an answer. After that I gave up."

"So, he moved out?"

"No, that's the odd thing. I looked in the window, and his furniture was still there. Sounds like a case for a missing-persons investigator."

"Possibly. Do you know what he did for a living?"

Terence gave him a quirky smile. "He called himself a puppet maker. His place was full of the darn things."

"Puppet maker? Could he have gone off to work on a film or an opera?"

"He said he did a lot of children's theatre back home, so I suppose it's possible opportunity came calling. I mean, I get jobs out of the blue and have to move away for a while, but I always leave a forwarding address."

"What do you know about him? Any family in the city?"

"No family here at all, as far as I know."

"What about friends? Anyone you could ask?"

Terence gave him a wry look. "He pretty much kept to himself. That's just what closeted men do, so there's nothing to explain when you run into people on the streets."

"Where did you meet?"

"At Zipperz on one of their retro disco nights. I got the feeling he didn't go out much, but Zipperz is dark and you can hang out in the corners without being seen. I offered to buy him a beer. It took a while to get him to come out of his shell, but he warmed up after that. It shook me when he disappeared. I really thought it was going somewhere."

"Did you report it to the police?"

Terence gave him a searching look. "Should I have?"

"Maybe he never left town."

Terence's mouth opened and closed. "You mean something might have happened to him?"

"At least two other men have gone missing recently. You must have seen the posters up around the neighbourhood."

"Come to think of it, I have. Wow. That's a scary thought."

"If he has no friends or family in the city, no one else will declare him missing. The police might never know. They'll just assume he left town for some reason. If anything happened to him, it would be better if they knew about it."

Terence sat back and shook his head. "Just my luck, I go out on a date with a good-looking guy and it turns into a missing-persons investigation."

"And it's just my luck that I end up saying scary-sounding things when I should be trying to be charming."

Terence laughed. "Oh, believe me — I'm charmed."

"Ditto."

A phone pinged with an incoming text. Terence checked his screen and gave Dan a rueful look. "I'm really sorry. I have to dash. That's not a staged exit line. I just got a note from my agent about an audition. It's in an hour."

"The life of an actor?"

"Sometimes. And here I thought you'd be the first one to dash when you saw my red hair." He held out a hand.

"It's been a pleasure, Dan. Shall we try this again sometime? Maybe something a little less rushed?"

"I'd like that."

"Good. I look forward to it."

FIVE

Two Brothers

It was Monday before Dan spoke to Donny again. He was seated in his office in a warehouse overlooking the Don Valley, thumbing his way through a case file that was proving particularly resistant, when his friend's name popped up on the call display.

"How's Prabin doing?" he asked without preamble.

"He's still pretty devastated about Randy. I told him he shouldn't hold it against himself for not meeting up with him the day he died, but he can't shake it."

"I know the feeling. I've beaten myself up for losing clients because I felt I wasn't paying attention to clues at the right time. It happens to cops, too. You overlook one thing and someone ends up dead. It haunts you, even though you know deep down there was nothing you could have done to change things."

There was a pause. For once, Donny wasn't smoking his way through the conversation like a forlorn sailor navigating by the pole star. "Domingo seems to think someone may be preying on gay men," he said at last. "Did she tell you?"

"Yes, she mentioned it the other day when we left your place."

"Have you seen the missing poster that was circulating for the past few months? The one for that hot leather dude?"

Dan closed the file and pushed it to one side. "Yeah, a guy named Joe. No last name. I tried looking him up. There wasn't much online about it."

"I seem to recall a similar poster being circulated in the summer."

"A dancer named Adam?"

"That sounds right."

"I found him online, too. Nothing conclusive, though. The police don't seem overly concerned."

Donny paused. "Prabin thinks there's another one."

"When?"

"Three days ago. He was contacted by the brothers of a guy named Nabil, to ask if he'd heard from him. He and Prabin work out together at the Y. Nabil hasn't been home since Friday night."

"Could he have stayed over at a boyfriend's house?"

"It's unlikely. Nabil's very closeted. Prabin says he's terrified of coming out to his family. He doesn't let things slip. But I guess he wasn't so successful at keeping his sexuality a secret."

"How so?"

"When they called Prabin, the brothers asked him outright if he knew Nabil was gay. Prabin didn't answer, but agreed to meet them. When he talked with them, he decided they weren't trying to find out if Nabil is gay. Rather, they were asking because they think his best bet of being found is by looking in the gay community."

Dan thought this over. "When Prabin's feeling a bit more stable, could you ask him to call me?"

"I can do better than that. He recommended you to the brothers. They want to hire you. Are you free?"

An hour later, Dan found himself seated in a brightly lit café beside Donny and Prabin. Across from them sat two earnest-looking Arab men. Amir, the older, appeared to be in his mid-thirties. He was well-groomed and on the thin side. His brother, Mustafa, looked a few years younger, possibly in his twenties. Mustafa did not seem to share Amir's style-conscious dress sense, however. A chubby boy with a gloomy expression, he wore a shape-less white shirt and black trousers. Both brothers sported full beards.

The downtown café was Donny's choice, and the broth-ers were cautiously checking out their surroundings. Amir seemed the more comfortable of the two, seated with his arm draped over the back of his chair. Mustafa, on the other hand, sat perched on the edge of his seat as though waiting for permission to leave.

"How long has your brother been missing?" Dan asked.

"Since Friday. Three days," Amir said.

"That's not unusually long."

"No, it's not long. But Nabil would not normally stay away overnight without letting one of us know."

"Has he ever done that before?"

Amir turned to his brother and they conversed briefly in Arabic.

"Occasionally," Amir said, turning back to Dan. "But only overnight. He usually returns home in the morning, saying he fell asleep at a party or some such thing."

"How did you know to contact Prabin when he disappeared?"

"We found his number on Nabil's computer," Amir explained.

"Wasn't it password encrypted?" Dan asked.

Amir glanced at Mustafa then back to Dan. "It was, but it was just his nickname: Nabs. We probably shouldn't have done it, but we went in."

"Is that how you found out he was gay?"

Dan saw Mustafa's eyes dart away at the word *gay*. In a police lineup, whether guilty or innocent, he would have been the one to draw suspicion to himself.

Amir nodded. "Pretty much that's how we confirmed it, but Mustafa and I knew what he was a long time ago. We just didn't discuss it with him."

"It can't be an easy thing in your culture," Dan said.

"It's not. But believe me when I say we love our brother more than we dislike what he is. We would never hurt him. We just want to know that he's safe."

"That's what most of my clients tell me. It's not always true, however."

"I give you our word of honour we would do nothing to harm Nabil. We just ask that your search be as discreet as possible."

"I don't know how discreet I can be if I'm looking for him in the gay neighbourhood," Dan said. "But if your

58

brother is gay, that's the obvious place to begin."

Amir held Dan's gaze. "Then you must do whatever is necessary. Inshallah."

"You must understand I won't agree to look for someone and return them to a family who would discriminate or harm them. I'm not a bounty hunter. And from what you're telling me, Nabil has done nothing wrong."

Amir held up a hand. "We understand that. For our part, we can tell you that no harm will ever come to Nabil from us. We love our brother. We just want him safe."

Mustafa's eyes met Dan's. He nodded. "It is so."

"Okay then, let me tell you my terms."

After the brothers had gone, Dan turned to Donny and Prabin. "What do you think? Are these guys legit?"

Prabin took a moment to answer. "I wasn't sure about Mustafa, but I felt okay about Amir. If you mean would they harm Nabil if he was returned to them, my gut feeling is no, they wouldn't."

"Donny?"

His friend stirred now for the first time since arriving at the café. "Call me suspicious, but I didn't like either of them. Those beards gave me the willies. How do you feel?"

Dan shook his head. "I couldn't get a read on them. They're like chatty cop/silent cop. Amir is friendly on the surface, but who's to say where his true feelings lie? Mustafa seemed as though he might have reservations about his brother's sexuality, but he wasn't going to come out with it. On the other hand, if I find Nabil and he says he doesn't want to be in contact with his family I would have to respect that.

I never force people together no matter who's paying me to do it." He gave Prabin a searching look. "What do you think the chances are that Nabil ran off to escape his brothers?"

Prabin shook his head. "I have no idea. I know he didn't want to come out to them for the obvious reasons. He seemed pretty frightened by the idea."

Dan took stock of this. "Is it possible he committed suicide?"

"Not the Nabil I know, but then again people can snap under pressure so I guess anything's possible."

"So, it's possible, but not probable. That's the distinction that matters in court, at least."

"If you want to put it that way, but the last time I saw him he seemed like his usual self. Then again, I only know Nabil as a gym buddy, so who knows what he's hiding behind his easygoing facade?"

"Everybody has something to hide," Dan said. "I think it's to the brothers' credit that they're coming forward about Nabil's sexuality. Too often families keep secrets that would help me find a person sooner rather than later."

"True. But in this case, there are other people who genuinely want him found, too. And I'm one of them."

"All right. Tell me everything you think you know about Nabil."

SIX

Leathermen

BACK IN HIS OFFICE, DAN laid the file with Nabil's name on his desk. He sat back and let his thoughts drift as he glanced out across the river. Joe, the missing man in the poster, had been a leatherman, while Adam was an exotic dancer, and Nabil a bodybuilder. Did the three have anything else in common besides a love of the physical?

Dan went online and trawled through a variety of web-sites for downtown bars till he found the link he wanted. Spearhead called itself a fraternity for "brothers under the skin." While others identified leather with sexual extrem-ism, Dan knew it for what it really was: a dress-up game for adults. Spearhead funded AIDS charities, raised awareness for social issues, and even organized an annual toys-for-tots drive as if to offset its darker associations.

He scrolled through the online photographs. He found a shot of Joe from when he'd competed in the Mr. Leatherman Toronto contest. There were no photos of Adam or Nabil, however, but Dan wasn't surprised to see the faces of a few old friends, including a rowdy photographer named Woody.

A decade earlier, not long after winning his first Mr. Leatherman competition, Woody had pursued him. Their heat indicator had been off the charts, though Dan found Woody's inability to commit off-putting. "You want a dozen lovers," Dan told him. "I just want one."

"Why restrict yourself?" Woody admonished him for his conservative thinking, but Dan was adamant.

"I want a stay-at-home companion," Dan told him. "Not a party boy."

Woody had laughed. "Yeah, I guess we're kinda mismatched that way."

Though Dan hadn't seen him recently, he remembered him fondly. He scrolled through his contacts list. Sure enough, Woody's number was there.

"It's Dan Sharp, Woody."

"Dan!" It was a near-explosion over the wires. "You sweet man, it's been a dog's age!"

"It has been quite a while. I'm not sure what happened. Everything seemed to hit warp speed a few years ago and nothing's slowed down since."

"You got that right! To what do I owe the pleasure?"

"I've got some questions about your community."

Woody laughed. "The gay community, the AIDS community, or the leather community?"

"The leather community for a starter. Got time for a coffee?"

"For the sexiest man alive, anything."

"No need for the flattery, but thanks."

It was a small establishment, Turkish, with brass decorations on the walls, colourful ceramic ornaments in every corner, and small, cozy booths for sharing. The owner, a jolly man with a rotund stomach, effused over them until they were comfortably seated.

"I bring you the best!" he exclaimed when they asked for coffee and pastries.

Dan gave his old friend the once-over. Woody's compact frame barely hinted at his powerful physique. And despite his youthful appearance, he'd been a fixture in the neighbourhood for nearly two decades. He was also one of the community's unofficial historians, showing up at events like a self-appointed archivist. It had started with AIDS, he told Dan. Losing so many friends had spurred him to document a world rapidly slipping away behind the curtains of hospitals and clinics. Eventually, the drug cocktails turned everything around and people began living longer than expected, but Woody's enthusiasm for documenting remained.

Coffee arrived with an assortment of delicacies. Woody sipped from his cup and popped a sticky-looking confection into his mouth. "So, what's the story, sexy guy?"

"I'm trying to find out about some men who might be involved in the leather scene here."

"If they're involved, then chances are I'd know them. Shoot."

"First is a guy named Joe. You might have seen his face on missing-persons posters for the past few months."

"For sure I saw the posters. Yeah, Joe's a leather guy. He was a Mr. Leatherman contender a few years back. I can't say when he stopped coming around. Maybe early in the spring? Hard to remember that far back, to be honest."

"How about a guy named Adam Carnivale? He's a dancer. There was a poster of him circulating in the summer."

Woody smoothed his moustache with his fingers as he considered. "Yeah, I recall the posters, but not the guy. He might have come around to the meetings once or twice, but I don't think he was a regular."

"What about a guy named Nabil Ahmad?"

"I know a guy named Nabil for sure. Don't recall his last name. Very handsome, a little bit shy."

Dan slid the picture Nabil's brothers had given him onto the table. "Is that him?"

Woody looked up with a curious expression. "That's him. What's this about? Have you got a crush on the guy?"

"No crush. He's missing, too."

Woody's expression darkened. "Oh."

"Are you in touch with him?"

Woody shrugged. "Not really. I see him around from time to time. We don't do Facebook or any of that shit. He's supposed to compete in the Mr. Leatherman contest this weekend."

That was puzzling, for a man said to be secretive about his sexuality. "When did you last see him?"

"Maybe a few weeks ago? It's hard to pin down. It would be a Friday. That's our regular meet-up night at George's Play. There's always a gang." He paused. "Is all this official? Did someone ask you to find these guys?"

"I've been asked to find Nabil by his family. I'm just trying to get a handle on things. As you said, it's hard to pin down. People move around. After a while you may not even remember they were ever there. I'm looking for the invisible thread between these men, if there is one. I thought it might have to do with the leather community."

"You mean like someone in the community's kidnapping them? That's a frightening thought."

"Did you hear about the doctor who was murdered last weekend?"

"Yeah, tragic." Woody shook his head. "But he wasn't part of the leather crowd, as far as I know. Did you hear differently?"

"No, but there could be something that connects them. There's nothing online that even says the police are acknowledging the gay angle. What about violence in the leather community?"

"I guess we're known for our sado-masochistic displays, but it's pretty much performance and posturing. No one's supposed to get hurt for real. There are code words and such, if things get out of hand. Maybe someone takes things too far once in a while, but it's not common."

"How about HIV?"

Woody nodded. "It's rampant. That's no surprise. Some of us are lucky to have made it to middle age. Many didn't. I just read a study claiming that leathermen are sixty-one percent more likely to have HIV than other gay men."

"That's pretty high."

"I'll say. Seems just like the bad old days." His gaze flickered away, over the unseen hordes who had not made it to middle age but continued to haunt the ones who'd managed that small miracle for themselves.

"Sixty-one percent." Dan considered. "Seems to be a thing people have for statistics at the moment. My son knows just about every murder stat going."

"Following in your footsteps?"

"Not that I know of. And I'm glad for that. He just has a head for what's going on in the city."

"That's cool." Woody bit into a slice of baklava. He studied Dan's face as he chewed. "It's been a while since you stepped in front of my camera. Care to do a little posing sometime?"

"I'm camera-shy these days, but thanks."

"That's too bad. You weren't always."

"People change."

"Yeah, true." He shrugged. "Well, if you have time at least come and see the contest. Who knows — maybe Nabil will show up."

"Good idea."

Dan typed the event into his phone calendar and finished his coffee.

"I've got to get back to work. Thanks for taking the time to chat."

"Any time. Always good to see you."

Woody leaned over the table and brought his face close to Dan's. Lips parted and they exchanged a kiss. Woody sat back with an ecstatic look.

"You still got it going on, dude!"

"So do you, Woody."

SEVEN

Lucky Charms

AMIR AHMAD'S FACE WAS IMPASSIVE as he placed a glass of water on the table in front of Dan. He turned and sat beside his brother, Mustafa. The only feature the two men had in common was their dark eyes, but where Amir's were sharp and inquisitive, Mustafa's were soft and worried.

"Thank you for coming so quickly," Amir said.

"It's always best to get started as soon as possible."

The house was surprisingly well kept for three cohabiting brothers, Dan noted. He studied a decorative weave with Arabic script hanging in a far corner. Amir followed his gaze.

"There are many who fear our religion because of the actions of a few." He looked at Dan. "Do you find it disturbing?"

"Not particularly. Perhaps Prabin told you my son's mother is Muslim."

Amir's eyes lit up. "Then you understand Muslim customs."

"Some, though I'm not comfortable with extremism of any sort."

"My brother and I are not extremists."

"Good to know."

"We have lived in Canada now for five years. Coming from Oman, however, there are many things we still do not understand about your country. We try, however, to be both good Muslims and good Canadians."

"Understood." Dan considered his words. "I didn't ask, but what is Nabil's citizenship status? Are there any visa issues, for instance?"

"No, there are no visa issues. All three of us are permanent residents. We are to become Canadian citizens next month." Amir gave Dan a conciliatory smile. "That is one of the reasons we are extremely anxious to have you find Nabil and bring him home. His name means 'noble' in Arabic."

"A good name." Dan nodded. "I'll do what I can. In the meantime, I'd like to see Nabil's room. I also need to check the contents of his computer."

The brothers exchanged a glance.

"If you don't think it is a violation of his rights." It was Mustafa who spoke, practically for the first time since Dan had arrived.

"Violation or not, it's necessary," Dan said carefully. "Sometimes you have to put the safety of the missing person ahead of their so-called civil rights. We all have secrets, but it's often those secrets that get us into trouble."

"Yes, of course," said Amir, with another look at Mustafa. "I want to reassert that whatever you find, our brother will come to no harm from us because of it. His safety is our chief concern."

They took him down the hall to Nabil's room. The furniture was unexceptional, vintage IKEA. Dirty laundry lay scattered on the floor, a half-unbuttoned shirt flung over the back of a chair. Hand weights were lined up neatly beneath the window in increasing sizes, with a long-handled skipping rope hung over the edge of the bedpost. A heavy bolt on the inside of the door said Nabil liked his privacy.

The brothers looked around, as though seeing the room through a stranger's eyes for the first time.

"Nabil is very messy for a good Muslim." It was Mustafa who spoke.

Dan sat on the bed and ran his finger along the spines of the books on the end table. About half the titles were in Arabic. One of the volumes had been turned inward. He pulled it out and flipped through a men's workout handbook. English, with plenty of well-lit photos of muscled men. Training manual or bedside erotica?

Amir ignored the book in Dan's hands and pointed to one of the others.

"This book is on purification of body, mind, and soul. The hadiths set out the rules of faith. There are many narratives about keeping the body clean and the home tidy. Cleanliness is said to be 'half of faith.' It does not mean only the physical self. It means having clean thoughts as well."

"In Christianity, we say that cleanliness is next to godliness."

"Yes, that is so. Good Muslims are told to purify and cleanse their bodies as well as their hearts before meeting our Lord."

And a gay Muslim with a leather fetish might have a very hard time doing that, Dan mused, returning the workout book to the shelf.

Amir fingered a chain draped over the corner of a dresser mirror. "He left his ta'wiz behind. That is unlike Nabil."

Dan glanced at the pendant. "It's to guard against the evil eye, isn't it?"

"Yes. Inside there are verses from the Quran inscribed on parchment. He had it for protection. This is an old-world tradition."

"So's the cross," Dan said. "It surprises me how people cling to the traditions that oppress them."

"Some would call it ignorance and superstition." Amir exchanged a look with his brother. "Nabil adapted well to his new life in Canada. Better than us. Perhaps we should not be surprised to learn there are many things he did not want to share."

In a far corner, a hand-carved wooden screen shielded a prayer mat from prying eyes. A wrinkled, sweat-stained T-shirt had been dropped on it, while a pair of running shoes lay upended against a nearby closet door. Hardly the actions of a devout man, Dan thought.

"Is it possible he was trying to distance himself from his religion?"

Mustafa bristled. "Please do not insult our brother in his home."

"I'm simply asking a question. How he reconciles his sexuality with his faith is his business. My concern is to find him."

Amir intervened. "Of course, this is Canada. We are all entitled to be who we want to be. Isn't that what you are saying? For instance, if certain people feel they want a Pride Parade, they are allowed to have a Pride Parade even if others oppose it."

"Yes, that's true."

"Yet if someone wants to have a Nazi parade, for some reason we are supposed to accept that that is not a viable option, despite whatever opinions we may hold."

"That's because there are laws about inciting hatred against others."

Amir looked at his brother. "Do you know what we are talking about, my brother?"

Mustafa shook his head.

"A Nazi parade. Do you know what this means?"

"A 'nasty' parade?"

Amir turned to Dan. "You see? This is what we have to contend with. You will forgive my brother. He is ignorant of many things in your culture."

Dan's gaze went back and forth between the two brothers. "It's appalling that someone living in Canada in the twenty-first century doesn't know what a Nazi is."

"Nevertheless, this is the reality some of us are dealing with. If it is haram — forbidden by Islamic law — it is sometimes just easier to ignore."

"As you said, 'ignorance and superstition.'"

Amir made a sign for his brother to follow him. "Come, Mustafa. We will leave Mr. Sharp to make his investigations."

They left him alone. Dan was surprised they were willing to give him unfettered access to Nabil's computer. Then again, it might be easier for them not to have to contemplate certain truths about their brother. In the course of his work, he'd uncovered many facts that had proved unpalatable to his clients. He couldn't afford to ignore them if he wanted to work to the best of his abilities.

He turned to the computer, a clunky old desktop model but with a sophisticated webcam. Nabil's screensaver was a lunar landscape of rocks and crevices that looked as uninhabitable as what Dan imagined his private life to have been, surrounded by two brothers who loved him but who could not understand him.

He touched the mouse and the rocks vanished, replaced by an orderly desktop. A folder with the wishful-sounding title *Maybe I Can Have It All* yielded a sub-folder labelled *Dreams*. Inside that were three JPEGs. The first was of a mansion in a tropical setting, the second a bright red Ferrari, and the third a cool blue yacht. *We all have to start somewhere*, Dan thought with a smile.

A folder labelled *Family* contained shots of a variety of domestic gatherings, with dozens of photos of Nabil and his brothers in an impressive garden, as well as an older couple Dan assumed were their parents. There was nothing out of the ordinary, just picture after picture of a shy-looking boy with a repressed vivacity, like a child who wanted to shout and be exuberant but had been taught to restrain himself at all costs. Even his school photograph showed a young man not entirely comfortable with himself, as though he'd learned to be fearful of revealing what lay beneath the surface in front of a camera.

It was the sub-grouping *Skin* that caught Dan's eye. Inside were shots of Nabil in leather gear. Hundreds, if not thousands of screen-capture images. The webcam. But here was a very different Nabil, at odds with the other photos. Arm bands framed his biceps, the skin oiled to a burnished chestnut. A studded vest curtained his chest, a coy invitation to follow the dark trail leading down to his slit of a navel, like a vaudeville muscleman. His hair had been styled and groomed into a jutting wave over his forehead. And around his neck, the ta'wiz. Here the drab wren turned into strutting peacock, the shy boy transformed into a crown prince of the erotic, fully in command of his world.

In the only nude, Nabil sat facing the camera, knees raised and hands clutching his feet, his genitals hidden behind muscular forearms. It was sexy and innocent, manly and boyish, at the same time. He looked assured — poised and balanced. Dan wondered who had taken the shot. Someone Nabil trusted, obviously. Possibly even someone who loved him.

He closed the folder and opened a daily calendar. Nabil had scheduled his daily gym sessions at the Y at varying times. And there was Prabin's phone number next to one of the entries, as the brothers had claimed. Nabil had also blocked off time in regular afternoon shifts. Dan considered their titles: *brownboy.com* and *iposeforyou.ca*. Prabin had said Nabil was a start-up business operator with his fingers in a number of pies, but they hadn't actually discussed his work. Dan was beginning to get an idea of the nature of Nabil's business ventures.

A cursory glance at both addresses showed they were pay-for-play sex sites. Soft porn, but still pricey, by the looks of it. There were always people willing to pay for a glimpse of a beautiful body.

The calendar contained personal notes as well. In March, he'd written: *Attended Almusawa, gay Muslim prayer group. Met H. Lots of us there, men and women praying together.*

The location changes from week to week. Of course, we are all risking our lives by being here. A few days later, he wrote: *H offered to help me with web services. Really knows his stuff! He helped me create sites for brownboy and iposeforyou.*

A month later, he wrote: *Went to Almusawa again. Very closeted bunch. I don't want to live like that. H asked me to stay after the meeting. Said we needed to get to know one another better now that the sites are operational. When everyone was gone, he came on to me. I turned him down and he became condescending. "After all I've done for you,"* he said. *I should have known there was a catch. What if he tries to blackmail me? Then again, I now know a few things about him. I could do as much damage to him as he could to me. Changed my password on the sites just to be sure.*

Dan skipped down. In May, Nabil had written: *Met S. I sent him flowers. He said he'd never received flowers before. A romantic nature.* And then a week later: *S very engaging tonight. Likes to get rough. Not what I was expecting. Called me his puppet. Said I was his toy and his plaything. Quite a conceited little ass under the skin.* And again: *I told S about my websites. He wasn't shocked at all. In fact, the next time we met he asked me to make a video for some guys he knows! I said I'd think about it just to intrigue him, but I'd never do it. Would I? Told me he has visa issues. I said I'd help him look into it.*

There were further entries with the Y and hours for the sites blocked off more frequently. *Must be a booming business,* Dan thought. Then: *H has been stalking me, showing up at the Y. It's as if he knows when I'll arrive.*

Not long after, Nabil wrote: *S not everything I thought he was. Very manipulative. I called him my string-puller and he laughed. It's my first real relationship, apart from R, who dropped me as soon as I got serious. I should have seen that one coming, but I am still naive. There is much to be learned about my new life in Canada.*

Dan turned to the beginning of the calendar, started five years earlier. The first entry read: *How can I continue this balancing act, half-Canadian and half-Muslim? Or am I just a fraud on both fronts? Do I resent Canadians for being blind to what goes on in the world? I flirted with that idea for a while, then turned my back on it. When I lived in Oman I did not know much of what went on in Canada. And moving here saved me from a disastrous marriage. Got out just in time! Speaking of balancing acts. How would I ever have pulled that one off? Yet lots of men do every day, even here in Canada.*

The entries spoke of an identity crisis writ large.

Dan turned back to the photographs. He found a selfie, taken with an upraised arm. In the background, slightly out of focus, a row of puppets dangled from a wire rack. He suddenly thought of Terence, the actor. One of his three Mr. Rights had been a puppet maker.

He snapped a picture of the photo with his phone and downloaded the calendar onto a USB stick. Turning, he saw a card tucked under the webcam: Hanani Sheikh — Sheikh IT! Designs.

H.

He put it in his pocket.

The brothers were seated in the same place when he came out of Nabil's room.

"Thanks for the look," Dan said. "It was helpful. I've got some leads for now, but there was too much data to go through. At some point, I'd like to come back and take the computer with me."

Amir consulted with Mustafa in Arabic then turned back to Dan. "My brother says there are tax records and personal papers on the computer that should not leave the house. We will copy these first and then you may remove it."

"Thank you." Dan waited. "Did Nabil ever mention someone who collected or made puppets?"

The brothers exchanged looks and shook their heads at the same time.

"No."

"How about someone name Hanani Sheikh? He might have been helping Nabil with his websites."

Again, the response was negative.

"Do you know how your brother made his money? What his businesses entailed?"

"Yes, he was tutoring university students," Amir said. "He seemed to do very well at it. Nabil's English is much better than ours."

The response seemed genuine.

"You said there were other times when Nabil did not come home overnight, but that he returned by morning. Is this correct?"

"Yes, once or twice he said he fell asleep at a party. That was most unlike him. He is, how do you say, a vigilant person. He does not let his guard down easily."

"I understand," Dan said. "Can you think of any other time when he stayed away longer than a single night?"

Amir took a deep breath, averting his gaze for a moment.

"I assure you it's always better if I know the truth," Dan said. "No matter how bad or embarrassing."

"There was one other time," Mustafa broke in. "Not in Canada, but back in Oman. Our parents arranged a marriage for Nabil when he was twenty-four years old. They thought he was old enough to be a man and that he was putting off the inevitable."

"They found a wife for him?" The *disastrous marriage* he'd written of.

"Yes. When they informed him of this, he ran away from home for a week. Only my brother and I knew where he had gone."

"Where did he go?"

"He went to stay at the home of our cousin Waseem."

"But he came back?"

"Yes," Mustafa said. "He came back because we had the letter of approval to emigrate to Canada. I went to inform him of this. Soon after, the marriage promise was annulled by our family."

"How did your parents feel about it?"

Amir shrugged. "They were ashamed of him for breaking the family's promise, but on the other hand they thought he would find a better wife in Canada."

"Wasn't it odd that they were trying to marry Nabil before you? You are the elder brother, are you not?"

Amir nodded. "I am the elder brother. And I am married. My wife is back in Oman, where I have two sons. One day, when I have enough money, I will bring them to Canada."

Five minutes later, Dan was sitting in his car. He had Terence on the phone.

"Dan! I meant to call you, but you beat me to it. How are things?"

"You first."

"Okay, I wanted to tell you that you're my good-luck charm."

"How so?"

"I got the part from the audition I went to right after meeting you. The said they loved my energy and my joyful disposition. I didn't tell them that it was because of the hot guy I had just met and that my normal disposition is gloomy."

"Somehow, I doubt that's true, but thanks for the compliment."

"So, yeah. That's all good. Unfortunately ..."

"Uh-oh."

"Yeah, big uh-oh. It's a TV series about Napoleon. It's being shot in France. I leave for four months starting next week."

"Oh, well, that's ..."

"Yeah. Not good for dating."

"So, I guess I'll see you next spring."

"Something like that. You know what they say. Chance of a lifetime and all that. Gotta take it when the taking's good. Sorry about the timing. I'm a slave to the powers that be. Now you. What's going on?"

"I'm on the trail of someone I thought you might be able to shed some light on."

"Me? Seriously? You think I can help you?"

"Possibly. You said you dated a puppet maker who disappeared."

Terence's voice was suddenly serious. "That's right. We had plans, but he disappeared. I never saw him again."

"What did you say his name was?"

"Sam."

S.

"Just Sam?"

"I never knew his last name. As I said, he was closeted. But he was very sweet, quite a simple soul. Exquisite manners."

"I've got what looks like a selfie in a room with puppets hanging in the background. I wondered if you could identify the place from the photograph."

"I could try."

"Hang on. I'll send it to you."

A moment later, Terence said, "It's his apartment, all right. How ... I mean ... who gave you this?"

"It was taken by a guy named Nabil who's gone missing. I was hired by his brothers to find him. He's gay, but closeted. I found this on his computer."

"Incredible." He seemed to be mulling this over. "So maybe the guy I was seeing was seeing someone else. I always thought that might have been why he never called back."

"When did you date him?"

"Last winter. It ended sometime in January when he disappeared."

"Interesting. This guy seemed to have dated him far more recently."

"He must have returned without telling me. But in that case his visa would have expired."

"Was he associated with the leather community by any chance?"

"Not that he mentioned. Are you sure it's the same guy?"

"Pretty sure. My client called him *S*. Said he had visa issues, just like your guy. How long did you and Sam date?"

"Oh, not long. A month, maybe?"

Dan gave a low laugh. "Maybe that's why he was Mr. Perfect. You never got the chance to know him in depth."

"Yeah. Maybe." Terence sounded sheepish.

EIGHT

Under Pressure

DAN ARRIVED AT DONNY AND Prabin's building at eight. A blast of cold air and snow blew in behind him as he entered. He stamped his feet and pressed the intercom. After a moment, he was buzzed in by an authoritarian snap of the lock. The sounds of the city receded as he passed through into the lobby's soft hush.

It didn't last. Behind him, a diminutive figure grabbed the door and raced inside. If he hadn't seen the wrinkled face and stubbly chin, Dan might have mistaken him for a teenager. He was dressed in a track suit that looked as though it hadn't been washed for some time. Dan got a whiff of something pungent as the man sped past.

The concierge looked up from behind a large desk, clocking the two of them together. "Hold on there."

Dan stopped and turned. The old man kept going toward the elevators, a force of nature humming a strange little ditty and staring brightly ahead as though he inhabited another dimension.

"You! Stop!"

The concierge practically vaulted himself over the counter to head off the intruder, who had begun pressing all the elevator buttons.

"Who are you visiting?" the concierge demanded.

The little man looked up at the tall figure bearing down on him and let out a scream, batting his head with his hands as though warding off a swarm of bees.

The elevator dinged. Before the gold-trimmed doors could open, however, the concierge grabbed the man by the arm and dragged him across the lobby, his captive screaming all the way.

"You're hurting him," Dan said loudly.

The concierge had by now assumed full-commando mode. "Mind your business!"

Dan pulled out his cell and dialed Donny's number, letting him know the situation.

Once he had forcibly evicted the intruder, the concierge returned to the lobby. He looked surprised to see Dan still there. "What's your business here?"

"I'm visiting friends. I was buzzed in. You were hurting that man."

His eyes narrowed. "That's your fault. You let that skanky bastard in."

"I didn't let the gentleman in. He came in behind me."

Just then the elevator doors opened and Donny came striding toward them. He took in Dan then looked over to the concierge. "What's going on?"

The concierge indicated Dan with a nod. "Is this your guest?"

"Yes."

"Your guest let in an undesirable. For the record."

"My guest is a private investigator. He's also a friend of the chief of police. For the record."

The man seemed to shrink a little at the words. "Make sure he behaves or I'll have to report you both."

Dan watched as Donny walked up to the concierge and stared him down, six inches from his face.

"This is my home. You are an employee here. If I can have you fired for your rudeness, I will."

There was a second when it could have gone either way, the concierge backing down or pushing forward, but just then the desk phone rang. He fumbled the receiver from its base and answered. His eyes flitted away from the two men, who seemed to have been dismissed or at least conveniently forgotten.

Dan silently followed Donny to the elevator and waited till the doors closed on them. "Nice point that, about the chief."

"Well, it's true. Sort of. Isn't it?"

"Calling him a 'friend' might be stretching it."

"Anyway, you know him."

"That at least is correct. And in case you're wondering, the guard was at fault. I thought he needed to be put in his place."

Donny gave him a sidelong glance. "I wasn't wondering. I know you. It's just that where others see a scrawny security guard flexing his muscles, you see the Four Horsemen of the Apocalypse. Do I even want to know what happened?"

"Apparently I let in an undesirable. I didn't mean to. He ran around until he got thrown out. End of story."

Donny took this in for a moment. "Is it possible you have a problem with authority figures?"

"Undoubtedly. But that's not really the issue. He was hurting that poor old man, who was obviously not in his right mind. He could have got rid of him without the strong-arm stuff."

"I'm just glad it wasn't Raúl."

"Raúl?"

"A very sexy Dominicano. This asshole is a homophobe. I saw him snickering at some old queen last week. I told him to wipe the grin off his face or I'd report him. He's been looking for a chance to bust my balls ever since, one black man to another."

"Sorry I gave it to him on a platter."

Donny cracked his knuckles and flexed his shoulders. "I'm kind of glad you did. Now I can happily go after him the next time he does anything."

The elevator doors opened onto a ghostly corridor that always reminded Dan of a mausoleum. Such were the realities of modern urban living.

Inside the condo was a different story. Expressionist art dominated, colourful, wild. A sultry jazz beat plied the airwaves. Prabin sat next to Domingo on the same leather couch they'd sat on after the memorial. The sky was clear, offering a backdrop overlooking the city's east end. In the distance, cars raced along the expressway with the harbour unfurling beyond. For a moment no one stirred in this still life with human figures.

Martini glasses sat perched on a Lucite coffee table, empty out of respect for Dan, who had stopped drinking abruptly several years earlier, leaving behind a blurred past of excess and self-abuse. The reformation had been at Kedrick's insistence, but with Donny's whole-hearted endorsement.

"Danny has been playing superhero in our lobby," Donny announced.

"Again?" It was Prabin who spoke. "The last time he visited, I swear I saw him fly across the room."

"He can't help it," Domingo said. "Wherever he goes, trouble follows. We just have to forgive him."

Donny brought out a tray of cheese and cured meats and set it on the coffee table. "I'm still trying to get over the last time, when he ordered the pool evacuated after some rowdy three-year-old used it as a toilet."

"That wasn't my fault," Dan protested.

"It never is. Things just seem to go a little bit crazy whenever you're around." He waved it all away with one hand. "What are you drinking? We've got San Pellegrino and every exotic juice you can think of — guava, mango, tamarind."

"Just coffee, please."

"That's boring."

"What can I say? I'm a boring guy."

"Hardly. As I never tire of telling people, my friend Danny is white but only on the outside."

Domingo whooped. "You got that right!"

Donny went back to the kitchen then returned, setting a steaming cup of coffee on the table. He clapped his hands. "All right, everyone. I call this meeting to order. We are convened to look into the matter of missing and murdered men from Toronto's gay ghetto. What do we know so far? Who wants to start?"

Prabin looked up. "I'll start. In the last year, at least two men have been declared missing and a third murdered. The first, a guy named Joe, was last seen by his friend Wendell on April fourth at Zipperz on Carlton Street. It was Wendell who distributed the posters around the neighbourhood. I called Wendell and made inquiries. He told me they had a dinner date the next night, but Joe never showed up."

Dan looked over. "Did you ask him Joe's last name? It might help me track more information."

Prabin shook his head. "I asked, but Wendell didn't know. He's new to the city and they'd only been friends for a couple of months. Apparently, Joe had lived here for about ten years. He had various jobs during that time, but was unemployed when he disappeared. Since then, there's been no word from him. Wendell is convinced something bad happened to him, but he has nothing to go on. He said I was the only one who called about the poster."

"Did he go to the police?"

"He dropped in at the station to report him missing, but as soon as he told them Joe was gay they dismissed him, saying he was probably on a weekend drug binge and would show up soon."

"Did Wendell mention drug use?" Dan asked.

Prabin nodded. "Wendell said Joe took recreational drugs, mostly light stuff, but it didn't seem to be an everyday habit. He never talked about dealers or scoring for the weekend or anything like that. He did say he thought Joe used steroids when working out, but whether that was excessive or minimal, he didn't know."

"Okay, good. Continue, please."

Prabin nodded and looked around at the others. "The second was a guy named Adam Carnivale, who worked as a stripper at Remington's. He disappeared sometime in the summer. We don't know much about him, including who put up the posters. I called the number, but it was disconnected. Last week, as we know, Randy Melchior was stabbed to death in a back lane off George Street. His body was dumped in an empty parking lot. So far no one has been charged. Then two days ago I was contacted by the brothers of Nabil Ahmad. Nabil and I are gym buddies. The brothers said Nabil hadn't been home since Friday evening. I asked about Nabil at the YMCA, but they wouldn't give out information about him. Instead, I confirmed with some gym mates who remember seeing him on Friday, the day his brothers said he disappeared. No one seems to recall seeing him after that."

"And as far as you know, Nabil wasn't into recreational drugs?"

"He never mentioned them to me, and he doesn't seem the type as far as I know him."

"What about steroids?"

Prabin shook his head. "He used to point out the steroid users at the Y. He was very critical of them and said they led to heart problems and mood disorders. He even dissuaded one of the young guys who go to the Y not to try them."

"Great work," Dan said. "Especially the YMCA check. If he was there Friday but not afterward then he likely disappeared from the neighbourhood as well."

"So, there are four men either missing or murdered," Domingo said softly.

"Possibly five," Dan corrected. "Your friend Terence Hardy, the actor, was seeing someone named Sam who vanished recently, leaving behind a furnished apartment and no forwarding address."

"Why only possibly?" Donny asked.

Dan smiled at his friend's perspicacity. "Because on Nabil Ahmad's computer calendar, he refers to someone he was dating recently as S. I think S is Sam." He pulled out his cellphone and passed it around. "I found this selfie of Nabil on his computer. There are puppets in the background. Terence confirmed it's Sam's apartment."

"Did any of the others know each other?" Domingo asked.

"In this little ghetto of ours, that's entirely possible," Donny said. He turned to Prabin. "You were friends with both Randy and Nabil. Did they know one another?"

"Not that I know of, but I wouldn't rule it out. Randy went to the Y, too, but not as obsessively as Nabil. Randy was more of a weekend guy. The other two, Adam and Joe, I know nothing about. And this is the first time I've heard of Sam."

"Here's a third possible commonality," Dan said. "They may all be associated with the leather community. Both Nabil and Joe were confirmed as part of the leather community by a friend of mine. Possibly Adam as well. I don't know about either Randy or Sam."

Prabin's brows contracted. "Randy wasn't into leather back in university, but people change. To be honest, though, I highly doubt it. He was about as preppie as they come. And those two crowds don't usually overlap, from what I know."

"Would you be comfortable asking his husband to confirm that?"

"Absolutely. I want to offer Nathan my condolences in person, so I'll find a way to bring it up."

Dan cocked his head. "Ask him about the Mr. Leatherman contest. Apparently Nabil is entered to compete in it."

"Really?" Prabin said. "I'm surprised to hear that."

"Then you might also be surprised to know that he makes money online posing on two soft porn websites." Prabin started to speak; Dan stopped him. "That's confidential, of course. It doesn't leave this room, but I think it may be relevant."

"I guess I don't really know this guy at all," Prabin said.

"Clearly, he isn't as closeted as you thought."

"True," Prabin concurred. "But there's closeted to your family and then there's closeted to everyone else. When you're from a minority culture the pressure to conform is huge. We're taught to hide our differences, not parade them."

"Back in the islands, you don't dare come out at all," Domingo said. "On my street we grew up with a girly-boy named Jimmy. We all knew he was different, but we just accepted it. As he got older, though, he became more defiant about his sexuality. He was clubbed to death at a party when he was eighteen."

"That's why we're all in Canada, isn't it?" Donny asked. "Compared to back home, this is Disneyland."

"You learn early not to rely on your family to protect you," Domingo continued. "I thought my brother would protect me from these things, but he didn't."

Dan turned to her. "In all the years I've known you, I've never heard you talk about a brother," he said.

"That's because I don't. So please don't ask."

Her expression made it clear that the subject was closed.

"The pressure to have kids is strong in the Indian community as well," Prabin added. "We're all taught to honour

our parents, and that means producing grandchildren for them. No matter who or what you are, family comes first. It's a sense of duty that gets ingrained in you from a very early age."

"That fits with what I learned about Nabil," Dan said. "My feeling is he was straddling two worlds and having a hard time doing it. According to his brothers, he disappeared once before back home in Oman when faced with an arranged marriage. That's why I wondered if he might find it easier to bolt from his life with his brothers than confront them."

Prabin nodded. "It's possible. Usually, with guys like Nabil, the brainwashing is so thorough it never really lets go. But I've met others who rejected everything about their former existence, completely detaching from their families. There's no halfway. It's all or nothing at all."

"For now, we'll assume Nabil didn't run away," Dan said. "Though I note that at least three of these men were immigrants. Which makes me wonder: what did these men *not* have in common?"

"Their socio-economic statuses," Prabin said. "Randy was a highly paid doctor and cancer researcher. Nabil referred to himself as a self-made entrepreneur, though now we know what that means. As you said, Adam was a stripper, and Wendell said Joe was unemployed at the time he disappeared."

"And Sam, apparently, was a puppet maker. Freelance artists don't make much money. What else?"

"Their ethnicity," Domingo said. "Randy was white Anglo-Saxon. Nabil is Middle Eastern. What about the others?"

"Hard to say," Prabin replied. "From the poster, Joe looks Italian or Portuguese. Joe's a common-enough name with either of those communities. Adam might be Greek, judging by his picture."

"I suggest we narrow it down to a probable Mediterranean background and leave it at that," Dan said. "Their body types varied greatly too. Joe and Nabil are bigger guys, weightlifters. Adam was a dancer with a great build. Randy seems to have been small and boyish with an average build. I don't know about Sam."

"Which tells us what?" Donny asked, eyeing the balcony for a potential cigarette break.

"It tells us that if the perpetrator is one and the same person then he doesn't have a specific type he targets."

"Is that odd?" Domingo asked.

"Some would say yes," Dan replied. "Gay men often have very specific types. Though we're assuming it's someone gay doing this."

"But murder is madness," Donny blurted out. "Does it have to make sense?"

"Even madness has its logic. My guess is what it really tells us is that there isn't just one perpetrator. This especially makes sense in light of the fact that we're looking at three or four disappearances, but only one confirmed murder. If they were all abducted and killed by the same person, why weren't their bodies dumped somewhere, too?"

"Maybe the killer was surprised in the act of killing Randy and didn't have a choice," Donny said. "In that case we can't know anything for sure until more bodies turn up."

Prabin winced.

"Sorry," Donny said, turning to him. "I sincerely hope they don't."

Domingo turned to Dan. "What do we do from here?"

"We're all connected with the community in some way. Sometimes the best thing is just to ask questions of anyone you know who might have heard something. The Mr. Leatherman contest is coming up. I'm going to be there. I'll also visit Remington's to ask about Adam. In the meantime, I'd like Prabin to follow up with Randy's husband to rule out any possible connection with the leather community."

Prabin nodded. "I'll contact Nathan right after this meeting."

"Good. Show him Nabil's photo and ask if he recognizes him from around the neighbourhood. Try to push Wendell for more information about Joe, too. In the time he knew him, he must have learned something about where he comes from, his cultural background, anything like that."

"Will do."

"Is there any other unfinished business?" Dan asked, looking around.

"Yes." Domingo smiled. "Is it too pushy to ask how your date went last week?"

"Date?" Donny cupped his ears with his hands and leaned in. "What date?"

Dan smiled. "My date with Domingo's friend Terence. And yes, it is pushy, but since you were behind it I will tell you that Terence is a very nice guy who will make someone a good husband one day."

"But not you?"

"Sadly, no. He just got a part in a TV series shooting in France. Neither of us is interested in doing the long-distance thing."

"But still a man of substance, would you say?"

"Definitely. I liked him immediately."

"So, I must be close to the mark. I've got a few others in mind if the first batch doesn't pan out."

Donny leaned back, arms crossed, and regarded his best friend. "Really. Has it come to this? You need an introduction? Why don't you just do it the old-fashioned way and slut around?"

"Not my style."

"No, it isn't, is it?" He made a face. "It's your Scottish heritage. There's always a whiff of the Presbytery whenever you enter the room."

"Don't pick on Danny. He's a nice boy," Domingo defended.

"I'm far too complicated to be nice," Dan growled.

Donny and Prabin rolled their eyes.

NINE

The Rose

THE NAKED YOUNG MAN HOLDING the red rose over his genitals seemed not to mind that he was on display on one of the city's busiest streets. Nor did he mind the afternoon's cold, with its occasional snowflake drifting past his steady gaze, his eyes focused on you, his intended target. *But only because he can't feel it,* Dan thought, as he strode past the larger-than-life poster and pulled open the doors of Remington's.

Inside, a skinny young man looked up from where he was bent over a pail, wringing out a mop. He was nowhere near as attractive as his outdoor colleague, a mane of shaggy hair framing a zit-spotted face beneath his baseball cap. Underpaid, minimum wage at best. Dan was reminded of himself at eighteen, a small-town boy escaping to the big city only to discover it was a lot harder to make things work there than it had been back home.

"Sorry, we're not open. The show's not for another hour," the boy announced softly with a look that said he hoped

Dan would turn and march back outside.

"I'm not here for the show," Dan said, pulling up a bar stool.

The young man stood, wiping his hands on his jeans. "I can't serve you a drink. The bartender's not here yet."

Dan pulled out his investigator's licence and placed a fifty-dollar bill on the counter, keeping his palm on it. "You can spare me the drink. What I'd really like is a chat."

The boy looked around nervously. "What about?"

"Adam Carnivale. He was a dancer here."

"Adam?" He eyed the bill. "I don't really know anything about him."

"But you knew him?"

"Sure. He was one of the best dancers in the place, till he disappeared."

"Was Adam his real name?"

"Uh ... we don't really ask the dancers their real names. It's not considered proper, you know?"

"Okay, so now I know Adam wasn't his real name. You see? You do know things."

"Sure, but —"

"So, if the dancers aren't known by their real names, is it fair to assume they aren't paid employees of the club?"

"Employees?"

"You, for instance. Do you get a weekly paycheque?"

The boy was looking more nervous by the second. "No, I get paid cash."

"So presumably you're not on a payroll somewhere. What's your name?"

"My name?"

"You do have a name, don't you?"

"Of course." The boy grinned. "Everybody has a name."

"But some people's names are proper and other's aren't."

"Yeah, it's kinda like that."

Dan held out his hand. "My name's Dan. What's yours?"

"Uh … it's Corby."

"Okay, Corby, here's the deal. I'm investigating the disappearance of Adam Carnivale, but I'm having trouble finding out about him because I don't know his real name. So how would I go about finding it out?"

Corby looked perplexed. "You can't. They don't allow it."

"So, no real name, no paycheque? They dance for tips, is that it?"

Corby nodded nervously. "Right. And, um, private dances."

"In the back rooms."

Corby glanced up at the ceiling. "Yeah, I guess."

"So, who doesn't allow them to use their real names?"

"The, uh, manager? He brings these guys in, but most of the time we don't even know who they are or where they're from. Some of them barely even speak English."

"What about Adam? Did he speak English?"

"I don't … uh, not really."

"If you were to guess, where do you think he might have been from?"

The boy wiped his hand across his forehead, leaving a smear of dirt. "Oh, gosh. I don't know. He had an accent. Maybe Russian or something, but I really couldn't say for sure. He and the manager used to speak the same language together."

Dan was inclined to believe the boy, if only because he looked too nervous not to be telling the truth.

"Okay, Corby. Now here's the prize-winning question. What is the name of the manager who brings in the talent? Does he have a real name?"

Corby grinned again, as though Dan were a stand-up comedian. "Sure, he's got a real name."

Dan waited a moment longer. Clearly, Corby did not have enough smarts to pick up his cues. "And his name is?"

"Zoltan."

"Zoltan who?"

"Zoltan Mirovic."

Serb, Dan thought, keeping his hand on the bill. To this boy, it might sound as if they were speaking Russian. "How do I know you're telling me the truth?"

Corby whirled around and grabbed something from a small container on the far side of the bar. He presented it to Dan with a satisfied smile. "That's how."

The card had a photo of the naked boy holding the rose on one side and the name *Zoltan Mirovic* with a website address below.

Dan pocketed the card and lifted his hand from the bill. "You win."

An hour later, back in his office, Dan turned on his computer and typed in Zoltan Mirovic's website. It showed the same boy on the poster outside the club, only this time the rose was slowly revolving. Fancy.

The large-print warning told him it was an elite members-only site. He was prompted to put in a credit card number with the assurance he would not be charged until after he had reviewed and agreed to the membership rules.

He made up a series of numbers and entered them. The rose grew and spun as the site considered his offering, finally rejecting the numbers with a flashing ERROR sign.

Dan was about to press cancel when he noticed a logo at the bottom of the page: Sheikh IT! Designs. Intriguing.

He inserted the USB stick with Nabil's calendar and downloaded it, going through the diary entries more thoroughly this time. There was a note about wanting to enter the leather contest. Here he mentioned the mysterious *R* again, saying he knew they would eventually run into one another, but that he would face that when the time came. So *R* was a leatherman, too.

From the calendar, Dan gathered that Nabil had had an on-and-off relationship with Sam from May through September. But what had started out with hope seemed to have gone sour. *I feel used.* S *plays me like a puppet*, Nabil had written. *No wonder, if he was a puppet maker*, Dan thought. At another point, he'd written: S *keeps pushing me to help him with his visa, but when I tell him these things take time he gets angry. I made the mistake of telling him I know where to go, but I just don't want to. I need to end this before it goes any further.*

Similarly, his feelings fluctuated with Hanani Sheikh, who at first designed websites for him then proceeded to stalk him when Nabil did not return his affection, though there was no further mention of the blackmail threat he'd feared.

Sam's name popped up again a few weeks before Nabil's disappearance; he'd reached out to Nabil for help with his visa again. S *said I was his last hope. Humbled myself and asked* H, Nabil had written. The follow-up had been brief: H *furious I asked by email. Told me never to contact him again.*

TEN

The Popular Choice

Dan looked up at the facade. The marquee read: TONIGHT — MR. LEATHERMAN TORONTO! He had spent many hours in this bar as a lonely young man, but almost none since becoming a father. Back then, when he was fuelled by alcohol and a newfound sense of optimism, the place had seemed to contain a world of amusement and good times. Now it was just another drab watering hole on the outside and a cheerless cavern on the inside.

Downstairs, a line of solitary figures stared at their reflections in the mirror behind the bar. These were the men who had long since given up the fight, knowing the world was a terrible place and only liquor could save them, finding their salvation at the bottom of a bottle. *All hail drink, our saviour and redeemer!*

Dan bypassed them and headed upstairs, where it took a moment to recognize the sweet, musky odour. *You know a leather bar is real when you can smell the rawhide*, Donny once told him.

The place was packed. He watched as several contestants arrived, discarding bulky winter wear to reveal the many variations on leather gear. The skin beneath that bound its wearers together. Here, the mood was cheerful, the camaraderie high. He'd be hard-pressed to find a murderous intent in this group, at least tonight.

Across the room, Woody raised his eyes from a video camera set atop a tripod. His face lit up. "Dan, my man! Thrilled you could make it!"

Dan took in his tapered black curves and heightened masculinity. The sleek sheen of animal pelt. He felt the same rush of infatuation he'd experienced on their first meeting. "You look great, Woody."

"Me? Just look at you! You could win this contest hands down."

"Not my scene, but thanks."

"Most of the guys are here," Woody said. "Not Nabil. Sorry."

"That's okay. I wasn't really expecting him to show."

"Grab a pint, why don't you? I'm almost set up. We're opening in five."

"I'm mostly a ginger ale man these days, but I'll get something. Anything for you?"

"Nah, I'm good, thanks."

A burst of raucous laughter erupted from the far end of the room. Heads turned to where half a dozen men were gathered around a diminutive figure. Dan was surprised to see Domingo's friend, Edie Foxe, at their centre. She wore a peaked cap and carried a riding crop, and was swatting playfully at several of the men. She wasn't the only woman at the event. Over in a corner, someone's plump grand-mother adjusted her leather skirt, while a third would have made a stand-in for rocker Joan Jett.

Dan had just taken a seat near the back when the lights dimmed. The audience applauded as the judges assembled to one side of the stage.

Woody waited till they were seated then grasped the microphone. "Welcome to the twenty-fifth annual Mr. Leatherman Toronto contest. I'm Woody Whitman, a former Mr. Leatherman winner. Tonight, we've got some great contenders for the title. Your applause may sway the opinions of the judges, so when I ask you to clap for each of the contestants, make sure they can hear you! The winner goes on to represent Toronto in the International Mr. Leatherman contest in Chicago, so let's send them our very best! Now let's bring out our guys."

The contestants marched on stage and lined up at the front. They ranged from fresh-faced striplings to older men with impressive musculature. But not one, Dan thought, would have rivalled the absent Nabil Ahmad for sheer physical presence.

With their sharp-brimmed caps and calf-length boots, they might have been an advance guard from the Third Reich or a squadron of Hells Angels. Some of the gear served no purpose other than to showcase the flesh on display. Straps to lift and divide, pouches to cup and square, thrusting everything forward. Clad only in his navy T-shirt and jeans, Dan felt like a pretender who'd broken uniform code among all those heavy-duty guys in their skins and gleaming studs.

Music swelled and spotlights narrowed as Woody announced the show's kick-off, "Pecs and Personality." *And who said leathermen don't have a sense of humour?* Dan mused. The crowd cheered as the half-dressed beauties preened and pranced like show ponies, stripping off their gear and striking their poses, while Woody's camera lovingly followed them around the stage. Despite the overt sexuality, the antics were as harmless as a Bettie Paige summer wear pin-up.

As the evening progressed, a youngster with black hair and slashing blue eyes caught the audience's attention, a thrill rippling through the crowd each time he stepped on stage. For once, however, age wasn't an issue. Some of the contestants were in their forties and fifties — leather-daddies who knew the routine. One man looked to be in his late sixties. He was a silver-haired monolith with a physique many younger men would envy. Another was a rawhide Quasimodo. His muscles bulged grotesquely, his veins taut beneath his skin, the flesh on his face twisted into rivulets. *Steroids,* Dan thought, recalling what Prabin had said about Nabil's pronouncements on performance-enhancing drugs.

During a break, Dan worked his way around the room, chatting up his fellow onlookers, flashing photos and asking whether they knew either Nabil or Joe. A trio of bystanders recalled Joe from the poster, but no one claimed to have known him well or intimately.

"These men are missing from the community," he offered before anyone could wonder why he was asking. "The police don't seem interested, so I'm looking into it. I'm a private investigator. I'm also gay."

"And incredibly sexy," one of the men offered to his face. "You should be up on stage with the others."

"Thanks," Dan said, tucking the photos back in his wallet, "but not for me."

The lights dimmed and the show resumed with a change of costume and another round of flexing. Speeches followed. Some of the topics were political, others personal. The older man told of having been rounded up in the infamous bathhouse raids of 1981, describing how men's wrists had been marked with indelible ink in a fashion eerily reminiscent of the treatment of Holocaust prisoners.

Woody returned to the microphone.

"You've seen our fab contestants. While the judges are tallying their marks, I want you to take a look around the audience. This is your chance to nominate anyone who isn't on stage. Let us know if you see someone you think should be up here."

Three men raised their hands. The first pointed to a youth on the far side of the room. He'd come dressed in full leather regalia, like a hopeful understudy waiting to play the part of a lifetime. Two others pointed at Dan.

"Over here!" one of them cried. "This one's a winner!"

"Let's bring them up," Woody said.

The youngster was only too happy to oblige, bounding on stage to enjoy his moment of celebrity.

Dan protested, but Woody smiled and shook his head. "We might have to get physical if you don't come willingly."

Three men hoisted him onto their shoulders and carried him up, depositing him in front of the crowd.

Woody turned to the men who'd brought him up. "Uh, guys — I think you forgot something. You know the rules. All contestants must wear some form of leather." He stripped off his vest and tossed it to them.

The crowd cheered as two of them wrestled Dan's T-shirt over his head and the third helped him don the vest.

Woody nodded approvingly. "I think we would very much like to see these guys here next year for real. Am I right?"

The cheering was raucous. Dan couldn't wait to escape.

The contest resumed and the elimination began. They were soon down to the finalists. Dan wasn't surprised to see the pretty, blue-eyed boy standing alongside the older man and a redhead with an impressive physique. The boy was declared second runner-up. The crowd grew silent. Woody announced the judges' choice — the older man was going on to the finals. The music swelled as the audience headed for the stage to congratulate the winners.

A commotion caught Dan's ears behind him. He turned and saw Edie Foxe fending off a drunken audience member. "Keep your hands off!" she commanded, slashing with her riding crop.

The offending drunk seemed not to have felt its bite. "C'mon — show us your tits. I know you're a guy!"

Three strikes across his face and he stumbled backward, fending off further blows with his hands. Edie stood before them, crop raised. "Anybody else?" she demanded.

"Edie, relax. He was only joking," said one of the men watching.

"Fuck you!" she said, and stormed off, shoving people aside as she went.

Not such an adolescent boy now, Dan thought.

A moment later he found himself face to face with Woody.

"Dan my man! How'd you enjoy it?"

"Great show. I especially enjoyed the visuals." He started to peel off the vest, but Woody stopped him.

"Keep it for now. It looks good on you. I'll call for it another time. I wanted you to meet this guy." He held out a hand to draw someone near. "Lucian, meet Dan. Dan's a private investigator. He wants to ask you about Joe."

It was the steroid queen, Dan noted. There was a frenetic look to his eyes, a mis-wiring of the synapses. Up close, his massive pectorals looked freakish.

"You knew Joe?"

"Yeah, I did. We dated a few times. He was a super guy."

Dan noted the use of the past tense. "Any idea what happened to him? Where he might have gone?"

Lucian shrugged his massive shoulders, reminding Dan of the Incredible Hulk. "Nah. No one's seen him for a while."

"Is it possible he moved away without telling anyone?"

"Could be."

"Can you recall when you last saw him?"

"A year ago, maybe more. I've been living in the States for a while. He was gone by the time I got back."

"Do you happen to remember his last name?"

He rubbed his chin and appeared to be putting an effort into thinking. "Nah. We didn't really do last names."

"Was he into anything kinky?"

The man laughed. "He was a leatherman. We're all into something kinky!" Then he grew serious. "But — yeah. Guy was on a suicide mission. When it came to anything sexual, he didn't do 'safe.' It was like he wanted to die. I wasn't all that surprised to hear when he went missing. I thought maybe he met his match, if you know what I mean."

Dan bristled at the man's callousness, but he wanted to hear more. "Was he popular around the scene?"

Lucian smirked. "You could say that. He certainly got around. He did a porno once."

"He was a porn actor?"

"Yeah, a starring role and everything. Oh, yeah. Joe was popular."

"Anything else you can remember about him?"

"Yeah, there was this one other thing he had about being strangled. He'd put his hands around your neck when you were about to come, thinking it would give you a lift. The first time he did it to me, I freaked out and popped him on the nose. He never tried it again, though I kind of wished he had."

His cracking knuckles could be heard over the noise of the crowd.

ELEVEN

All That Stuff

DAN STUMBLED OUT OF BED and headed downstairs, thinking he was making enough noise to wake the dead. It was still dark outside, the daylight an hour away. This was a time that could yield some of his best thinking, or make him wish afterward that he'd slept in.

In the kitchen, Ralph looked up from his bed.

"It's early. Go back to sleep, Ralphie."

Ralph thumped his tail twice against the floor then laid his head back down. But his eyes stayed open so as not to miss anything.

Dan opened the fridge and peered inside. Sometimes, when Ked wasn't around, he had a Coke for breakfast. It was a habit he'd started when he stopped drinking. The first month had been hell. He sometimes downed four in a row to get the monster out of his mind, scraping his stomach raw in the process. Whatever it took to forget his cravings. *Then again, who said caffeine was any better,* he thought, turning on the coffee maker.

His need for self-flagellation only seemed to increase with age, the propensity for tolerating self-inflicted punishment growing stronger, though the methods might differ. Sometimes he wondered if that was why he couldn't forge a lasting relationship. Then he stopped himself and thought of Donny, Prabin, Domingo, and Ked's mother, Kendra. He could, it seemed, with the right sort of person. Tellingly, those relationships were more often than not with outsiders of some sort. Friends who understood otherness. He'd always felt like an outsider.

A text from Donny alerted him to a follow-up article on Randy Melchior's murder. CCTV footage had captured the doctor in a 7-Eleven just a block from where his body was found. Dan clicked on the link and watched a young man and woman enter the store moments after Randy. Randy made his purchase, a chocolate bar, then exited. The pair followed him out.

They'd been identified by an elderly woman as the couple who stole her purse at knifepoint in another part of town on the same day. The girl had stopped her to ask directions when the boy attacked her from behind. It seemed the duo was on a holdup spree, only in Randy's case it ended in murder.

A blurry image lifted from the footage showed the young suspects in close up. There was nothing especially memorable or remarkable about them. *Don't hardened criminals have nifty Facebook photos to use these days?* Dan wondered.

He recalled Domingo's prediction that the crime would prove to have been perpetrated by two people. She'd also predicted drugs were involved. Once again, she was bang on. According to the article the pair were drug addicts. In truth, he liked it when she was right, even if he didn't admit it.

The first time she'd helped him with a case, he'd been skeptical. The second time, he admitted it embarrassed him to ask for her assistance. "You're not the only PI who ever used a psychic to catch a criminal," she told him. "Or to run a government. William Lyon Mackenzie King used to hold seances to ask his dead mother's advice while he was prime minister."

Dan stared at her open-mouthed for so long she burst into laughter. "Nice to have a private senatorial committee on the other side," was all he could think to say.

His cell rang, interrupting his thoughts.

"So, what do you think?" Donny asked breathily.

"What do I think?" Dan repeated as he fumbled his coffee cup with one hand and juggled the phone with the other. "I think coffee should be given intravenously."

"I was referring to the story. Did you read it?"

"I read it. It looks highly unlikely that the people behind Randy's murder are the same people behind the disappearances." He took a sip. "But I didn't see anything saying those two were apprehended. Did you?"

"No. But at least they know now who they're looking for."

"Meanwhile, they're still out on the streets doing god knows what to other hapless victims. People have no idea how dangerous drug users have become. And it seems as though there are far more of them now than ever."

"But she was right."

Dan played dumb. "She?"

"Domingo!"

"Oh."

"She was right about what she said. She said it would be two people, one to distract and the other to attack. Drugs, too. She even got that right."

"Uh-huh."

Donny snorted. "You don't fool me. I know you secretly enjoy it when she's right. Have you followed up on your leathermen angle?"

"Yes, I did. I went to the contest last night."

"And?"

"I got crowned Mr. Wannabe Leatherman or some such."

"Are you kidding me?"

"Do I ever?"

"No, you're not really capable of it. You are the most annoyingly literal person I have ever met. But apart from your so-called coronation, what did you discover?"

"I discovered that Nabil Ahmad probably had a good shot at becoming Mr. Leatherman Toronto. He was stunning in that peculiar garb they wear. There were a few other contenders, but Nabil would have aced it in the looks department. From his photos alone, you can tell he has charisma to burn."

"Whoa! Do you think he was kidnapped to give someone else a shot at the title? I mean, that's like something out of *Whatever Happened to Baby Jane?*"

"Out of what?"

Donny spluttered. "The picture that put Bette Davis and Joan Crawford back on the cultural map and single-handedly invented the psycho-biddy genre!"

"Oh, that. You know I don't do campy B movies."

"You don't know what you're missing."

"Yes, I do. And that's why I avoid them. But no, I don't think Nabil was taken out of the contest to give someone else a chance to win the title."

"Hmm. Actually …"

"Yes? Actually?"

"Sorry, I was wrong. The film I should have compared it to is *Willing to Kill: The Texas Cheerleader Story*, about the mother of a cheerleader who hires a hit man to kill the mother of her daughter's rival —"

"Well, I'm not going to watch that one either. But still no, so it doesn't matter."

"Then what do you think is really going on?"

"I met one of the contestants last night — big guy, massively on steroids. Lucian something or other. He knew Joe, the guy who disappeared last spring. He said Joe was into dangerous sex. Said he liked to fake-strangle his tricks."

"Charming. I wonder how you bring that up on a first date." He paused. "This Lucian guy — could he have anything to do with the disappearances?"

"I don't think so. He was living away when Joe disappeared and said he just found out about it when he got back. He didn't seem too surprised, though. Or sympathetic. What exactly do those drugs do to your brain?"

"No idea. Hope I never find out."

Dan heard a noise behind him and turned to see Ked enter the kitchen, his eyes glazed, hair a broomstick of angry straw. He glanced down at Dan's cellphone as though recognizing the source of a bad smell or maybe wishing it harm.

"Say hello," Dan commanded. "It's not nice to listen in without identifying yourself."

Ked rolled his eyes. "Duh. I'm not CSIS, Dad." His voice was a croak. To the phone, he said, "Hello, Uncle Donny."

"Hey, Ked! How are you?"

"Asleep. How are you?"

"I'm good. Lester says he saw you and Elizabeth at his concert the other night."

"Oh, yeah! It was awesome," Ked said, suddenly coming to life. "Those guys are amazing. Say hi to Lester for me."

"Will do."

"I'll let my dad talk again."

"Keep cool, dude."

"Yo, commander."

"See?" Dan said to his son. "It's not that hard to be lively in the morning."

"Yeah, okay," Ked said, and he went off to stare at the coffee machine.

Dan turned back to the phone. "Anyway, I'm still following up on the leather angle. I think we're on the right track with that one. We'll just have to see what turns up."

"All right. I won't impose on your cheery father-son morning. I'll check in with you later."

Dan ended the call. He turned to see Ked leaning against the counter and eyeing him. "What's up?"

"Dad, it's not good to carry all that stuff around by yourself."

"What stuff?"

"All that stuff about dead people and murderers and people who disappear and everything."

"Oh, that. You're right. Sometimes it gets to be a bit much. The horrible things people are capable of doing to other people." He stopped. "Anyway, that's why I have you. I can't tell you all of it, but I occasionally tell you things I think you need to know."

"So, unload."

"Okay, it's like this ..."

TWELVE

Second Coming

AN HOUR LATER, DAN RESOLVED to go to his office. It was a ten-minute walk through cold, blustery winds, but he knew he'd be better able to concentrate out of the house. Before he could reach his office, Prabin called on his cell.

"Got some news for you. I talked to this Wendell guy again. We met for coffee and I showed him Nabil's picture. Said he looked familiar, but couldn't swear to it. I asked more about Joe and he told me Joe was in a porn movie, but didn't know the title of it or even if he used his real name, though he doubted it."

"I heard the same thing from one of the contestants at the leathermen contest last night."

"Wendell said Joe got into the film after being invited by a bartender at Zipperz —"

Dan felt a stab of excitement. "Which is where Joe was last seen."

"Exactly."

"Did he say which bartender? There must be a half dozen or more."

"Yes. He said Joe talked about a guy named Sasha."

Again, S.

"I've met him," Prabin continued. "Little guy, eastern European. But tough. Looks like a bodyguard, if it's the one I'm thinking of. He's the front for something called Star-X Productions."

"Then I guess I'll be making a stop off at Zipperz later this afternoon." He paused. "I'm sorry to put you through all this after Randy."

"Never mind. All I care is that we find Nabil."

"I'm doing my best."

"I know you are. And thank you."

A text dinged. Dan caught Woody's name on the screen.

"Sounds like the world needs you," Prabin said.

"It needs a lot more than I can give it."

Prabin laughed. "Anyway, I'll let you go."

"Okay. Let me know if you hear anything else."

"Oh, I will. I definitely will."

The line clicked off. Dan turned to his text: *Hey, buddy. It's pretty chilly out. How's about a little get together so I can reclaim my vest and we can share some body heat? Doing anything tonight?*

It was Sunday. Ked was having dinner with Elizabeth's family, which meant the house would be free all evening. Not that Dan hid things from Ked. That had never been part of their father-son arrangement. Honesty on both sides had always been their style. He would never ask Ked to stay out so he could entertain a guest, although Ked had once asked him to vacate so he could host a party of school friends. It was at that point he'd realized his son was growing up fast.

Free tonight, he texted back. *I'll throw an extra log on the fire.*

See you then, came the reply. No set time or request for an address. That was Woody all over. Slipping in and out of his life when it pleased him. A man of sweet, if inconstant, affection. Easy to catch, but impossible to hold.

At the office, Dan trudged up the unshovelled steps and along the half-lit hallways. More often than not, because of his late evenings and weekend hours, he was the only person in the building. It made for an eerie setting — like waking to find yourself alone in an abandoned spaceship where all the machinery still operated, lights flashing and pipes clanking, thousands of light years away from everything in space.

He opened Nabil's file and called the number on the card he'd found in his room. It was the weekend, so he didn't expect an answer, but a cultivated male voice picked up.

"I'm looking for Hanani Sheikh."

"Yes, that's me. How may I help you?"

"A friend recommended you as a website designer. He said you were the best there is."

"That's quite a recommendation, but yes, it's true. I'm the best." He laughed. "Is yours a commercial site?"

"Its purpose is more advertising than sales, but it is commercially oriented."

"What is it you intend to advertise?"

"I guess you could call it a club. I sell memberships, that sort of thing."

"I see. Then you'll probably require some sort of application to accept credit cards or PayPal. Or am I mistaken?"

"No, you're bang on."

"Then I would suggest an appointment. We can set up a time to discuss your needs."

"I'm free any time. Where are you located? I could pop over now, if you like."

There was a pause. "Who did you say your friend was who recommended me?"

"Nabil Ahmad."

"I don't recall the name."

"Funny — he said you did some sites for him. Brown-boy-dot-com? I-pose-for-you-dot-ca?"

"Possibly. I don't remember." Dan heard pages being turned in the background. "I'm very sorry, but I don't seem to have anything available in the next few weeks."

"What about after that?"

"After that I'm leaving on a business trip that could take some time. If you like, I can refer you to someone else."

"No, it's fine," Dan said, and hung up.

Curious business that turned down potential customers.

At four, Dan finished up at the office, closed down his computer, and headed out. The wind had died down, but the snow continued. Woody would be over in a few hours. In the meantime, there was still time for a visit to Zipperz.

Dan entered and looked around. The place was nearly empty. He took a seat at the bar and the bartender came over, a big man with a friendly face.

"What's your pleasure?"

"Scotch on the rocks."

The man made the drink and placed it in front of Dan. Dan paid and left a ten-dollar bill sitting on the counter from his change. The man eyed it.

"It's yours," Dan said. "I know how hard you guys work."

"Thanks."

Dan made a show of picking up the glass, swirling it around and sniffing it. "It's the good stuff," he said.

The bartender pushed a rag across the wood countertop. "You looked like the classy sort," he said with a wink.

"Thanks." He glanced around at the few solitary figures whiling away their time in the late afternoon, people too lonely or too bored to go home. "Sasha not in today?" Dan asked.

The bartender looked up. "Nah, Sasha's not in. He took a trip back home."

"Bulgaria, was it?"

"No, Bosnia."

"Yeah, that's right."

"You could try him on Tuesday."

"I heard he could get me into a porn flick." Dan made a show of looking around the bar. "I bet he must meet some interesting clientele in here. Does he get lots of promising stars here?"

"Oh, yeah!" The big man laughed. "All kinds. I bet he'd love to have a look at you. Definitely come back Tuesday, if you're interested."

Ralph did a hopeful little dance when Dan got back to the house. Dan leashed him and they headed out. The urgency of Ralph's need became apparent when he squatted right outside the front door. Dan had to step aside to not get his boots splattered.

"Okay, Ralphie — let's make this quick. It's too cold to stay out long and we're both old men now."

Ralph clearly didn't agree. He sniffed at the snow, wagging his tail like it was the best thing he'd seen all day. Dan relented and made an extra long circuit with him.

On their return, he fed Ralph then headed upstairs to a hall closet, searching through a long-unopened box of CDs. He still remembered the leatherman's favourites: Foreigner, Aerosmith, Heart. Woody was a lot of things, but subtle wasn't one of them.

The doorbell rang a few minutes before nine. When Dan opened the door, Woody thrust a six-pack of beer forward and planted a kiss on Dan's lips. *No, definitely not subtle*, Dan thought.

Woody cocked an ear and gave a listen. A tune thrashed in the background. "They're playing our song," he joked, looking around. "Still love this place. Always feels like home to me."

Dan stopped to consider how many times he'd actually been over and laughed when he recalled. He watched as Woody kicked the snow from his boots then stripped off his jacket and slung it over the banister. He'd come dressed in jeans and a black T under the layers. No leather tonight, but all the right bulges in all the right places. There wasn't much use in trying to resist. They were upstairs before Dan knew what was happening. Woody led the way to the bedroom, as though he were over every other day instead of just twice in ten years.

Lying in a tangle of limbs, Dan thought briefly of the hors d'oeuvres he'd left on the counter under the bright lights — olives, cheese, and caviar — and wondered if he should interrupt to put them in the fridge, but with Woody's hands all over him the thought disappeared before he could turn it to action.

Afterward, Dan watched as Woody held up a glass of wine, the firelight glinting off his skin. He remembered all he'd once felt for this man and all he had hoped would come of it. Outside, the snow fell silently.

"I used to wish I could domesticate you, Woody."

Woody pulled him closer. "Yeah, so did I, though we both knew it wasn't gonna happen. But if anyone could have done it, it would've been you. I just needed to be that bird that refused to live in the cage."

"I didn't want to put you in a cage. I just wanted to wrestle you to earth once in a while."

Woody laughed. "These days I could just about manage it. Once in a while. Maybe."

"That almost sounds like an invitation to try."

"You know me — you can always try. You just gotta take it when it comes. But I'll always be there for you if you need me."

"Good to know. Me, too."

"Of that I have no doubt. You are one solid guy." Woody scooped a dollop of caviar onto a cracker and popped it into his mouth, considering as he chewed. "Weird stuff, but I like it."

Silence spread through the room, broken occasionally by the snapping of the fire.

Woody shifted in Dan's arms. "I was thinking about

those guys you asked about. I hadn't thought about Joe for a while. But I just remembered something about him. He told me once he thought someone was after him."

"After him why?"

"I'm not sure. He was always a little paranoid. Afraid his family would find out about him, too."

Dan thought of Nabil's brothers.

"Particularly because of the porn, I think. I mean, he thought he was being brave to do it, but he was really afraid someone would find out."

"Does the name Star-X Productions ring any bells?"

"Sure. They're getting pretty big these days. Lots of local stars, I hear. Some of their stuff is pretty kinky. And I mean far-out weird, even for me."

"Do you know if Joe used his real name in the video?"

Woody gave him an odd look. "Nobody uses their real name in those films. That would be suicide, I think. Anyway, Joe wasn't his real name. It was like Saleem or something."

"Saleem?"

Yet another S.

"Yeah, I think that's right."

Dan sat upright. "Are you sure?"

"Pretty sure. Why?"

"Was he Muslim?"

"I think so."

Dan thought about the entry in Nabil's calendar. "Do you know whether he went to a gay Muslim prayer group?"

Woody shook his head. "I doubt it. Joe wasn't a believer. He spent his entire life casting off his background once he realized he was gay. He said it took a lot of courage. Believe me, he was glad to be rid of them. It was his second chance at life, he said, and he wasn't going to get back on his knees for any religion." He gave a belly laugh at his joke.

Dan remained by the fire after Woody left. Outside, the flurries were slowing, but the wind had begun to howl down the chimney as if it had things to say. By morning the snow would be hardened to a crust. His mind drifted with the large wet flakes.

He texted Terence: *I'm curious about Sam, your puppet maker. Was he Muslim, by any chance?* The reply was almost immediate: *Yes — he was Iranian. Getting somewhere with this?*

I think so, Dan texted back.

Startled, he got up and wandered around the room till Ralph looked at him with something like concern.

"It's okay, Ralphie, I'm not going crazy."

He went upstairs to his computer and pulled up the link for the community noticeboard. *I suggest we narrow it down to a probable Mediterranean background and leave it at that,* Dan had said. But yes, looking at him now, Joe could easily be Muslim. And so could Adam, coming from Bosnia.

Leaving Randy out of the equation, all the others seemed to fit into one category: Adam, Joe, Sam, and Nabil. He paced for a bit then sat and stared at the screen. *Who would want to harm gay Muslims?* he asked himself over and over. Dan thought of someone he could ask.

He texted: *It's Dan Sharp. Wondering if you might have half an hour for me to bend your ear. Any time tomorrow is good.* The reply came a few minutes later. Dan groaned. Five-thirty in the morning wasn't his preferred meeting time by a long shot, but when the mountain was willing to come to you, you didn't stop to question the timing.

He was brushing his teeth and getting ready for bed when a second text followed on the heels of the first. It was from Domingo: *Up for a morning coffee? I've got some eligible bachelors to tell you about!*

Dan texted back: *It'll have to wait. I've already got a date with Mr. Big.*

THIRTEEN

Mr. Big

DAN RECOGNIZED THE PLACE ON his approach, though he hadn't been there in a while. It was one of those nondescript diners where at any given time of day you might find yourself rubbing shoulders with all levels of society: civil servants leaving work, heiresses in disguise, gangsters fresh from an assignation, local celebrities mingling with the hoi polloi, and even young Muslim girls out for a lark without their hijabs before returning home to a strict observance of Sharia law.

He checked his watch. It was 5:12. He'd been a bit overzealous in his arrival, not to mention aggressive in his driving. Mornings were never his favourite time of day. The fact that he did his best sleuthing at night seemed to confirm that.

At that hour, there was only a handful of customers in the place. It looked like an antechamber for the underworld, a waiting room for the newly dead. Over at a far table a cabal of old men, withered seers, sat sweating over beer steins preserved from last night's festivities as though foretelling the future in froth. From the pile of dirty dishes set before them, they might have been making their way through the menu for the better part of the evening, the last meal of the condemned. In another age, they would certainly have added to the ambient fug with deep exhalations, cigarettes passing from trembling fingers to wobbling lips and back again. Shipwrecked and cast away in this modern era, their lungs resented every drag denied them. As it was, one of the group suffered from a hearty cough that sounded just a notch away from a death rattle.

Dan was reminded how whenever men gathered in public the conversation tended to focus on the material, as though they couldn't countenance intangibles or conceive of anything that smacked of abstraction. This bunch seemed to be in some sort of mystical state over cars, how well or badly they drove, their constant need for fuel and oil, and an inexplicable conspiracy that kept them putting winter tires on each fall only to remove them again in spring once the snow was passed. He passed them on his way to a booth, leaving them to their questioning minds.

The only other person in the place, an older woman, sat talking to the walls in a sibilant hiss, commenting on the weather, people she hadn't seen for some time, news from home. Her grey hair was perfectly combed and tucked beneath a coif. A thin wool sweater clung to her bird-like shoulders. Half nun, half harpy. Her claw-like hands seemed unable to grip, dropping utensils onto the table and occasionally sending them clattering to the floor with a sound that made Dan start each time, though the men at the other table seemed not to notice. With a full plate of food set before her, she obviously had means, otherwise the staff might not have been so willing to indulge her peculiarities.

Noises from the back of the diner indicated the presence of kitchen staff, though none had yet shown to greet him. Then again, it could have been thieves ransacking the larder or raccoons helping themselves to human food.

To Dan, everything seemed smaller than he remembered, as though some sort of shrinking ray had been scanned over the place since his last visit. He thought he recognized the busboy on his approach, but the visual didn't fit the memory.

"You look different," Dan said, without knowing how or why.

The man set a glass of water and a menu on the table and patted his waistline. "Bariatric surgery — a hundred-and-forty pounds gone just like that."

Suddenly Dan saw him as he had been, jolly, hearty, and triple-large. Now his jaw-line sagged, his face was gaunt as if an invisible plague had decimated his body, eating him away from within. Fittingly, he was dressed all in black, a sombre spectre come to join the feast.

"Mandy'll be out in just a sec," he said before hurrying off.

It was another five minutes before Mandy appeared, patting the golden curls on her head with one hand and carrying an order pad with the other. Her hairdo seemed to be in imitation of some popular singer, though Dan couldn't bring to mind who she was trying to be in a forlorn effort to brighten her early shift. At a guess, he might have said she looked like Dolly Parton circa 1978, though whatever plastic surgery she'd endured to facilitate the crossover had not held up as well as Dolly's.

"Coffee, hon?" She raised a pot and flashed her white-as-snow dentures.

"Thanks."

She turned his cup and poured. "What can I get ya ta eat?"

"Pie," he said. "Apple."

"Ice cream on top?"

"Yes, good. Thanks."

She was back in less than a minute with the largest slice of pie Dan could recall ever being served. A giant mound of ice cream slid off to the side. She looked concerned by Dan's surprised expression. He took a bite and smiled to reassure her all was well.

At 5:29 the front door opened with a soft click. A cool gust blew through the place. The chief clocked Dan the moment he entered. He came over and dropped wearily onto the seat as though impersonating someone much heavier, a diminished sovereign exhausted by the daily rituals and unable to rise to his station in life. Or perhaps he really was that tired old man, Dan thought, and the facade he put on every day — that of a resilient police chief — was the real impersonation, an impressive sleight-of-hand performed over and over on a daily basis, of which few were privileged to witness the behind-scenes reality.

Dan had once done the chief a favour and, tit for tat, the chief had done him one in return. It didn't mean they were best buddies or even that they had each other's backs, though Dan suspected the latter might be true if push came to shove. For now, at least, it simply meant he could confide in him and ask questions others might not dare. Hard questions that elicited hard answers. If there was one thing Dan knew about the chief, it was that he wasn't afraid to admit when he made a mistake. It was the sort of blatant honesty that impressed Dan and encouraged trust. How far it extended was impossible to say.

Dan hadn't seen the chief in a couple of years, but judging by his looks, they hadn't been good ones. He'd never stopped to wonder if police chiefs suffered from burnout and PTSD, but of course they would. Then again, they were on the city payroll and would at least have something to fall back on if they ever cracked up. Dan never let the recurring bouts of traumatic stress he suffered hold him back, though they increased his anxiety and played havoc with his workload. Still, he could happily have done without the ongoing nightmares about the people he failed to save — the ones who eluded his grasp and ended up suicides or worse — or the nagging inner voice whispering in his ear to say his life had been lived in vain and that he was just taking up space on the planet. Some days it felt like that was all there was, but for a few bright spots like his son and his friends.

When Mandy returned she seemed unnerved by the chief's presence. Maybe she was on the Ten Most Wanted list and one glance from the chief would put her behind bars for the rest of her life. Golden curls notwithstanding, her disguise had been seen through. Dan made a mental note to suggest putting the faces of fugitives on coffee cups in diners the way they did with missing kids on milk cartons.

She took the chief's order, her sweaty fingers fumbling the pencil like a five-year-old learning her alphabet. Then she was gone back to the kitchen where she would no doubt report the presence of heavy brass in the diner.

The chief held out his hand. Dan saw a distinctive tremble. "My nerves are shot," he said. "My wife's leaving me. After thirty-six years, she wants out."

"I'm sorry," Dan said.

"I said, 'Do you want a career? Something to do with your time while I'm at work?' But that wasn't it." He eyed Dan like a stand-up comic waiting to deliver the punchline. "Said she can't take it no more. Doesn't want me to be on the force, doesn't like it when I'm in the public eye. She can't stand it. All these years and she never told me."

They sat in silence a moment as though neither of them could think of a worthy follow-up to the statement.

Mandy returned with the chief's coffee, fumbling the saucer and slopping the coffee onto the table. The chief's hand shot out and deflected her arm like a mountain lion taking a swipe at a careless coyote. Instinctive, reactive. Dan could imagine him killing like that. Without a second glance over his shoulder.

"I'm so sorry!" Mandy exclaimed, mortified at having imperilled such an important customer. After all, it wasn't every day one got to serve royalty.

The chief looked up from the stain on the white cloth and faked a smile. Noblesse oblige. "I'll live."

Dan wondered if there were days when the chief thought he might prefer the alternative. It would be tough having to constantly deflect not just coffee, but also the harshest criticism from both outspoken city officials and the public, your every action mirroring a landscape of anxiety and demands as unending as the flow from Niagara

Falls. Perhaps being on the public payroll wasn't as easy as it sounded.

"You know why I like this place?" the chief asked after Mandy had sopped up the spill and returned to the kitchen.

"The decor?"

The chief looked around as though he'd never considered it. "Not really." He gestured over his shoulder. "You see that high-rise across the street?"

Dan looked to the window and nodded.

"There's a water tower on the roof. Just imagine, a place in downtown Toronto with a water tower on its roof." He shrugged, as though it were all but incomprehensible. "Anyway, my last shift as a detective on the street I get a call — they want me to climb to the top of the friggin' tower and talk down a psychiatric patient. Skinny little thing in a nightdress. No shoes." The chief's gaze drifted off, all misty and faraway, making Dan expect a sad ending to the story. "Anyway, I talked her down, so all good on that end." He paused, dumped cream into his coffee and stirred. "God, I miss those days. But we're not here to do therapy on me. I guess you got something you want to tell me."

"Not tell. Ask."

The chief looked up with a wary expression. "Is it to do with the murder of that doctor last week?"

He'd do well to be wary. The pressure to arrest the suspects had to be enormous. Or perhaps free speech was on the chief's endangered-species list at present. In any case, he had no choice but to press on. The worst that could happen was that the chief would tell him the information was off limits.

"Not directly," he said. "Though it might be connected. Your officers may not notice these things, but there was a poster pasted around the gay community of a man who vanished from a bar back in spring. There was another one in the summer. Then a week and a half ago a third man was reported by his brothers as having vanished without a word that he was going anywhere. He didn't frequent the bars, but he was a regular at the downtown Y. I've been hired by his family to find him."

"Okay." The chief stirred the coffee, tasted it then set the cup down with something like disdain written on his face. "I've been coming here for thirteen years and they have yet to make a good cup of coffee."

"Have you thought of trying another place?"

"It's not the place I want to change, just the coffee." He grunted. "So, go on."

"Recently I learned about yet another gay man who disappeared, maybe end of last year. A guy who makes puppets, apparently, though I can't say for sure if he's really missing. But for the record I don't think these disappearances have anything to do with the murder of Doctor Melchior. It sounds like Melchior was a casualty of street violence, not homophobia. But with these others, my concern is that someone may purposely be targeting gay men."

The chief looked gloomily around, as though bad news was waiting to waylay him at every corner. Did his wife badger him about unsolved crimes? Ask him about drug busts gone wrong, perpetrators of violence against women? Dan could imagine him turning to her and saying, *Hey! I don't ask you about every stain on the tablecloth, do I?*

"For the record, I had heard about the two poster guys. But not the others. And yes, Melchior was the victim of casual street violence." The chief looked off for a second. "Okay, I can tell you a little something on that one. But keep it to yourself." He shrugged. "You always do, so I don't know why I bother telling you that. You're a credit to your profession, such as it is."

Dan smiled at the backhanded compliment.

"You may have heard about the CCTV footage?" His eyebrows went up. Dan nodded. "Good. We're not ready to release details just yet, but we know where these two are holed up. Check the news this evening." He nodded — message delivered. "The problem with the disappearances, as I'm sure you know, is making connections between missing men without the bodies turning up. Dead men tell no tales. Neither do missing ones. Have you found any connection between the vics?"

"Possibly. Two of them were involved in the leather community."

"Rough crowd, I hear. But it's an interesting point. Thanks for bringing it to my attention."

"The man I'm looking for also had a pay-for-play online sex site. One of the others was an exotic dancer and a third appeared in porn films. Have you heard of a Toronto-based company called Star-X Productions?"

The chief grunted. "The local porn industry is no longer a cute little diversion for bored suburbanites. It strikes me I've seen something on your Star-X cross my desk recently. We know these companies hire illegals. They work sex shows for under-the-table money, not just in the gay community. We've got multiple strip clubs in the city, but most of them say they're private clubs so we can't just walk in on them. It's hard to keep tabs on all of them."

"What about a guy named Zoltan Mirovic? Have you heard of him?"

The chief took a little longer to reply this time. Dan wondered what he was holding back. At last, he said simply, "Again, sounds familiar. I'll look into it. Anything else?"

Dan looked carefully at the chief. The little he knew of the man could be put on the back of a postage stamp. "There is something else. It strikes me that, apart from the murdered doctor, all of the men are Muslim."

The chief's spoon cracked against the tabletop. "Shit!" He stared at Dan with baleful eyes. "Are you telling me someone is kidnapping Muslims in this town?"

"Not just any Muslims. *Gay* Muslims."

"But why target gay Muslims? They're already pariahs in their own community." He looked across the room as though the answer might lie on the TV screen silently broadcasting weather reports, traffic updates, stock exchange results, and the news, simultaneously. Finally, he turned back to Dan. "So, we're looking for someone who targets gay Muslims because they're easy to isolate and victimize. Is that what you're saying?"

Dan shook his head. "It's not that simple. I think we're looking for a man who may hate gays in general, but has a vendetta against gay Muslims in particular."

Dan saw the click.

"A Muslim targeting other Muslims?"

"Yes, specifically because they're gay."

"Holy shit. It's a fucking fatwa." The chief sat back. "I came here this morning thinking my life couldn't get worse. And now you're telling me I've got Muslims killing other Muslims because they're gay. That's going to cause a media frenzy."

"No doubt," Dan said.

The chief's mind was already churning through the possibilities. "If you're right and we keep it quiet, then how can we warn other potential vics? And if we don't and someone else disappears or gets killed, this could get a lot worse."

"That's what I think," Dan said. "There's a meeting group for LGBTQ Muslims. At least one of the men was involved with them briefly. I'm going to contact them and see if we can't get the word out that way at least."

The chief looked skeptical. "It's a start, I guess."

Mandy arrived with the breakfast special, a mountain of hash browns in a pool of grease piled alongside three fried eggs, and set it on the table.

The chief looked down at his plate. "Why do I order this shit?"

"To keep yourself alive," Dan said, noting Mandy's grateful look at his reply.

The chief looked up at him with baleful eyes. "Remind me again — what's the point of that?"

FOURTEEN

Resistance

IT WAS A LITTLE PAST seven by the time Dan left the diner and headed over to Church Street. Half of the faces he encountered looked fatigued from lack of sleep, forced out of bed to get to work on time. The other half were glassy-eyed from being out all night and only now slowly wending their way home. He wasn't sure which group he pitied more.

Two men in their twenties, one fat and one thin, stood outside Starbucks arguing.

"Meth is something I only use once in a while as a little pick-me-up," the larger one explained to his companion. "That way I can't get addicted."

"Yeah, dream on," said his skinny friend. "I can't tell you how many times I've seen you passed out in the baths. You probably don't even remember when you're high."

The other looked indignant. "Well, at least I'm not a full-time junkie like you."

"I like getting high. I'm just not in denial about it."

Dan passed by, shaking his head.

He paused inside the entrance to Second Cup to look over a community billboard covered with invitations to LGBTQ groups alongside bicycles for sale and notices for drag bingo. Dan scanned the circulars till he found the one he wanted: *Almusawa — Equality*. He took a shot of the invitation to the all-gender Muslim support group and was about to turn away when he caught sight of a card tucked into the corner: *Edie Foxe — Sexual Contortionist*. He recalled her attack on the drunken man at the leatherman contest. *You are on my radar far more often than I would expect*, he thought.

He lined up and ordered a coffee and muffin. Funny how life seemed to take him from one coffee shop to another. He chose a plush armchair on the upper level and sent a text to Terence, asking if he remembered the address of the puppet maker. Next, he dialed Almusawa. An authoritarian-sounding message directed him to leave his name and contact info. It felt as if he were applying for a job.

He sipped his coffee and surveyed the other customers. They seemed by and large an unremarkable bunch. If it weren't for the high percentage of men, he might not have known he was in a gay establishment. It was ironic how ordinary the ghetto had become. After Stonewall and AIDS, the community had settled for some sort of hyper normalcy, as though fitting in with the social fabric was what they'd wanted all along. If so, it simply meant becoming invisible in the long run. He couldn't remember the last time he'd heard of a queer protest or boycott. Now it was all gaybies and marriage. Even the corporations were far too concerned with soliciting the support of the LGBTQ community to risk offending it. Even a company as solidly establishment as IBM, which once refused its employees same-sex spousal benefits, now proudly proclaimed to have been the first to offer what was simply the status quo when all was said and done. And thanks very much. Scratch the surface, however, and Dan knew you'd find a struggle by gay rights activists in the background forcing the corporation to its knees and setting off a landslide of change around the world. And it had all begun in Toronto, where the world's first legal same-sex marriage took place. So how could it be that someone was killing gay Muslims in this great country of history-making social reforms and cultural freedoms?

His phone rang, startling him out of his reflections.

"You called about Almusawa," a woman's voice said.

"That's correct."

"What's your interest in the group?"

"My name is Dan Sharp. I'm a private investigator —"

"Are you with the police?"

"No, I'm —"

"Are you Muslim?"

"No. I'm the father of a son with a Muslim woman."

"Is the son a practising Muslim?"

"No, but if I could just explain —"

"This group is for practising Muslims who wish to pray in peace."

"I understand. I'm phoning because I'm concerned for the safety of your members." This was met with silence, so he went on. "The gay male members of your group in particular —"

"If you are talking about the recent murder of a gay doctor then you are mistaken. He was not a Muslim. Someone may be targeting gay men, but that does not mean they are targeting gay Muslims."

"There are at least three, and possibly four, Muslim men who have gone missing from the community. I don't think they're connected with the doctor's murder. I was hoping for a chance to address your group to see —"

"It's a violent world out there. Many LGBTQ people are being hurt right now. It's not just Muslims who are being attacked. What does your wife think?"

Dan felt his ire rising, but he held back. "I don't have a wife."

"You just said —"

"I said I fathered a child with a Muslim woman. I'm not married. I'm gay."

"But you are not Muslim. I cannot invite you to speak to my group. I have to be concerned for their safety. We are like a resistance group during the war. I cannot risk exposing the members for fear of their safety."

I could do with a little less resistance from you, Dan thought.

"How do I know you are not trying to find out who our members are?"

"I'm not interested in finding out who your members are," Dan said. "Perhaps you could speak on my behalf and inform them. At least one of the men who disappeared attended your group."

"Who is that?"

"His name was Nabil Ahmad."

"I don't recognize that name."

138

"Perhaps for the very reasons you just mentioned. He might have given an alias."

"That is his right. But we do not want outsiders interfering with the group. No, I will not allow you to speak to our members. Goodbye."

She hung up.

Dan sighed and looked down at his coffee. His stomach rebelled. There was such a thing as too much caffeine. He put the cup aside and did a search for the group online. There were several full-colour pictures of the group's founder, who he assumed was the woman he had been speaking to. She certainly seemed to like publicity for someone who claimed to want to remain anonymous. From what he could tell, she was a high school teacher. Paranoid, too, by the sounds of it, but then she no doubt had her reasons for that.

A text dinged. It was from Terence. *Good timing*, it read. *You caught me just as I'm about to board my flight for Paris.* It included the information he wanted, an address right in the downtown core for a building called the Viking. He'd attached a photograph of Sam with a grinning Terence looking over his shoulder. *In case it helps*, he'd added. Dan looked over the photo. *Smitten* was how Dan interpreted the look on Terence's face. The young man was attractive, but not highly memorable. The sort of face you would overlook in a crowd. *I won't forget you*, Terence concluded. *Hope you're still single when I get back. Hmmm … I don't mean that in a bad way. Au revoir — for now!*

Dan smiled at the last remark.

†

He ditched his coffee and headed up Church Street, pausing as he reached Cawthra Square Park with its AIDS memorial. The granite markers listed the names of the plague's dead beginning in 1981, proliferating through the crisis years from 1986 to 1996 before slowing again. A final untouched panel waited down the line like a hoped-for ending to the disease, or perhaps just the end of time. Dan doubted either would be coming soon, but even if they did, he reasoned, the memorial keepers could just as easily keep things going by inscribing the names of those felled by violence, either from others or self-inflicted.

Farther up the street, rainbow-coloured bands painted on the pavement showed through a dusting of snow, marking the limits of the gay neighbourhood. Not a yellow brick road leading to the Emerald City, but more like a warning you'd reached the end of the safe zone. In some ways, he thought of the ghetto as a psychological concentration camp. He recalled the woman on the phone and how she let fear define her world.

When he was younger he'd participated in Pride parades because they symbolized struggle in the face of oppression. He didn't mind that they were now more about celebration than activism, though he still recalled an argument with a friend who insisted that with the arrival of same-sex spousal benefits, and the right to marry, all was well. *That's First-World tunnel vision,* he'd snapped. *Until you can safely walk down any street in any country in the world holding hands with anyone you choose, then all is definitely not well. Any fool could figure that out.* Severing yet another relationship with a well-meaning but obtuse person.

Branches stretched overhead, skeletal fingers grasping for warmth from the receding sun. April wasn't the cruellest month, he thought. December was.

The puppet maker's building was a mixed-use, three-storey walk-up on Gloucester Street. From outside there seemed nothing unusual about it. In a foyer that barely allowed for room to turn around, Dan cast his eye down the list of residents: K. Smith, David T., Fred's Bicycle Repair, Carrie the Friendly Dog Walker. A transient-sounding bunch at best. There was just one full name in the lot, a Miss Prudence E. Fulcher. With a name like that, Dan was willing to bet she was nearing her centenary. There was a blank for apartment 102, where Terence had said Sam lived. With the current low-vacancy rates, empty apartments in downtown Toronto were all but unheard of.

He tried the door, wondering why such a heavy-duty electronic system was needed to guard an unassuming apartment walk-up. Drug addicts, perhaps. Or break-ins. At that time of day, with pedestrians coming and going, he couldn't risk being seen tripping the lock.

Flagstones led alongside the building, a narrow pathway looking like it was perpetually in shadow. Dan glanced over his shoulder then headed down the walk, leaving tread marks in the unsullied snow. Never mind, he reasoned, they'd be gone with the next storm.

There were just two windows on the ground floor, starting a little above eye level. He got a good grip on the sill nearest him and hoisted himself up, using a hand to darken the reflection of the winter sky. It yielded a view of a sparsely furnished apartment with a sofa and a reclining chair positioned in front of a wide-screen TV. Two wooden chairs sat cockeyed at a kitchen table shoved against a wall. It was all thrift-shop decor, the home of someone who had little inclination toward design. The only thing adding a note of interest was the two marijuana plants carefully positioned to catch the falling light.

Dan lowered himself and took a breath. Time was telling on him. Ten years earlier it wouldn't have been an effort, but now he paused before continuing. Thankfully, there were no dogs to avoid. Or at least none making their presence known yet. A surprise of that order was something he could happily do without.

He moved along to the next window, waited for his heart to stop pounding, then hoisted himself up again. Here the view was blocked by thick brocade curtains. Through a chink he could just make out another room off to the right. This apartment appeared larger than the other.

Dan eased himself down and walked around to the back. The building was narrow, with only a single window on each floor. He looked around carefully. A three-door garage stood at the end of the drive. It was locked and the windows darkened.

Gripping the sill, he raised himself up and peered in. The curtains were open, but it took a while for his eyes to adjust. He felt a sudden chill as he caught sight of a row of puppets hanging from a wire strung across the room.

That was all the time he had to contemplate the discovery. He felt his grip torn from him. His hands were scraped raw and he fell backward, hitting the ground, the breath knocked from him. Before he could fathom what had happened, someone was on top of him, pummelling his head and chest. Iron hands gripped his Adam's apple, a pair of knees crushing the breath out of him.

Instinctively he fought back, adrenaline and shock adding to the fight. He was bigger than his attacker, but the other was wiry and had the advantage of surprise. Dan pried the strangling grip from his throat, peeling back the fingers one at a time. It took almost a minute to get on top and subdue his opponent.

"Whoa! Whoa!" he cried as the man flailed with his fists each time Dan got a hand loose.

"Who are you? What the fuck are you doing?"

"It's okay," Dan said, trying for casual as much as might be possible under the circumstances. "I'm looking for a friend."

"Who are you looking for?"

"A guy named Sam."

Dan felt the struggling ease up. "I'm going to let you go now," he said. "Don't try anything or I'll hit you a lot harder."

He let his attacker get to his feet, guarding himself from a surprise blow, but the man had given in. Dan looked him over. He wasn't big, but he'd put up an impressive fight.

"Who are you?" the man demanded, wheezing and brushing the snow from his clothes.

"My name is Sean Peterson. I'm a private investigator. I'm looking for Sam in apartment 102. I've been trying to get in touch with him. He doesn't answer his email or his texts."

"He moved," the man said.

"Okay, fair enough. Your turn. Who are you and how do you know he moved?"

The man scowled, wiping the snot from his nose. "I'm the super here."

Dan was beginning to see the light. "Can you tell me when you last saw him?"

"Few months ago. Maybe a little longer."

"Do you know where he went?"

"No idea." He shrugged. "It happens sometimes. In the city you can just disappear."

"Is it possible he comes and goes without being seen?"

The man shook his head. "Not a chance. I'd hear him if he did. I live in the other apartment on the ground floor."

"So, he just left his things here?"

The super hesitated. "His rent is paid up for six months. It's not my business if he isn't here."

Dan looked at him, calculating his chances. "Would you let me in just to look around his apartment?"

The man's eyebrows went up. "No way! I can't do that."

"You're the super. You would have spare keys to all the units in case of floods, things like that."

"Yeah, but —"

"I have reason to believe he was abducted."

"Abducted? You mean, like kidnapped?" He stared warily at Dan. "Still, I don't have a good excuse for going inside —"

"The man's missing. He could be lying dead in there on the floor or in his bed."

"I could lose my job."

Dan thought of the marijuana plants he'd spied through the other window. It wasn't the sort of thing a building superintendent would want on his record if he hoped to keep his job.

"I could come back with a warrant," Dan said, wondering if the chief would go along with this.

A fearful look crossed the super's face. "A warrant? You mean, like the police?"

"I'd have to go through legal channels, of course. It might take a day or two, but I could do it and come back with the police. They'd want to investigate the entire building."

"I couldn't let them do that."

"You wouldn't have a choice."

That seemed to tip the balance in Dan's favour.

"Show me your ID."

Dan pulled out his wallet and flipped it open to the brass slug he kept for occasions like this, hoping the man wouldn't take too close a look at the generic insignia. He didn't.

"All right," the man said hesitantly. "But just a quick look. And you can't touch anything."

"Agreed."

Dan waited while the super went into his apartment then emerged a moment later with a large antique key.

"That's an unusual key," Dan said.

He laughed. "Yeah, right? They're all like this. This place has all the original hardware, locks and all. The owners are restoration freaks."

They went down the hall to the end apartment. A quick knock reverberated back from inside. There was no response.

"I'm Reggie," the super said, extending his hand, as though the past few minutes had been simply a prelude to their introduction.

"Pleased to meet you, Reggie. Hope I didn't hurt you back there."

"Nah, I'm good." Reggie gave an unexpected giggle. "Hope I didn't hurt you either."

"I'm tough."

"Yeah, I can see. And built."

Dan caught the flirtatious tone.

"You gay?" Reggie asked, inserting the key in the lock.

"Yes."

"I thought so. I can usually tell." Reggie pushed the door open and stood there framed by darkness. He frowned. "This better not get me in trouble."

"You're looking after the well-being of your tenant. It won't get you in trouble."

The door closed behind them as Reggie fumbled for the switch. He clicked it and the room sprang into view. They were in a sumptuously decorated apartment. Dan saw the swelling curves of a couch, richly upholstered, with hand-carved arms and legs. On the far side of the room, a sideboard with a glossy walnut veneer kept company with a hand-painted armoire. Someone with taste lived here.

A door at the far end was closed. Dan went over and knocked. Again, there was no answer. He looked back at the super.

Reggie gave a resigned shrug. "Go ahead."

Dan pushed the door open. He was met with more gloom, this time of the sepulchral variety. He strode over to the window and parted the brocade curtains until light flooded the room. A row of puppets hung from a wire, their mouths caught in a silent scream. Hand-carved, outfitted in dapper costumes with miniature buttons and jewellery — this was the work of a master craftsman.

There were others, two-dimensional animal shapes, lions, water buffalo, tigers, hanging from invisible wires and floating in space. Shadow puppets. Dan held up his phone and took a shot. The flash lit up the room, making the outlines quiver against the walls. Forms given the semblance of life.

Framed photographs showed a family in a Middle Eastern city. Laughing, happy people whose likeness from another time had been carefully preserved. The entire room had the feel of a museum. Of things maintained and kept in darkness, not to let them fade or decay. Likewise with the bookcase pressed up against a wall, its volumes encased in richly grained leather. Arabic script ran along the spines like the ones on Nabil's shelves. The pages were thick and unevenly cut in a style that had gone out of fashion in the middle of the last century, along with filigree passkeys and shadow puppets.

He picked one up and flicked it open. Inside the cover, in flowing English script, was the name Sam Bashir, written three times, as though someone had been practising his signature.

Dan replaced the book and stood at the window looking out at the snow, sullied where he and Reggie had grappled after his fall, but pure and crisp in the distance. He turned back to the room. Wherever he went, the puppet eyes followed him.

It was a zoo without a zookeeper. *Where did you go?* he wondered.

Dan returned and looked over the sitting room. A chair had been pushed right up to the divan. Anyone sitting in it would have touched knees with the sofa. A lone candle rested on a side table, as if an impromptu vigil had been set, someone worriedly watching the death of a loved one.

He turned to Reggie, waiting in the centre of the room. "What's he like?"

"Who?"

"Sam."

The super's eyes flashed suspicion. "I thought you said you knew him."

"Not well."

Reggie seemed to accept the answer. He sneered. "He's an ass. Pretentious little twit. But he doesn't cause me no problems. That's all that matters."

"Is he rich?"

Reggie turned to look around the apartment, as though it had just dawned on him that the furniture was beyond the reach of ordinary tastes and bank accounts. He shrugged. "He said his family had money."

"Did he say where they were from?"

He shook his head. "One of those Middle East countries."

"Iran? Iraq?"

"Yeah, one of them."

"What about visitors? Boyfriends? Girlfriends?"

"Nah, don't think so. As I said, he's quiet."

"Those puppets. Is he a collector?"

Reggie shrugged. "Said he made them, I think."

Dan went into the kitchen and turned on the light. The refrigerator emitted a quiet hum. He opened it and looked inside. A couple of bottles of carbonated water kept company with sealed cartons of juice and a tin of kippers. Nothing perishable. It was almost as if he'd known he was going away.

"All right, thanks for this."

They stood outside in the hallway while Reggie locked the door, clearly glad to be out of the apartment.

"Can I get your phone number?" Dan asked. "In case I think of anything else I want to ask?"

Reggie looked him up and down. "Do you have a card?"

"I left it at home."

"Okay. Let me get one of mine."

He opened his door and went over to a desk, searching amid the clutter. Dan's eyes picked out the pot plants beneath the window. Reggie caught his glance.

"It's medicinal," he said.

"Yeah, I'm cool."

"It's Sean, right? Sean Peterson?"

"That's right."

"Okay. Come around sometime. You like to smoke? We can get high."

"Not when I'm on the job." Dan looked at the card: REGGIE KANE, Superintendent. "Thanks for this."

"Private investigator, eh? Is that like security?"

"Not really. I don't guard things. I look for missing people."

Reggie looked impressed. "Oh, yeah? 'Cause, you know, I think about what I'm gonna do when I leave this place. It's all right here, don't get me wrong, but I don't want to be a superintendent forever." He laughed as though they shared a joke.

"Well, the good thing about it is that I make my own hours. The bad thing is that if I'm feeling lazy and don't find work, I don't have an income."

"Oh yeah. That wouldn't be so good. Still … I gotta do something eventually. I can't stay here forever." Reggie looked as if he were staring through the bars of a cage. "I'd make a great detective. I see things, eh? People don't think I see them, but I do."

"What sort of things?"

"All sorts. There are some real characters in this building. Drug dealers and whatnot. There's even a guy who makes his own porn." Reggie giggled again. "It's not exactly a high-class establishment, if you know what I mean."

"Porn?"

Reggie giggled. "Yeah. Real characters coming and going at all hours."

Dan nodded. "Maybe you could let me know if you see anything you think I should know about."

"I might." Reggie eyed him, wary again. "So, you don't think you'll need to get a search warrant now, right?"

"I don't think the police are going to need to have a look now that I've been here."

"That's good. I mean, you can't trust cops, right?"

Especially not when you've got something to hide, Dan thought.

They walked to the entrance. Reggie looked him over again. "So, you're gay."

"Yes, as I said."

"Single?"

Better to nip this one in the bud, Dan thought. "No. I'm married."

"Where's your ring?"

Dan groaned inwardly. "I never wear it on the job. Better not to give any outward clues."

Reggie seemed to consider this. "Like spies," he said.

"Kind of."

The idea seemed to intrigue him. "Cool. I get it."

As they stood there, the front door opened and a frenzied-looking man came in. *Furtive* was the word that came to mind. Drug dealer, possibly. Worried expression, beady eyes. Small frame, ponytail. Dan's inner camera took shots. The man glanced at Dan and Reggie, brushing the snow off his jacket, then scurried up the stairs.

"That's the porn guy. His name's Xavier." Reggie glanced up the dark stairwell after the vanished figure.

You'd be useless at keeping secrets, Dan thought.

He turned and glanced over the tenancy list again. There, right at the bottom, was the name he'd missed: Star-X Productions. He nodded to Reggie and stepped out into the sunlight where a cold breeze hit him square in the face. *Early winter and home-style pornographers*, he thought. *I'm getting too old for this shit.*

FIFTEEN

Trolling

"I WAS JUST LEAVING WHEN the pornographer showed up. He was seriously devious-looking," Dan said to the three faces watching him.

No one spoke for a moment. At last Prabin asked, "So are you thinking there's a connection between Star-X Productions and the missing men?"

"I'm saying I wouldn't be surprised to find a connection. Sam's apartment is in the same building. We know Nabil visited him there. It sounds like Joe is in one of their videos. Adam was an exotic dancer, so it's possible he performed for them, too."

"You think this guy is making snuff videos?" Donny asked.

"Trust you to go to the darkest interpretation possible," Prabin groused.

Dan considered this. "If he is, I doubt he'd make snuff videos and then label them with the company name. I looked up their website. From what I can tell they're a small-time porn studio with a taste for kink. If they're doing anything that radical, it would have to be distributed elsewhere. Online would be the best bet."

Donny turned to Domingo. "What do you think?"

She shrugged. "What's the saying? A fox doesn't hunt in its own backyard. I think it would be too close to home to kidnap someone right downstairs from where you live."

"Don't they say most violent crimes are committed by someone the victim knows?" Donny asked.

"That's true," Dan said. "The percentage is even higher with sexual crimes."

Domingo sat back and crossed her arms. "Okay, I'm not arguing with you guys. I'm just here as a sounding board."

"That's what we're all here for at present," Dan reminded them. "There's still not much to go on, but Nabil operated his own sex sites online. And his diary mentioned that Sam asked if he'd be interested in making a video for some guys he knew."

"Well, that's all very colourful and *Maltese Falcon*-ish, but I'm still not sure where it leaves us." It was Donny who spoke. "Where is this Sam?"

"I don't know," Dan said. "He seems to have vanished with all the others. If he's still here then he's illegal, so we can assume he's gone underground. He was pressuring Nabil to help him with his visa. But he may have the key to what happened to these men who disappeared. I'd like to find him and see what he knows. There was also a mention of someone with the initial *H* who made websites for Nabil. I think that's a guy named Hanani Sheikh. It sounds like he's the go-to guy for fake visas. Nabil asked him for help with Sam's visa. Sheikh also designed a website for Zoltan Mirovic. Mirovic is in charge of talent at Remington's."

"I know Hanani Sheikh," Prabin said. "He used to show up at the gym whenever Nabil got there. It was as if he knew Nabil's schedule."

"Nabil called him a stalker in his diary."

"That fits. He was a creep. I got a chill the first time I saw him."

"Then he's got to be our guy," Donny asked. "First he stalks, then he kills."

"Possibly, but we don't have anything to tie him to the others," Dan said. He turned to Domingo. "What do you think?"

"I've been considering," she said. "We're looking for someone who lives in the shadows. He's a manipulator, but he operates from behind the scenes. This man is a master of disguise."

"Yes," Dan said. "That sounds right. He prowls. In bars, in gyms. But always silently, invisibly. He's in plain sight, but nobody notices him. That's how he gets away with it."

"I can tell you this, too," Domingo said. "The killer is cruel and arrogant. He thinks he's smarter than everyone. He speaks of others with contempt. He likes to brag because he thinks he can get away with it."

"That fits with the profile I'm building in my mind," Dan said.

"He'll be hard to track down then," Prabin said.

Donny nodded. "I should say so. Especially without a name for us to go on."

Prabin looked at Dan. "You and I could go out prowling in the bars and see if we find anyone suspicious. If he's going after Muslim guys then I could pass."

Donny's face took on an expression of horror. "Oh, great, you want to track down a serial kidnapper and potential murderer. And worse, you want to use yourself as bait."

"Dan would be there," he said. "I wouldn't do anything crazy."

Donny turned to Dan. "Aren't there police officers who do this kind of thing?"

Dan nodded. "There are. Better that they pose as human bait for kidnappers than roust the prostitutes on Church Street by posing as johns. Then again," he reflected, "if they're not really gay, they probably wouldn't have a clue how to blend in."

"See?" Prabin eyed Donny. "They wouldn't get it right."

"Forget it. That's not happening," Donny said, as Domingo and Dan traded amused looks over his shoulder.

Prabin shook his head. "I can see it now — one of the cops gets groped while waiting for a beer and trouble ensues. That'd out him for sure. Have you ever seen two gay guys fighting in a gay bar?"

"No, not with fists," Domingo said. "But I've seen a couple of drag queens going at it with their tongues. Blood was spilled without a single blow."

Donny's expression hardened. "I'd sooner face a drag queen than a serial killer. But I won't have Prabin facing either of them, if I can help it."

"I hope we won't have to resort to that," Dan said reassuringly. "And for the record, I had breakfast with the chief of police this morning to ask his advice."

"Ah! So that's your Mr. Big," Domingo said.

"Yes, that's him. I might be able to convince him to put an undercover officer in the bars. There's got to be at least one gay cop on the force. But for now, he's got his hands full with catching Randy's killers."

"Did he tell you anything?" Prabin asked. "Are they getting close to an arrest?"

Dan nodded. "Sounds like it. He said they're focusing on the two kids on the CCTV footage at the convenience store. So, we should give credit where credit is due." He looked to Domingo. "You were bang on in what you said. Two perpetrators who were trying to score drug money."

"Just call me the Voodoo Queen of Toronto," Domingo said.

"Oh, she's one of the Voodoo ladies, all right," Donny said. "You don't want her turning the evil eye on you! Back home, they'd be *waaay* afraid of her."

"In any case," Dan said, "I feel reassured whenever you speak your mind. You might even have me believing in these things one day. What do you think we should do from here?"

She sat quietly for a moment. "Just keep on sleuthing," she said at last. "Something's going to turn up very quickly. It will tell you you're on the right track. Then things will start to get tricky."

As Dan was leaving, Ked texted to say he and his mother had a movie night planned. Dan stopped off at a convenience store on Church Street to pick up snacks. On exiting, he saw a young man on the corner. For one startling moment he thought it was Kedrick, but the boy turned and Dan caught his features full-on. They were similar, maybe even enough to be mistaken for brothers, but this young man's eyes were full of longing. Dan recognized the look of someone wanting to be let into the club. A kid trying to come out and wishing someone would give him a helping hand.

The only problem was, he looked Middle Eastern. How to cross life's hurdles when your culture was dead set against them? Back home, he'd be facing death threats. Here, he might just get away with it if he kept it a secret from his family.

The boy looked up to the awning of a popular bar as though to say, *I'm thinking of going in there. What do you have to say about that?* Dan stopped to consider what he would have wanted to be told at that age: *Go somewhere else? Come back another day if you still feel strongly about it?*

No, that wouldn't do it.

At least these kids have bars, Dan reminded himself. There were no gay bars in Sudbury when he was making his first half-hearted attempts at coming out. Somehow, word got round that if you went to a certain place near a train trestle you might meet someone to have sex with. He had no idea how or when he learned this, it was just one of the devious things that kids shared, but it proved true.

The first few times, he wouldn't allow himself to get close to the men hovering in shadows. He was terrified, having heard that all queers were criminals and drug addicts. Still, something drew him back there. Eventually, the ones he met were kind and polite. He never felt threatened by them. But by others, yes. Like the gang of boys who came with baseball bats. Dan had just been approached by a tall, skinny man with acne a few years older than him when their conversation was interrupted by yelling and crashing in the bush. Two other men darted off, but the man he was with shook his head.

"Don't run," he said. "They're more frightened if you stand up to them."

He reached down and picked up a branch, hefting it for weight. It proved solid. When the boys saw Dan and the man at his side, they jeered.

"Faggots!" one of the kids yelled, a scrawny ruffian with eyes the colour of dung.

"These faggots aren't afraid of you," Dan's companion countered.

The boys circled and threw rocks, but didn't advance. The stand-off held for less than a minute. At a signal from their leader, they ran off. It had been Dan's first lesson in self-respect. And one he wouldn't soon forget.

He looked at the boy standing on the corner outside the bar.

"Thinking of going in there?" Dan asked.

The boy looked up, terrified. But he nodded.

"That bar is for older men." Dan pointed across the street. "That one is for younger people. Or if you go up the street to the 519 Community Centre, you can ask to talk to one of the counsellors about the gay community in general. It might be a better starting point."

"Thanks," the boy said, looking relieved.

"You're welcome. Take care."

SIXTEEN

Dangerous Things

DAN HAD JUST ARRIVED HOME when Ked came in the door brandishing a DVD.

"I let mom pick the movie," Ked proudly informed him. "I didn't think she wanted to watch *Zombieland*."

"Good thinking." Dan grinned as Kendra walked in behind him, cool and collected, a fresh breeze wafting through the room.

"I told him I didn't mind. Woody Harrelson is cute," Kendra said, "but he insisted."

"Argue not with the youth of this generation," Dan advised.

"So anyway, we got *Terminator Salvation*," Ked informed him.

"A huge improvement, I'm sure."

They settled in. The movie opened on a present-day execution before throwing forward to a time when machines ruled the earth, ruthlessly hunting down the last humans.

They were so lethal, in fact, it would have been a miracle if anyone survived their relentless destruction. Lost lands, savaged hopes, the future of the human race heading for the dustbin. *Ho-hum*, Dan thought.

Afterward, they tuned the TV to the local news. It was the third item in. Dan reached for the remote as Randy Melchior's smiling face filled the screen.

"That's Prabin's friend," he explained as the volume swelled.

The chief had been as good as his word. The newscaster detailed the arrests of two young people charged with the doctor's murder. Grainy footage showed a pair of ordinary-looking teens, a boy and a girl, inside a convenience store a block from where Randy's body had been found. Seconds later they left right behind him.

"The suspects will appear in a Toronto court on Monday on charges of first-degree murder." The newscaster turned to face a second camera. "Police are also investigating the disappearance of a man from the Church-Wellesley neighbourhood ..."

Dan's interest was piqued as Joe's face flashed on the screen. It was the photo from the poster.

"... Saleem Mansouri was last seen at a bar called Zipperz in April of this year. Known to friends as Joe, Mansouri's disappearance is not believed to be related to the murder of Doctor Melchior. Police are asking anyone with information that might help trace his whereabouts to come forward."

There was no mention of a Muslim connection or of other missing men. The chief was playing it safe. The newscaster moved on to a contentious vote at city hall.

Dan turned off the television.

"Does first-degree murder mean it was planned?" Ked asked.

"Yes, it does," Dan said. "You saw those two people leave the store right after the victim. What the prosecutor will have to prove is that they planned to kill and not just rob him. Otherwise it's second-degree murder."

"You said he was Prabin's friend?" Kendra asked.

"An ex, actually. Prabin and Randy went to Queen's together. They had just got back in touch recently after not seeing each other for ten years."

Kendra looked at Dan. "At least he can be thankful they got back in touch before he died."

"I don't think Prabin sees it that way. He's concerned that he didn't make a better effort to spend time with him."

"And now there are others missing," she said quietly, finishing his thoughts.

"Yes, and they won't be the last. From what I can see, these men are targets because they're not properly integrated into the community. At the same time, they're estranged from their own communities. They don't belong anywhere."

"It's not uncommon for immigrants to feel that way," Kendra said. "Nostalgia's a dangerous thing. A part of you always wants to go home again, to make peace with the past. I still dream of the olive trees in our backyard in Damascus. There was a bright blue sky over the city the day I left. The night before, I set my pet finch free. I put the cage out in the garden and let it fly away. In the morning, it was back in the cage. But I was determined not to be that bird."

"Will you ever go back?" Ked asked, watching his mother carefully, as though she had just revealed herself to be someone very different from who he thought she was.

"One day you and I will go there for a visit. But it won't be for a long time, sweetheart." She turned to Dan. "Armand said when he went back last year it broke his heart to see the destruction and the people panicking as they tried to flee. He knew there was nothing he could do to help them. I'm afraid the worst is still to come."

Dan's cellphone interrupted them. It was Prabin.

"You saw the news? About Randy and the other guy, Joe?"

Dan stepped out into the hall. "I saw it."

"They were playing it pretty safe."

"My guess is the chief doesn't want to alert the killer that they're drawing lines and connecting dots. It might be better this way for now."

"I want to do something," Prabin declared firmly. "The sort of thing we talked about the other day."

"It could be very risky."

"I know. I want to do it anyway."

Dan peeked back in to where Kendra and Ked sat talking. "It's a family night here. How about we meet tomorrow to talk it over?"

"Let's do that."

"I'll be in touch," he said. He hung up and went back to the living room.

Kendra looked up. "Everything okay?"

"I hope so." His eyes went back and forth between Kendra and Ked. Ked was busy tapping out messages on his phone. Dan hoped he was too absorbed in his task to listen. "Prabin thinks we should stake out the bar where the missing man disappeared."

"The man on TV?" Kendra shivered. "That sounds dangerous!"

Ked's eyes flickered over, registered "adult" conversations then flickered away again.

"He's adamant. I doubt anything could happen to him in a public place, if we do it. In any case, I'll be there to make sure no one tries anything."

She shook her head. "Famous last words. And he's not a trained sleuth like you."

"That's what worries me."

"Be careful, Dan."

Dan packed up the snacks, putting lids on containers. He was standing at the sink doing the dishes when he felt a presence and turned to see his son's eyes on him.

"Why do you always have to get involved in dangerous things?" Ked asked.

"I'm sorry if it worries you. I'm sure you know most of what I do isn't dangerous at all. And it helps other people, which is very important. But if I were in the army or the police force, it would be a similar situation. Sometimes danger comes with the territory. Still, I don't take unnecessary risks."

"I know." Ked nodded, but didn't look quite convinced.

Dan felt shaken by his son's expression as Ked turned and left the room.

SEVENTEEN

Pumping Iron

THE AIR WAS CHILL, THE morning traffic snarl just beginning, when Dan arrived at the lobby of the downtown YMCA. The young woman at the desk was unwilling to give him any information on the attendance of a fellow member until he produced his investigator's licence. On seeing it, she stiffened as though he'd pulled a handgun and demanded cash.

"I'll have to see the manager," she said, turning to a back office.

An older woman in a beige sweater and wool skirt emerged, smiling, everybody's favourite aunt, and asked whether he was with the police. *If I were*, Dan thought, *I'd have pulled out a badge instead of this card*. He took stock of her appearance: tidy, composed, and sure of her place in the world. Threatening her with a warrant wasn't going to work, though she might stop short of telling him to "bring it on" if he dared. When he told her that the member in question, Nabil Ahmad, was missing, and that he was looking into the disappearance for Nabil's brothers, her demeanour changed.

"I remember him. Nice man. I'm sorry to hear that," she said. "Is it serious?"

How to answer that? he wondered. Did she mean "serious" as in the difference between a head cold and cancer? There was no such thing as a partial disappearance, so yes, it was serious, but he refrained from saying so.

Instead, he smiled and assured her they were simply following all leads at present. Her expression said she wanted to ask more, but she hesitated, perhaps out of politeness.

She smiled lightly then said, "I hope this has nothing to do with the posters I've been seeing around the neighbourhood, the ones with the other missing men."

"We hope not, too." It was the best reassurance Dan could give at present.

A quick look at her records showed Nabil had not been to the Y since two Fridays ago, the day of his disappearance. This jibed with what Prabin had said and with Nabil's online calendar. Until then, however, he'd been in nearly every day for as far back as the records indicated. A devoted bodybuilder. It showed in the photos Dan had seen.

He thanked her for her co-operation. She nodded, concern written on her face, but clearly hopeful that would be the full quotient of excitement she had to face that day.

Dan found Prabin upstairs dressed in workout clothes. No slacker, he'd been at it for half an hour already. His efforts showed in the dark patches beneath his arms and the sheen on his forehead. Normally clean-shaven, he was sporting a two-day growth of facial hair. It looked good on him.

The tinny beat of dance music competed with the clank of metal as members lumbered between benches and machines, pumping and pushing their way to perfection before heading off to offices and cubicles and the everyday, imperfect world of work. While the rest of humanity lay in bed, these juggernauts rode the pilgrimage to physical supremacy, desired by many but achieved by few, forsaking sleep and rest in their efforts to attain the ideals of the Greeks. All that just to look good on a beach.

Prabin had snagged a prime corner where they could talk without being overheard. Dan spotted him while he hefted a monster barbell.

They talked between sets. Prabin was adamant: the bottom line was that he wanted to help Dan in his search for Nabil and the other missing men.

"If the chief were serious," he said, "he'd let the public know they're looking for three gay Muslims, not just one guy who disappeared from the Church-Wellesley neighbourhood six months ago."

"Not necessarily. We don't even know if all the men are still missing. It's possible they've shown up elsewhere. Their friends claim they disappeared, but what if one of them got nabbed for selling drugs and ended up in jail? There could be plenty of reasons why they didn't announce their departures. We still don't even know their full names."

Prabin looked unconvinced.

"There's also the possibility that the chief might not have been able to secure permission from the men's families to bring the matter to public attention. Nabil's brothers don't want him to be outed, especially if he turns up and suddenly finds all his friends and relations now know he's gay."

"But that's not helping things."

Dan shook his head. "No, it's not. But in a perfect world where we can be who and what we are without fear of consequences, there wouldn't be gay kidnappings and killings."

A trainer in a torn T-shirt and worn jeans strained beneath a barbell, his muscles ripped as he demonstrated proper form to a skinny man who'd come dressed in a pricey blue track suit. The women in the room looked overly serious in this male-dominated world. The others, mostly men in their twenties and thirties, sweated through their workouts. Three of them sported facial hair. They might have been Muslim. Any one of them could have been the man behind the disappearances.

"I guess that's where we come in," Prabin said.

"Maybe," Dan said. "I still don't like the idea of deceiving Donny. It puts me in a difficult position personally."

Prabin shrugged. "I'll square it with Donny when the time comes. This is my decision. I'd prefer not to do it on my own, but I will if I have to."

Dan sighed. Talking to Prabin was a bit like arguing with Ked. "Then let's strategize. I still don't know how to go about setting you up to be potentially abducted in a bar full of strangers. How do we know who's interested in meeting Muslim men?"

Prabin grinned. "If you weren't so white you would know it's not that hard. When I go out to bars, I can tell instantly who's interested in a brown boy like me and who is not. You know the expression 'fats and femmes need not apply'? That goes for non-whites, too. I'm aware that I am not to everyone's taste, but conversely I'm also very aware when I am. It's in the eyes."

"So, should I assume anyone who doesn't look at me is not interested in white guys?"

Prabin's grin faltered. "Touché."

"More to the point, you're saying we should go out to the bars and let you get picked up by total strangers? I think Donny would crucify me for doing that no matter what the intention."

"Not just any bars. We'll go to the bars where the men were last seen. That way at least we'd get an idea of who is interested in me. I'll leave the rest up to you as my chaperone."

"As your pimp, you mean. Then what?"

"I don't know. Don't you have some sixth sense giving you spidery tingles that tell you when you've been approached by a killer?"

Dan shook his head. "If I didn't know you were an intelligent man, you might have me wondering."

"But I am intelligent. Look — I grew a beard."

"Ah, that's the reason. I thought maybe your razor was rusty. Still, it's going to take more than facial hair to convince someone you're Muslim."

"What else can we do? If I'm approached and it feels a bit dicey, I'll just play it cool and see what the guy suggests. If he asks for a name and number to set up a coffee date then he's probably legit. But if he asks to meet me in some dark dungeon, then sure as shooting, that's our guy."

"Unless he's an S&M master. In which case he'll

just want to torture you, not kill you. Then where would you be?"

"True, but if we're right in assuming the guy we're looking for is Muslim, too, then it should be easier to narrow down."

"Even if he is, not every Muslim is going to look like a stereotypical Muslim."

"Domingo agrees with you on that."

"You want Domingo to give us a physical description? That's a little far out for me, but if you want to give it a try then go ahead."

"I already asked her."

Dan stared. Prabin nodded.

"She said our guy is a shape-shifter. He appears as whatever you want him to be. Young to the old, old to the young. She said he's a man without a soul. He takes the form of whatever's around him."

"Then maybe what we need is a mirror to see if he casts a reflection."

"That's vampires."

"In any case, this is out of my league. I deal in hard-core facts."

Prabin hefted a hundred-pound barbell as though it were a Popsicle stick. He carried it over to the bench and placed it on the frame. "I'm counting on you to take me seriously, Dan. This one's for Randy."

"Hold on a second. This is not about payback time. You are not an action hero."

Prabin looked hurt.

"If we do this, I've got your back. But you have to assure me you understand this is not a game."

Prabin nodded. "I understand perfectly."

"Good. Then we'll have to figure out when and where to begin the hunt for this mysterious abductor."

"Hunt for a killer, you mean," Prabin said. "I think it's time to call him a killer. I hope I'm wrong, but I don't think those men are coming back. Maybe not even Nabil."

He grabbed the bar and pressed.

Dan was at his office by ten o'clock. There were three messages waiting. The first was from the leader of Almusawa. She'd seen the news item about Joe the previous evening. This time she left her name — Khaleda — and a request for him to call back.

The second message was from Nabil's brother Amir. He and Mustafa were hoping for further news. Dan knew to interpret that as saying they wanted him to give them something hopeful to cling to.

The final message came from Domingo to say she'd mentioned Dan to someone named John, who would contact him to set up an appointment. She made it sound like a consultation for hair removal or a dental treatment. John might seem a little eccentric, she warned, but he was very good-looking. *I don't give points for looks*, Dan caught himself thinking.

He phoned Khaleda first. It was the same off-putting voice he remembered from the previous day, only this time it was less strident. She told him that on seeing the news report she'd called her group members to discuss the matter. They were willing to give Dan a chance to tell them what he knew. Their next meeting was that afternoon. It was short notice, she realized, but would he like to join them? Yes, he would do that.

He phoned Nabil's brothers next. Amir answered. As he'd anticipated, they were anxious to hear any news Dan had of their brother. They, too, had seen the report and were more concerned than ever. Did he think Nabil should be added to an official missing-persons list?

"That's up to you," Dan said. "I can still keep looking for him even if you choose to inform the police. They won't be as discreet, but they can certainly help widen the search."

"We will discuss it, my brother and I. In the meantime, Mustafa has transferred the information from Nabil's computer to his own. You may take it with you, if you like."

"Yes, I would. I'll drop by this afternoon to get it."

He turned to his laptop and checked his email. Most of what tumbled from out of the ether appeared to be junk, which was par for most of his work days. He sorted through the garbage, sending it to spam, the IT version of purgatory. At the bottom he found a message from Domingo's latest project: John.

John had included a picture. Domingo had been right — he was impressive-looking. A bodybuilder with massive pectorals and ripped abs, he was wrapped only in a plush white towel. His tongue wagged flirtatiously at the side of his mouth as he held up the camera to a mirror. Evidently he enjoyed posing as a sex kitten. Dan's expectations were plummeting, but he made the call.

The voice that answered sounded distrustful. Dan was reminded of his initial conversation with Khaleda.

For Domingo's sake, however, he was willing to give the guy a chance.

"What do you do again?" John demanded.

"I'm a private investigator."

There was a pause. "What do you investigate?"

"Whatever I agree to take on."

"Like my ex-boyfriend, for instance?"

Humour? Possibly.

"We could discuss it."

"You might come in handy. Is Dan your real name?"

"Of course. Isn't John yours?"

"No. I never give out my real name till the third date. If there is one."

Dan considered several choice answers, but thought of Domingo and held his tongue. "Well, I guess I'll have to wait and see then."

"Who else are you dating?"

"Listen, why don't we get together to discuss these things?"

"Okay. I can schedule you in for next Friday at two."

"That's a week and a half away," Dan said.

"My workout regime is very demanding."

Dan slumped in his chair. He looked over the sleek torso and that salacious tongue. "Not a good time for me," he said.

"When are you free?" John inquired.

"Probably not for a while. Let's just leave it open for now."

"Something pressing going on in the investigating world?"

"Actually, it's my part-time gig," Dan said.

"What's that?"

"Led Zeppelin tribute band. I've got rehearsals coming up."

There was a suspicious silence. John sniffed. "Really?"

"Sure. I'm a dead ringer for Jimmy Page. What say I give you a call when my schedule settles down?"

The line clicked off.

EIGHTEEN

Blunders

MUSTAFA MET HIM AT THE door and ushered him in with the barest of greetings. Amir emerged from the kitchen carrying a tray set with a pot of tea and three cups. He smiled on seeing Dan. As before, the brothers sat side by side on the couch, with Dan across from them in a straight-backed chair. Eyes met and held across the table.

Mustafa waved the cup aside when Amir offered it to him. Perhaps he didn't drink tea with non-believers. Or maybe just not with gay private investigators. Dan was beginning to dislike his quiet, sour looks. At least he could deal with Amir.

"We have considered your request for a list of places our brother may have frequented," said the elder brother. "I am afraid it is very short. There is a mosque we all attend on Danforth Avenue near Donlands Avenue." He hesitated. "Though Nabil was less inclined to go the last year."

"I know it," Dan said. "That's not far from my neighbourhood. I will check in there."

"As well, we know he attends a gym in the downtown area, but we do not know which one."

"It's the YMCA. That is where he met Prabin. I've been there already. He hasn't been seen since the day you last heard from him. I will keep checking, however, in case he turns up."

He quickly brought them up to date, detailing his visit to the Mr. Leatherman contest, but leaving them to figure out the cultural context. Next he told them of his breakfast with the chief of police and how that meeting had resulted in the news item they watched on television. From their expressions, Dan couldn't tell if they were impressed or frightened.

The brothers exchanged a few words in Arabic, their faces impossible to read. Amir might have been instructing Mustafa on how to make tea or he might have been saying they couldn't trust Dan now that they knew he was friendly with the chief.

"I should also let you know," Dan began, "that on looking into Nabil's business affairs, it seems he was operating some websites —"

"Yes, yes — we know of these," Amir said hastily. "He was tutoring young students."

"No," Dan said. "He was operating sites where he posed for money."

Mustafa looked perplexed.

"Sex sites," Dan explained. "People paid to see him show his body on camera."

Mustafa's face struggled to contain his emotions. "These are not the actions of a decent Muslim," he said at last.

"Is it true?" Amir asked.

"Yes, it is," Dan told him. "The only reason I mention it is that his disappearance may be connected to someone he met on one of the sites. There would be records of credit card transactions. That may be beyond my scope to investigate, but the police would be able to look into it. I'm also looking into a man named Hanani Sheikh. He was the designer who created the sites your brother worked on."

"And who is he, apart from being a web designer?" Amir asked.

"Nobody special, as far as I can tell, but he seemed to have an interest in your brother that extended beyond his business affairs."

The brother sat, digesting these revelations. Neither spoke for a moment.

"There's one other thing," Dan said. "I found a reference to a gay prayer group in Nabil's journal. Almusawa. I spoke with the leader, but she didn't recognize his name. He probably used a pseudonym. I have a meeting with them this afternoon. I'd like to show Nabil's photograph to the members to see if anyone recognizes him."

Amir nodded. "Then, yes. It must be done. My brother and I have discussed this already. Please, do whatever you can. It is now more than a week since we have heard from Nabil. We are beginning to give up hope. Every day we wake up to an empty house."

"I understand what you're going through," Dan said.

He followed them down the hall to Nabil's room. Inside, nothing looked as though it had changed since his last visit.

The computer was on. He touched the mouse and the screensaver vanished. As he pointed the cursor to the power button to turn it off, something caught his eye. The desktop configuration looked different.

The folder containing Nabil's photographs was missing.

"Did some of the files get moved around?" Dan asked.

"Mustafa removed all our personal information, but nothing else," Amir said with a glance at his brother.

"I seem to recall some photos from the other day that aren't here now," Dan told them. Mustafa fidgeted nervously under his gaze. "Pictures of Nabil."

Amir said something to Mustafa in Arabic then turned to Dan. "Perhaps they are in another folder. Or else you mistook one directory for another. We all make these blunders from time to time."

Dan shrugged. "Possibly."

His eye caught on the silver ta'wiz. He picked it up by the cord, letting the amulet rest in his palm. Along one side, a sickle moon cradled three five-pointed stars within the open end of the sickle. A slender piece of hope.

"'Prosperous are the believers,'" Dan quoted.

"Inshallah," replied Mustafa. *If God wills.*

"What's inside this?"

"It is a marriage dua from our parents to Nabil. It is their fervent wish that he marry."

"Were they pressuring him?"

Amir nodded. "Yes, I believe they were."

Dan thought of Domingo's tale of violence, ending in the death of the young man in her community.

"May I borrow it?"

"If you wish."

"Thank you." Dan pocketed the trinket and unplugged the computer. "Do you want a receipt for this?" he asked.

The brothers looked to one another again, shaking their heads.

"It is fine," Amir said. "Please tell us about this group. When will you meet with them?"

"This afternoon, if all goes well."

"And you will tell us what you learn?"

"I will."

"Inshallah."

NINETEEN

Mu'tazili

DAN SHOWED UP PRECISELY HALF an hour before the group meeting. The woman who met him at the door was surprisingly young and petite. From her formidable presence on the phone, he'd been expecting someone more commanding and ferocious-looking.

"Hi, I'm Dan."

She actually smiled. "I'm Khaleda. Please come in."

The apartment had a stunning view of the city sweeping westward from Yonge Street. Black thatched roofs, the sudden rush of green at Queen's Park, high towers to the south curving around the lake. The living room was appointed with tasteful modern furniture — monochromatic, uniform — with here and there a dash of colour in hand-carved end tables and Hamsa cushions embroidered with Fatima's lucky hand. Atop a bookcase, ornate silver frames showed smiling faces. Young, brave, resilient-looking all.

She invited him to sit. A ceramic pot sat on a silver salver, emitting aromatic fumes. More tea. At least with Muslims he didn't have to keep turning down alcohol. She poured and handed him a cup.

Finally, she spoke. "One of the members thought I should ask you to participate in the prayer session before speaking to us. She felt it would show that you are in earnest. I assured her it wasn't necessary. I looked you up. It seems you are known in the community. You have done good work for us. I am impressed."

"Thank you."

"You may, however, be wondering who I am."

"I did my research, as well. I know you're a teacher and an author of several books. I also know you fled from Iran." He caught her eye. "If that's the correct verb."

She nodded. "Oh, yes. I fled. I left in the middle of the night. My life was definitely at risk."

"Because you write about gender and sexuality in Islam."

Her eyes told him she was pleased to hear this.

"That and more. I was considered a Mu'tazili — a heretic. Mu'tazila was a school of theology that flourished from the eighth through the tenth centuries. The word means 'to separate from.' Though that is a misunderstanding of what I write. I have not separated from my faith; I merely disagree with some of its fundamental teachings. For instance, it is considered heretical to suggest that the Quran was not uncreated and therefore not co-existent with God."

"I'm sorry — you've lost me."

"Traditional wisdom suggests that the Quran, like God, has always existed. Mu'tazilites believed that God came first and created the Quran. That was a radical philosophical position back then, though one we might think reasonable today when we consider that if the Quran is God's word then God must have preceded his own speech. Others have pointed out inconsistencies in the Quran, such as the sun going around the earth, to prove that the Quran was created at a time when our understanding of the world was faulty and limited."

"Like unicorns in the Bible," Dan suggested.

Khaleda smiled. "Yes, exactly. Scientific investigation, of course, has always been hindered by teachings of various religions. No one wants the inconsistencies of their views pointed out."

Dan thought of his Aunt Marge, a devout Jehovah's Witness. She'd taken him to a Witness meeting where, during a discussion, he'd asked whether the dinosaurs had come before or after the tribes of Israel. The answer had started off a lifetime of questioning when he realized most believers had a habit of cherry-picking their way through books of faith to bolster their prejudices, disregarding anything that didn't fit their ideology, all the while turning religion into a hating machine.

"My faith is important to me," Khaleda continued. "I've written secular views arguing that the words of God are accessible to reason. It's my way of reclaiming Islam from the extremists. There are progressive Muslims, but the voices of the extremists drown us out. We don't fly planes into buildings or behead prisoners; we want a better world, so we aren't considered newsworthy."

She sipped from her cup as casually as if she'd been speaking of simple things like weather patterns or traffic congestion.

"And it was this that made you a Mu'tazili?"

"Yes. When my book came out I soon found myself under attack in my own country. There were death threats. I feared for my life. I knew it was just a matter of time before someone tried to kill me. So I came to Canada."

Once again, she made it sound like child's play, something as simple as identifying a problem and finding a solution.

"Here, I discovered I could be as outspoken as I wanted. It was here also that I came out." She looked around the room. "So now I try to make a safe space for others who want to follow the faith and also follow their own inclinations of sexuality. As the Quran says, 'To save one person is to save all of humanity.'"

"Noble sentiments."

She nodded. "Yes, but as you know, we must put those sentiments into action, not just talk about them."

A buzzer sounded. She put down her cup.

"The others are arriving."

Over the next quarter hour, the buzzer sounded repeatedly as eight women and four men arrived for the meeting. There were no hijabs or thobes, just plain Western dress. Jeans and slacks, T-shirts and blouses. Thoroughly modern Muslims.

Dan had expected resistance or skepticism, but in fact they seemed eager to hear him. He explained how he'd noticed the poster for the first missing man then quickly learned of others who had vanished, leading him to the conclusion that someone was preying on men who were both Muslim and gay.

"And you are sure these men are gay?" asked a young woman named Shenaz.

"What I know is that they all had some association with the community. As for their all being Muslim, that's only conjecture at this point, but I'm pretty confident that I'm right."

An older man with a gloomy expression spoke up. "I only heard about one man who was missing. Why are the other disappearances not on the news?"

"That's a good question," Dan said. "As far as I can be sure, no one has put the pieces together till now. I brought my theory to the chief of police two days ago. He doesn't think I'm wrong, but he's not ready to jump to conclusions. Until he has anything further to go on, he's reluctant to say that they're connected. For now, they're simply being viewed as random disappearances."

"It's not very reassuring to hear this," Shenaz said. "Do they not think Muslims are worth worrying about?"

"I don't believe that's true in his case," Dan said. "But until now no one has come forward from any of the men's families to confirm that they're missing."

"So you are saying we are victims because of our silence?"

"I'm saying it helps to be open, even if you believe the police aren't always on your side."

Dan brought out Nabil's photograph. Heads began to nod.

"He was here about six months ago," Khaleda confirmed. "He didn't give his name. That's not uncommon for people who are trying to see whether they fit in with our group. Then later, if they trust us enough to come back" — here she smiled at one of the women — "more is revealed when the group's commonalities are shared with one another."

She turned back to the photo. "He came only twice. He seemed nice, but I could tell he was displeased about something. When I tried to talk to him after the prayers, he left without saying what it was he hadn't liked. I never really gave it much thought after that. The group is not for everyone."

"I thought he was homophobic," said one of the men. "It was as if he didn't want to be one of us."

Dan nodded. "You might be right. He's closeted and lives with two brothers who suspected he was gay but didn't really want to face what he was until he disappeared."

"We're not allowed to come out to our families," said one of the women. "They want to hear us talk about getting married and how much we want to have babies. Anything else is forbidden. They think *we* are the radicals." She put a hand on the arms of two women seated on either side of her. "Try to talk about things like polyamorous relationships and they would have you declared insane."

The women laughed lightly.

"But oddly," said another, "it's fine to talk about transitioning from one sex to another. I'm trans, but somehow that's seen as preferable to being gay. If you're a man, you're supposed to desire women, not men. It's better to have a sex reassignment than to be gay." She shrugged. "For me, it was like — hey, yeah! That's what I want. But for others it's just another form of oppression."

"In Iran and through much of the Middle East," Khaleda said, "there are gangs who round up gays and lesbians. They run fake LGBTQ websites and lure their victims to meeting places. Then they are killed."

"In Nazi Germany," Dan said, "they were called pansy catchers. Men who lured gay men into compromising situations then had them arrested and sent to concentration camps with pink triangles identifying their orientation."

"Heretics. Mu'tazili," Khaleda said. "Those of us who go against the accepted order are always the first to die."

"What about someone named Hanani Sheikh?" Dan asked. "Is he a member of your group?"

Eyes searched one another.

"Why do you ask?" It was Khaleda who had spoken.

"Nabil wrote about him in a calendar. He said he met him here."

She hesitated. "Hanani was a member, but I asked him not to return. He seemed to treat the group as a dating service. I doubted his sincerity in attending."

Dan looked around at the others and saw a faint smile on several of the men's faces.

An attractive young man with long eyelashes spoke up. "He poses as a devout man, but really he's just a lech. He was a pest."

"Did he ever discuss arranging fake papers for people having trouble with visas?"

"Yes." Khaleda nodded. "Though it's a difficult subject. I would prefer to discuss it with you in private."

"Fair enough," Dan said. "Did any of you ever see Nabil outside of the prayer meeting?"

"I used to see him at the Y all the time," said another of the men. "But after he came to the meeting here he pretended not to remember me. I think he was afraid I would out him."

Dan stood. "Thank you. I won't take up any more of your time." He slid Nabil's photo across the coffee table. "I'll leave this here, in case any of you see him again. For now,

I'd like to remind you to be extra careful of strangers. We don't have any idea who is behind these disappearances, so unless you know a few basic facts about people you meet — who their friends are, where they work — please exercise caution. Don't take any unnecessary risks."

He saw his statement cast a pall over the group. The heretics and Mu'tazilites. When really they were just people who simply wanted to love in the only way available to them.

TWENTY

Betrayal

Fifteen minutes later Dan was back at his office. He stood quietly looking out the window over the Don Valley, thinking of what he'd learned from Khaleda and her group, until screeching tires and honking horns on the parkway brought his reveries to an abrupt halt.

He set up Nabil's computer and turned it on. The missing folder bothered him. The childhood photos were still there, but the shots of Nabil in his leather gear were missing. He wondered what else might have been erased. From what he could tell, the calendar was still intact. Dan read it through again but it brought no further revelations.

He was not sure what to make of it all, but he did know what to do about the missing folder. He called Donny and asked to speak to Lester.

Lester came on the line. "Hey, Uncle Dan."

"I've got a little challenge for you. Can you restore some files that were deleted from a hard drive?"

"As long as the drive hasn't been wiped clean. But if they were just deleted and no one wrote over them yet, then yeah. I can find them for you."

"I'll drop it off tomorrow morning."

"Cool."

There was a knock on the door. He looked over to the smoked-glass window and made out a familiar outline. When he opened the door, Kendra smiled at him.

"Believe it or not, I was in your neighbourhood."

"That's not something I hear very often. No one is ever in my neighbourhood on purpose. In fact, most people avoid it. What's up?"

She held up an insulated bag with a rooster logo.

"Lunch, if you have time. And in case you're wondering, I have no ulterior motives."

"Do I look suspicious?"

"No, but I know how your brain works, so I just wanted to reassure you."

Kendra sauntered into the office and looked around. Things seemed to meet her expectations, or at least not to disappoint them any more than usual. She turned to the coffee table and proceeded to pull a variety of containers from the bags, opening them and doling out paper plates, chopsticks, and napkins.

Dan told her of his meeting with the members of Almusawa as well as Prabin's inclination to go ahead with his plan for staking out the bars.

She listened in silence, a worried expression on her face.

"Look after him," was all she said.

They ate and then cleared up the mess. Dan was making lattes on the office Faema when his phone rang. He ignored it and let it go to messages. A moment later it rang again. He glanced at the screen. It was Khaleda calling a second time.

"Dan Sharp."

There was a moment's hesitation, then Khaleda spoke. "You betrayed us!"

It took a second before Dan found his voice. "What's happened?"

"We've been stalked. Someone showed up at my apartment at the end of the prayer meeting."

"Who showed up?"

Dan exchanged glances with Kendra.

"He didn't give his name. He pounded on my door and when I opened it he began screaming that we had destroyed his brother Nabil. I said I didn't know what he was talking about."

"Did he threaten you or do anything violent? Is anyone hurt?"

"No, but we were all very frightened."

"Describe him to me."

"Twenty-something ... bearded ... dressed in old-fashioned clothes."

"Mustafa," Dan said. "It was Nabil Ahmad's younger brother. I'm sorry. I never gave out any personal information. He must have followed me."

"You're a private investigator. Don't you know when you're being followed?" Khaleda's voice was on the edge of hysterics again. "My god! I knew I would never be safe anywhere and you've just proved it to me."

"I'm sorry. I know this is an unforgivable breach of your privacy. I don't think you or your members are in danger, but let me phone Nabil's brothers and sort this out."

"You must do something. This is terrible!"

Dan hung up and explained to Kendra what had just happened.

"She's right — it is terrible. The poor woman. She's probably terrified."

"Considering the precautions she takes to ensure the safety of her group, I have no doubt she is. Give me a moment while I phone the brothers."

Kendra sat on the couch as Dan dialed Nabil's home. Amir answered. When Dan explained the situation, Amir took a breath.

"I am sorry," he said. "This is unforgivable. I'm sure he didn't mean to hurt —"

He broke off. Dan heard a flurry of impassioned Arabic and put the call on speaker. The argument died after a brief exchange, followed by a door slamming in the background. Amir came back on the phone.

"I heartily apologize for Mustafa's actions. Yes, he admits it was him. He said he followed you to the meeting because he thought he might find Nabil there."

"I would have told you if Nabil was there," Dan said angrily.

"Yes, I understand this, but my brother does not. Please — forgive him for this outrage. I will ensure he never does anything like this again."

"It's not me who has to forgive him. He disrupted a peaceful gathering and those people may want to press charges."

Amir muttered something in Arabic that Dan took as an injunction against such a thing from coming to pass.

"Let's hope it doesn't come to that," he said. "If anything further like this happens, I will drop the case."

Dan heard a sharp intake of breath.

"Please do not do that," Amir said. "I will speak with Mustafa."

The conversation ended. Dan turned to Kendra.

"Your life is so colourful compared to mine," she said with a timid smile.

"It's not by choice."

"From what I heard, I gather the brother who went to the apartment — Mustafa? — was not pleased to find men and women without head scarves gathered together in prayer. To him that was an abomination. It's the sort of Western behaviour that devout Muslims abhor."

"Did you get a sense that he might try to go back and harm them?"

Kendra frowned. "Hard to say. He sounded angry, that's for sure. Is he the violent type?"

"I can't tell. He seems very simple, but sometimes those are the worst. They brood in silence and nurture imaginary slights. Whenever I'm at their house, Mustafa lets the other brother speak. It's as if he doesn't want to reveal his thoughts."

"That fits with what I heard. He kept saying their brother Nabil was a good Muslim and a wonderful boy growing up, but since coming to Canada he has changed. If this Mustafa gets upset because men and women are praying together then what sort of things could he possibly find acceptable about North American life? Our ways must seem positively evil to him."

She looked at her watch.

"I have to go. I'm sorry."

"I'll call you later."

Dan waited till she left then phoned Khaleda back. She hadn't calmed down. Her strident voice was back. She seemed to consider him personally responsible for what had occurred. He apologized again and promised to have a face-to-face talk with the brothers and explain that what Mustafa had done would get him in far more trouble than he could possibly deal with if he targeted the group in any way again.

He was sad it had ended this way. Obviously, whatever chance he might have had for learning more about Hanani and his trade in citizenship documents, whether legal or illegal, was gone.

He'd just closed his office and headed down the hall when his cell rang. It was Prabin calling to remind him they were set to go out to the bars that evening.

TWENTY-ONE

Pulling the Strings

IT SEEMED LIKE AGES SINCE DAN had agreed to accompany Prabin to the bars to round up a potential killer. Back then it hadn't seemed like such an insane idea. Now he wasn't sure, but so far Prabin showed no signs of wanting to back out.

Outside, a blustery darkness had fallen on the sort of chill wintry evening when the sun disappeared by five o'clock and solemn crowds made their way home from work, the odd straggler stopping in at a bar or a coffee shop, fending off the day's gloomy end. Dan tried to think when he'd last been away for a sun vacation. It took a while to recall a Costa Rican excursion nearly a decade earlier. He wished he were there now, but there was work to be done and this was no time to let his mind get in a rut. Still, he reminded himself, it should be simple. As long as they both kept their wits about them, what could go wrong?

Prabin was waiting for him at Starbucks. His beard was approaching full-blown proportions. More than that, he'd found a leather vest, donning it as part of his trolling outfit. A good method actor always came outfitted for the part.

"I'd talk you out of this if I could," Dan told him.

Prabin shook his head. "You know it's not going to happen. The train has already left the platform."

"And you're on it."

"I am. But if you want to give me a pep talk, go ahead if it will make you feel any better."

"It might. In any case, you already know what I'm going to say. Don't do anything heroic. The moment you get the feeling someone is trying something strange then you alert me."

"I promise not to do anything stupid. I don't want to end up dead."

Prabin was to enter the bar first. Dan would follow after fifteen minutes, locate Prabin, then wander off without making contact. He would always be available, no more than a room away at any time. Neither of them was to leave the bar without alerting the other.

When Dan felt certain they were on the same page, he pulled the ta'wiz from his pocket and held it up to the light.

"Put this on."

"What is it?"

"It's called a ta'wiz. It's a lucky amulet."

Prabin grinned. "You think I need good luck?"

"Not you. Your Muslim alter-ego. Other Muslims will know exactly what it is."

Prabin's eyes lit up. "Where did you get it?"

"It was Nabil's. I borrowed it from his brothers."

Prabin's smile vanished. He held the pendant aloft and closed the clasp behind his neck, leaving it resting perfectly on his throat. Soft, vulnerable. Dan already regretted giving it to him.

"How does it look?"

"It's fine. All set?"

"All set."

"I'll see you there."

After a quarter of an hour, Dan left the coffee shop and made his way down the street to Zipperz. An imposing figure in black leather stood on the doorstep smacking his hands together to keep them from getting cold. The bouncer gave him a once-over and nodded him inside.

The notes of a baby grand cascaded through the room. Over in the corner, a pianist provided distraction to any number of lonely souls willing to part with a few dollars tossed into a goldfish bowl in exchange for a snatch of their favourite tune. Nostalgia came cheap to some; to others it was priceless.

Dan made his way to the back of the bar, parting the heavy curtains separating Zipperz from its evil twin, Cellblock. On one side a singalong piano bar, and on the other a full-scale disco. As the evening progressed, the singers were forced to find up-tempo numbers to compete with the sounds battering the walls from the adjoining room. Dancing queens and karaoke lovers made for uneasy bedfellows.

Prabin sat alone on the far side of the room, a half-empty beer bottle in front of him. Dan ignored him and continued down the hall to the bathroom, splashed water on his face, then left. Lights glittered over the half dozen men prancing on the steel floor, a magic carpet floating them to their dreams. Though long dead, Sylvester sang his heart out and reigned supreme in the Stardust ballroom, sprinkling the dancers with glittering memories. Dan caught a last sight of Prabin dancing with a young man as he stepped back through the curtain, the beat shifting abruptly from feeling mighty real to a sentimental ballad about a rose blooming bravely through the snow.

The patrons were mostly men, with here and there a woman, all of whom shared one quality: loneliness. Young, old, and in-between, these were the ones who couldn't bear their empty rooms and empty beds. Dan had thought Prabin's suggestion to go out mid-week misguided, as greater numbers of partyers went out on the weekends and the possibility of a killer blending in with the crowd higher. Now he realized Prabin was correct in saying that people who went out mid-week were likelier targets, more desperate for company and less likely to be accompanied by friends. A predator's dream, in other words.

The drinks and laughs and singalong numbers were all about one thing: people disguising their emptiness. Dan knew the feeling, the urge to chug back one drink after another until you blotted out the feelings, the unwanted emotions, the corrosive fallout of going home alone.

The hilarity may have been a front, but it was loud. At that hour they were all just one step away from Alcoholics Anonymous, but the rowdier they got the less anonymous they seemed. Come on, get happy. Let's chase those blues away. After three drinks, everyone was a talent waiting to be discovered. After four, all propriety went out the window. Dan felt a hand squeeze his butt. Proof that sticking to soda water was best.

He turned and mustered a polite smile. "Thanks, but I'm not interested."

The man leering at him was drunk, but not too drunk to hope for a ride on life's endless merry-go-round. "Oh, sweetie, loosen up and live a little! You don't know what you're missing."

It was a variation on a hundred lines Dan had heard over the years, none of them compelling enough to make him take its speaker seriously.

"I'll take your word for it, but I'm still not interested."

The man's expression changed to a snarl. "Asshole. You look like a waste of time anyway." He stalked off, haughty and bitter.

Dan leaned on the counter and watched the crowd. As usual, there was far too much ice in his glass. He listened as funereal ballads crashed headlong into up-tempo numbers that in turn gave way to weepy blues songs. What the evening needed was a theme.

He'd just bought his second drink when a familiar face entered the bar. Scruffy and dissolute. This was Reggie's pornography-director tenant.

Dan watched him lean into one of the bartenders, a small man with an impressive build. The bartender nodded to a clean-cut young man at the far end of the bar. Dan knew the type: naive, but with a natural sex appeal, and looking for validation in the form of flattery or anything else that came their way. Money didn't hurt either. The director considered the boy for a moment before heading over to introduce himself. After a few minutes of conversation, he offered the youngster a card, then left. The boy turned the card over with a look of excitement mingled with disbelief.

Dan finished his drink and waited till the bartender caught his eye.

"More soda? Or you want to try something stronger this time?"

The accent was thick, Eastern European.

"I'll stick with soda," Dan said.

"Sure thing."

"Did I recognize a director over here a minute or two ago?" Dan asked when he returned with his drink, once again piled high with ice.

"Sure you did. He is a big name in local porn."

"Xavier Something?"

"This is correct. Xavier Egeli." He gave Dan a knowing look and leaned in. "Are you looking to get into the biz? If you like, I can set you up with him."

"I might be interested."

"Very good — here is my card. I am Sasha."

"I'm Sean."

"Great, Sean. Give me a call sometime."

Dan looked down at the image of the boy holding the rose.

He headed to the far side of the room. From there he had a vantage point to see the entire bar. The space had filled up considerably. He watched in the mirror as Xavier headed for the back room. There was something feral about him that was only enhanced by the ponytail hanging down his back. The curtains parted and he disappeared like a duck slipping underwater.

Dan was tempted to head inside, but held his curiosity in check. Prabin knew not to do anything dangerous. After ten minutes, when the pornographer hadn't returned and there was no text from Prabin, Dan got up and headed for the curtained entrance. On the other side, the lights had gone down considerably. Apart from the dance floor, the room was in shadow. Prabin was nowhere to be seen.

He wandered past the DJ booth. Still no sign of Prabin. Nor could he see Egeli. The only other place they could be was in the washroom. Dan headed down the hall, aware that he might appear to be searching for someone. There would be time later for apologies if he disrupted anything.

There was no one in sight. Two of the stalls were open, the last one closed. The smell of crystal meth wafted up from behind the door. Dan knocked. A startled voice called out. "Busy, man."

"Sorry," Dan said, rushing back out.

Out in the hallway, he looked around, fighting panic. Then he remembered the outdoor smoker's patio. Turning left, he walked straight into the path of the drunk he'd rebuffed earlier, clearly a tad more drunk now.

The man locked eyes with Dan, pushing him with one hand. "Think you're too good for everyone else, do you?"

Dan wrenched the hand aside. The drunk let out a shriek worthy of any beer hall floozy.

Timing was not with him. Just then the bouncer appeared, saw Dan's hand on the other's wrist and grabbed his arm.

"Problem?" he demanded.

"No problem," Dan said. "I was just removing this man's hand from me."

"He pushed me," the other lied.

"I think you both need to take this outside," the bouncer said, releasing Dan.

"I was just going to find my friend on the patio and leave," Dan said.

The bouncer looked him over. It was obvious Dan could prove to be a handful if he wanted to. On another day, the leather-clad doorkeeper might have been more inclined to get rough and see what happened, but today he seemed to think it not worth his while.

"All right — get your friend and leave." He turned to the drunk. "And you, don't start anything. If you're past your limit then it's time to go."

Clearly a regular.

The drunk drew up to his full height. "I'm not past my limit. I know when it's time to go."

"Then make sure you do."

Dan pushed open the back door and stepped onto the patio. It was covered in a dusting of snow. Footprints led to the street entrance. Dan unlatched the gate and looked out, but there was no sign of Prabin. He reached for his phone and sent a text: *Where are you?*

Back inside, the bouncer stood at the end of the hall watching him.

"Your friend gone?"

Dan shrugged. "Seems to have. Do you mind if I just have a look around inside for him?"

"Fine with me. Stay away from that little creep. He's a troublemaker."

Dan nodded. "Will do. Thanks."

He'd just passed through the curtain when his phone

beeped. Dan looked down: *Sorry for alarming you. All good here. I'm back at Starbucks.* He buttoned his coat and left.

Prabin sat on a stool by the window. He looked up sheepishly when Dan entered. "I'm sorry for leaving without you," he said. "Donny called twice. The first time I ignored it. The second time I thought I'd better answer, since he'd be wondering where I was. I didn't want him to hear the music, so I exited by the patio. When I tried to get back in, the gate had latched behind me. There was a lineup outside the front door and they wouldn't let me back in."

"I was worried. I saw the pornographer from the apartment where Sam lived, but he vanished around the same time as you."

"Actually, someone did approach me."

"Greasy looking guy with a ponytail? On the small side?"

"No, just a cute kid. I danced with him a little to get in to the club vibe. He was watching me from across the room for a while before coming over. He seemed very interested in this thing." He pulled the ta'wiz out from his collar. "I couldn't remember the name of it. I was kicking myself."

"What did you say to him?"

"Nothing. He spoke to me in Arabic. I don't know a single word. When I told him I didn't speak the language, he took off."

"No harm done then, I guess."

TWENTY-TWO

The Nature of Evil

IN THE MORNING, DAN DROPPED Nabil's computer off at Donny's. Lester was waiting for him. He'd taken the day off school to accomplish the task Dan had set out for him. Dan didn't argue with him or try to talk him out of it.

Lester had become a handsome, respectful young man. Dan smiled to think of the dirty, distrustful kid he'd hijacked off the streets three years earlier, setting him on a path that would lead to something positive. It had led to an interest in music. *Give a misguided kid a goal*, Dan thought, recalling his own redemption following the birth of his son, *and you give him a second chance.*

"Do what you can," Dan told him. "Anything you come up with may be helpful."

"I won't disappoint you, Uncle Dan," Lester said. "This is child's play."

Dan had low expectations, but by afternoon he had a message from Lester saying he'd salvaged four deleted folders and had emailed their contents. "I can also tell you that someone has been monitoring this computer remotely," he added. "Could be a hacker, but it looks friendly. Ever heard of Sheikh IT! Designs?" he asked.

Oh yes, I have, Dan thought, as he opened the attached files.

The first contained tax data, which jibed with what Amir told him. He deleted that without opening it. The second folder contained detailed plans for a business deal that went sour. There were a few angry outbursts in two emails between Nabil and a potential partner. That in itself might be worth looking into, he noted.

It was the third folder that caused him to pause. In it was the same nude photograph he'd found both sexy and boyish. He studied it again: Nabil faced the camera, his hands gripping his feet, revealing everything and nothing at the same time. It was intimate and sweet, the sort of photograph where you would have to be fond of the photographer to allow it to be taken. And the photographer, no doubt, would have to be fond of you.

Alongside the photo, Nabil had saved an email thread. The first message in it said, *To my little imp — hope you enjoy the attached!* The second, Nabil's reply, thanked the photographer: *R. Whitman*.

The *R* from the diaries who broke Nabil's heart. The same *R* he knew he'd run into when he entered the leather contest.

Woody Whitman's first name was Robert.

Dan's mind went into overdrive. Why had his leather-wearing friend not mentioned photographing Nabil? There could, of course, have been a dozen good reasons, the chief among them being an affair he hadn't wanted to reveal. But to Dan it seemed a serious omission considering the circumstances in which he'd asked if Woody knew Nabil. And then there was Woody's evasive reply: *I see him around from time to time.*

The fourth folder was of even greater interest, containing a scan of Sam Bashir's visitor's visa showing an expiry date from early that year. An appended email to Hanani Sheikh asked him, as a friend, to do whatever he could as a favour to Nabil. Dan recalled the special request Nabil had humbled himself to ask, and thus Sheikh's fury that Nabil had emailed him. But it still didn't answer the question of whether the designer had supplied the document in question.

Dan called the number on Hanani Sheikh's business card.

"Mr. Sheikh, it's Dan Sharp again. I called earlier about setting up a website."

"I told you I am very busy. I can't help you. I run a small business all by myself and take on my clients when and as I choose. You need to stop pestering me."

"Then I suggest you make a space for me in your busy little schedule before I go to the police with information that will put you out of business for good."

The premises did not look like the opulent preserves of someone who made his living exploiting other peoples' misery, but Dan was more than willing to give Hanani the benefit of the doubt and let him prove he was as rotten as he believed him to be.

Just a stone's throw from Yonge and Bloor, at the heart of the city, Sheikh IT! Designs was one of the smallest, dingiest office spaces Dan had seen in years. His own, above a warehouse in the city's east end, was palatial compared to this squalid two-room affair over a pizza joint, whose neighbours included an Indigenous HIV agency, an ethnic actors' studio, and a tarot card reader. Maybe Domingo should give them a whirl, Dan thought, as he climbed the grimy set of stairs, avoiding the broken tiles on every other step.

He knocked and entered. The inside of the office was little better than the hallway. The walls were a lurid orange. There was no receptionist to greet him. A thin, bespectacled man who looked like a private school headmaster came out of a small room at the back and looked Dan over.

"Dan Sharp?"

"Yes."

"I'm Hanani Sheikh. Come in," he said simply, indicating a battered desk and chair at the back. "Please let's get to the point. I see no reason to waste your time or mine."

Dan sat and placed a USB stick on the desk. "The contents of this device were taken from the hard drive of Nabil Ahmad's computer. I understand that, among other things, you created websites for Mr. Ahmad."

"I run a design company, Mr. Sharp. Are you implying that there is something illegal in that?" Hanani looked at Dan over his glasses. "Has he done something I need to be careful about associating myself with?"

"Not unless you've done something wrong."

"No, nothing."

"You planted software on his computer allowing you to access it remotely. You read his calendar. I have a witness who works out with Nabil Ahmad who saw you arrive at the YMCA within minutes nearly every time Nabil was scheduled. It's called stalking."

"It's called a coincidence."

"Like hell it's a coincidence!"

Hanani removed his glasses and pinched the bridge of his nose. "I was only trying to help him."

"Help him how?"

"Help him sort himself out. He's living a duplicitous life. He's gay, but he's in deep denial." Hanani glared at him. "What do you want? Money? Did Nabil hire you to squeeze me? I have nothing. I am an honest businessman."

"An honest businessman who supplies fake visas. Nabil emailed you a copy of Sam Bashir's visa and asked for your help."

For a moment, Hanani looked frightened. Then his face took on a shrewd look. His composure was back. "And was there a reply from me agreeing to do it? No, there wasn't. Because I never supplied him with anything. And if it ever comes down to it, it will be his word against mine." He pointed to the doorway. "Get out. You're wasting your time. Tell that idiot Nabil to stop bothering me."

Dan paused. Unless he was faking it, Hanani didn't know Nabil was missing. But it had been worth a try. "I can still report you. A quick government search will show whether such a document was ever used. Bureaucrats love these things. They'll put you out of business forever."

"Go ahead and search. Someone else may have supplied him with a visa, but it wasn't me." He leaned across his desk. "I know who you are. I've done my research. I have to say, I was impressed with what I found. When you called, I thought, *Whatever he wants from me, this is a man I do not have to be afraid of.* But I wasn't expecting this cheap attempt at extortion. Let me ask you something. Do you know what happens to people like us in the Middle East?"

"I can guess."

"They bury us up to our necks in the sand. Then they stand back and throw rocks at us until we're dead. So go ahead and report me, if that's what you intend to do. You'll be closing the door on a lot of refugees. I am their only hope. Look around you. Do I look like I'm getting rich doing this? If someone has money, I take it. If they don't, I spend my own. I give people their lives back."

"How do you know they're legit?"

"I don't have time to worry about that. To me, if they're gay then they're legit."

Dan eyed him. "Does that go for Zoltan Mirovic's underpaid dancers as well?"

Hanani had the good manners to look embarrassed. "We can't all be so choosy about our clientele."

Dan left undecided about whether Hanani had anything to do with the disappearances, though he wasn't ready to rule him out entirely. He had just returned to his office when a knock came at the door. It opened of its own accord. In strode the chief of police hugging a small box, with an exasperated look on his face.

"Three flights up? Why doesn't this place have an elevator?"

"Luck of the draw."

He looked around, taking in the furniture and all the other trappings of Dan's life as a private investigator. "This is what you prefer to working for me as an officer of the law?"

Dan smiled. "I call my own shots. Could I do that working for you?"

The chief seemed to consider this. "Nah. Maybe not."

"Busy men like you don't usually make house calls."

"No, they don't. I'm making an exception with you."

He set the box on Dan's desk, reached in, and brought out a handful of DVDs. He tried unsuccessfully to place them neatly in a pile, but the slippery covers erupted from his hands and spilled across the surface. Naked bodies lay everywhere, their titles silently screaming up at them. *All male action. Hard-core! Double penetration. Triple action!*

Dan looked up. "If I didn't know better, I'd think you were flirting with me."

"Yeah, well … as I said, my wife left me. I might be open to suggestions, but keep it to yourself. For now, I suggest you look through these and see if you recognize any of the men you're looking for."

Dan sat back and crossed his arms. "Why me? Don't you have any gay cops to do this sort of thing?"

"A couple, yeah, but I'm afraid they'd get too engrossed and miss the point. No pun intended. The straight ones would just turn a blind eye to anything they don't want to see." He paused. "Not to mention I'm kinda embarrassed to ask some of my guys to watch this stuff, so I figured you're the best choice."

Dan reached for one of the cases: *A Clear and Present Danger.* A youngster dressed in a naval uniform and tied to a chair recoiled from the advances of an older man sporting an impressive erection. *A submarine like that* would *constitute a threat*, Dan mused.

He turned it over. On the back: *Star-X Productions!* Beneath it, the now-familiar boy with his rose.

The chief shrugged. "You mentioned the name Zoltan Mirovic. He runs it. Mirovic made a living in the black market during the war in Bosnia. He was rumoured to be associated with a death camp where inmates were forced to kill one another with hammers, but nothing was proved. When the war ended and the good times dried up, he came over here to avoid criminal charges. Lucky us. Now he's transformed himself into a purveyor of kinky videos. On the surface, it's just your local pornographer marketing his wares online to anyone desperate enough to pay for that shit. All quite legal in today's world, of course. But there's a bigger side to it. We suspect he's running a flesh trade in illegals, narcotics, all that stuff that keeps me up at night and makes my wife want to leave me."

Dan thought of Hanani Sheikh's underground railway. "If he's using illegals, is it possible some of the missing men are being offered papers in exchange for their work?"

"You're a smart cookie, Mr. Sharp. You really should be a cop and work for me." He looked down at the DVD cases. "Why not start there?"

Dan studied him. "Is this an official request you're making?"

The chief shook his head. "Officially, I have to tell you to stay far away from this one. Mirovic and his cronies are about as evil as it gets."

"And unofficially?"

"I know you. You never do what you're told. It's what I like best about you." He winked. "Have a look through these and see what you can find. If those missing men are in here, I want to be the first to know."

Dan squared the DVDs into a pile, running his fingers down the titles. Was the chief so naive as to think you had to watch them to know who was in them? Maybe there were other reasons his wife wanted to leave.

One by one, he examined the covers. *Sugar Is Sweet, Boy Meets Toy, Man O'War*. Not exactly literary efforts. He was almost at the bottom of the pile when he saw Joe's face on the back of a DVD entitled *1001 Arabian Knights*. He was credited as Joe Slayed.

He slipped the shiny disc into his laptop. After a jangly fanfare, a sultry voice told of a young man's exploitation at the hands of a thousand-and-one well-endowed Arabs. These, the narrator explained, were a few of his favourite episodes. Cut to: a diaphanous curtain, a thin youth lying naked on a bed beneath a canopy. The music turned horror-flick cheesy as a shadowy figure approached. Dan fast-forwarded through the early sequences, as thuggish-looking men in skimpy costumes took advantage of the young man, whose attempts to resist were all but non-existent. *Either he's a lousy actor or he's drugged*, Dan thought.

In the final scene, the young man, who had clearly not learned to sleep elsewhere, was awakened by a man with a scimitar. This was Joe. Once again, the boy submitted to his aggressor's assault. After a racy sex sequence, Joe put his hands around his neck and began to squeeze. Here, at least, the action looked real as the young man thrashed then lay still. The camera pulled back to reveal his inert body until fadeout.

Naughty urban fantasy or something more? Dan wondered. He thought of Donny's comments about snuff videos. No production company would distribute a real-life snuff scene, despite what he'd just watched. As the credits rolled, Dan read the fine print about all actors being of legal age plus a disclaimer that the violence had been simulated.

He turned to the remaining DVDs. It was the next-to-last case that caught his eye. There, Edie Foxe appeared before him in all her coquettish, contortionist spectacularity. *BOI Meets BOY* promised "a gender-bending S&M queer fuck." *Whatever that is*, Dan thought as he popped it into his laptop.

The opening images were blurry. In a darkened room, the camera panned across a four-poster bed with several coils of ropes in view. Then it turned to Edie, who appeared in her boi drag. She seemed to be watching someone just out of range of the lens. Her heavy-lidded eyes made her look like a silent-film vamp.

"Hi," said a breathy male voice from off-screen.

"Who are you?" Edie asked.

Her deep voice and Eastern-bloc accent fit the scene well, like Bela Lugosi in his vampire drag.

"Just a friend."

"What do you want?"

A skinny male figure edged into view. "Do you like rope play?"

Edie turned and regarded the ropes, as though she might have thought she was there for some other purpose.

"Yes."

"What do you like to do?"

"I like to submit," she replied.

"Do I have your permission to hurt you?"

"Try me," she replied.

Dan fast-forwarded to the next scene. They were both naked now. The boy was scrawny, but he had an impressive erection. Edie lay face-down, her ankles and wrists secured to the bedposts. She'd been gagged, rendering further dialogue unnecessary, though her captor seemed determined to fill in the blanks for the unimaginative.

"I'm going to hurt you now," he said, slapping her buttocks hard enough to leave handprints.

Unlike the youth in the previous DVD, Edie's reactions were believable. She writhed and moaned, twisting her head from side to side. Her eyes flashed in what looked like genuine fear. The lights narrowed till they focused on her pearl-white skin.

She struggled as the boy entered her roughly, without a condom. Dan thought of Woody's comment about the prevalence of HIV in the S&M scene. Perhaps the risk was part of the allure.

He fast-forwarded again. He was nearing the end of the video. The boy bent and whispered in her ear. Dan was unable to hear the dialogue. Edie looked panicked. She struggled and tried to pull free of her bonds as the boy vanished off-screen. When he returned, he brandished a metal rod that emitted an orange glow. His hands were gloved.

Somewhere out there in the darkness, Dan knew, there was a camera operator, a director, lighting people. If anything went wrong or got out of hand then they would be there to stop it. None of this was real. It couldn't be.

He watched as the boy pressed the metal against Edie's back. Her screams were audible despite the gag. She writhed in an impressive display of pain then lay still. The boy did this three times in succession, each time leaving a long red stain on her skin. If Dan hadn't known better he would have sworn they were real.

TWENTY-THREE

Secrets and Lies

DAN PUSHED THE DVDs ASIDE and sat gazing at the whitened trees across the river, their branches dusted with snow. There was something peaceful and annihilating in how it enveloped the city, transforming sidewalks and rooftops, filling streets and slowing traffic.

He pulled a card from the pile on his desk and dialed the number.

"Hello, Reggie, this is Sean Peterson. The private investigator." There was silence on the other end. "Hello?"

"Is that really your name?"

Now it was Dan's turn to reply with silence.

"I looked you up, you know. There's no one by that name doing what you say you're doing. Not in this city, anyway."

Dan sighed. Most people weren't as diligent as Reggie, or if they were they preferred not to confront him with his inevitable lies.

"You're right, it's not my real name. I don't always give it out for reasons of privacy and client confidentiality."

"You could've trusted me." The voice was hurt and distrustful.

"I apologize. If you knew the nature of my work you would understand why I can't always do that."

"Was any of it true? Do you even know Sam — the guy you said you were looking for?"

"I am a private investigator. I was hired by clients to look into the disappearance of a man who knew Sam. I thought perhaps I could find a clue to what happened to my client if I could see whether Sam still lived at the same address."

"So you don't really know him?"

"No."

Reggie seemed to be mulling this over. "What's your real name?"

"Sharp. It's Dan Sharp."

Dan heard tapping.

"I'm looking you up as we speak, so it better be real." There was a pause. "Okay. That's your site. At least now I know you're a real person. What do you want?"

"I'd like more information."

"I told you all I know about Sam. There's nothing more to tell. He's gone and I don't know when he's coming back."

"That's okay. I'm not looking into him at the moment. I was wondering — if I came over in person, would you answer some questions about your other tenants?"

"I'm kinda busy right now —"

"I can pay for your time."

That seemed to settle the matter.

†

Dan showed up bearing a pen and notebook. Reggie might not have been the sharpest pencil in the case, but he was the kind to respond to visual clues. In fact, it turned out to be a good choice. The super clocked the notebook in Dan's hand and nodded.

"That's good," he said. "Because I was going to say you can't record anything I say in case it gets me in trouble later."

He opened his door and Dan followed him inside the sparsely furnished apartment. The air was heavy with pot smoke.

"If you prefer, I won't write down anything at all. That way there's no record this conversation ever happened. You could deny I was ever here, if that makes you feel better."

Reggie shook his head. "No, it's okay. Write down whatever you want. Just don't make me sound weird."

Dan held out the cash they'd agreed to on the phone. Reggie looked at him contemptuously as he pocketed the bills.

"You didn't really need to pay me, you know. I would've talked to you for free."

He giggled.

Dan wondered if it would even be worth interviewing him while he was stoned, but he'd come this far already. Who knew when he'd have another chance in the future. "A deal's a deal. Do you mind if I sit?" he asked, indicating a footstool.

Reggie made a gesture that seemed to take in much of the room. "Wherever you like. I ain't gonna stop you."

"Thank you."

Dan sat and looked carefully at Reggie. "The other day when I was here —"

"When you were trespassing."

"Yes. The other day — after you let me look in Sam's apartment, which I very much appreciated — just as I was leaving there was another tenant coming in the front door. You said he was a pornographer."

Reggie sneered. "Low-life son of a bitch."

"I saw him in a bar a few nights ago. Do you know Zipperz?"

The look on Reggie's face showed confusion. Dan thought at first he was surprised to learn that his tenant had been in a gay bar, but then the super said, "I thought you said you weren't single."

"I'm not single. I still go out once in a while," Dan replied carefully.

Reggie smirked. "So you have an open relationship? I know all about that."

"Whatever you want to call it. Anyway, I was out a few nights ago and I saw your tenant. The one who was at the door when I was leaving."

"I can't let you in his place, too," Reggie spat out. "What do you think I am?"

Dan put up his hands to ward off further protest. "I wasn't going to ask you to let me in. I just wondered if you could tell me about him."

"Okay, so what do you want to know? His name's Xavier. Xavier Egeli. I can tell you that much."

"I already know that, thanks." He placed Nabil's and Joe's photos on the table. "Do you recognize either of these guys?"

Reggie looked at them quickly and shrugged. He pointed to Joe. "This guy was in posters around the bars a while back. Never saw the other guy."

Dan pointed to Joe's photo. "Sure you don't recognize him from around here?"

Reggie scratched his head. "Nah. I don't think so."

"The reason I'm asking is because he was in a Star-X video. Are you ever around when they make the videos?"

"Sometimes I see guys waiting in the hallway. And once in a while there are these heavy-duty lights outside his door. I mean, I'm the super, right? I know about all the shit that goes on around here."

"What about the other one?" He pointed to Nabil's photo.

"Nah. Like I told you." He stopped and regarded Dan. "So what's all this about, anyway? Is it because the guy you're after was in one of Xavier's films?"

"That, and I wanted to get a better sense of why at least one of the men who vanished had been in Sam's apartment."

Reggie's eyes looked as though they might pop. "For real? How do you know that?"

"I saw a photograph."

Reggie's look was pure doom. "So the police will be coming here, one way or another, is what you're saying."

Dan shook his head. "No, not necessarily. I'm just trying to piece some of the story together and figure out where it leads."

Reggie's hand slammed down on the coffee table. "Shit! These freaks are going to get me in trouble." He looked around crazily, his gaze lighting on the pot plants. He nodded. "This is all my boss's fault. He lets this crap go on up there. They're even filming in the basement. It's getting out of hand."

"The basement? Is that the industrial door at the other end of the hall?"

"That's the one. They shouldn't be down there. Other tenants use it, too."

"Would you show it to me?" Dan asked.

"What? The basement?"

Reggie looked frightened. "Why? What do you think you'll find?"

"Hopefully nothing."

Reggie's eyes moved over to a rack of keys hanging beside the fridge. "What do I get for it?"

"If we go over the hour, like I promised, then another fifty."

"How about something else?"

"Like what?"

"Like a date? Come out and have a drink with me sometime."

"All right."

"When?" Reggie snapped.

"You choose."

"Friday. No one's around on the weekend. They don't bother me unless it's an emergency."

"Okay, sure."

"You promise?"

"I promise."

Reggie sprang up and grabbed a flashlight and a set of keys. "Let's go."

Dan followed him down the hall. Reggie took a moment to unlock the heavy door. It swung open into darkness. A retrofit light switch clacked under his fingers and a dim bulb of iron-age wattage flickered on. The stairs were worn, showing deep grooves where footstep had followed footstep for who knew how many decades.

"Don't touch the walls," Reggie warned. "You'll get dusty."

They were pea-soup green, bilious and flaking with silicate dust like a festering wound, as though the wall had bubbled. The building was old, probably mid-nineteenth century, from sometime after the Great Fire of 1849 when promises to build out of brick instead of wood got you a better chance of getting your application passed.

It was cold. Their breath lit up the space. The air had a peculiar quality, as though they were breathing in something unsavoury. The silence felt oppressive until a furnace chugged on, an eerie, octopus-like contraption feeding its many arms up through the ceiling and filling the space with a heavy thrumming. At the centre of its bulk, an orange glow seeped around the edges of the intake door.

"Is that thing even legal?" Dan asked, thinking it a wonder it hadn't burned the place down.

He recalled furnaces like this back in Sudbury, tucked away in the basements of houses built on rock. You found them wrapped in huge rolls of insulation. The risk of asbestos contamination was high until legislation made it illegal.

"Not for much longer. We have to get rid of it. The city, eh?"

They plunged on till they came to an old door built of wood planks with an iron grill. It swung open at Reggie's touch. The cold seeped through even more now. It was like a morgue.

Spiders had claimed lineage here, creating webs and tunnels coated in mica dust where no self-respecting fly would venture. Dan remembered the adage he'd learned as a child. If you had ants in your house, get some spiders; if you had spiders, get some mice; if you had mice, get a cat. It went on from there, a zoological ladder up the food chain. And if you had humans, then what?

They twisted and wound their way through dingy rooms lit by overhead bulbs overlooked by the passage of time. Dan kept his eyes open, but saw nothing unusual in the assortment of tools and boxes and debris scattered about, the detritus of lives left behind. At the far end of the corridor they arrived at another solid wood door. Someone had had a moment of inspiration and painted it blue, the single bright note in all the greyness surrounding them. In honour of what, it was impossible to say.

A hefty padlock lay across the latch.

"This is the locker room," Reggie was saying. "These are personal, eh?"

He unlocked it, slid the door open, and switched on the overhead fluorescent light. It fluttered on, revealing a row of metal doors lined up one after another. Some opened onto empty space. Others were secured with a variety of locks, both massive and flimsy, just begging to be broken into, Dan thought.

"The tenants keep their belongings down here?"

"Every apartment has a locker. No one can get in but the owner."

"Which is Star-X's?"

"That one." Reggie pointed to a scarred door secured with a heavy bolt.

Dan tried the lock, but it held. "Which is Sam's?"

Reggie hesitated then pointed out another door farther down. "That one, I think."

The lock hung in the clasp, but wasn't secured. Dan slipped it off and opened the door. Reggie stepped in and switched on his flashlight. It barely illuminated the room. The space was empty. Dust motes hung in the air like miniature planets orbiting a feeble sun.

"Did he ever keep anything in here?"

Reggie looked around. "There used to be several large boxes. Then one day they were gone. I never knew what was in them."

Dan wasn't sure what he'd expected to find, but it felt anticlimactic, as though he were missing something obvious. The furnace chugged off and an eerie silence resumed as they made their way back through the maze of corridors, following the long, gloomy passage. From the floor above, a voice called Reggie's name.

A large silver-haired man stood at the top of the stairs, flicking the unclasped lock. His eyes glittered, green and luminous, like a predatory animal's.

"You should be more careful. I could have locked you in down there," he said as Reggie emerged from the gloom with Dan behind him.

His accent was similar to Edie Foxe's, but cultivated as though to disguise its origins. The clothes he wore were tailored and expensive. He filled them well, a man assured of his place in the world. There was a subdued strength beneath the cloth, a hint of muscle under the fat, like an indulgent man in good shape who had let himself go out of boredom.

Prabin had asked Dan whether he could detect the presence of a killer. This man felt close.

The man exchanged a look with Dan. It felt oddly intimate. He smiled as though they might be friends. "And you are?"

"He's the furnace inspector," Reggie interjected.

The man's expression turned dismissive.

"We'll be in compliance soon," he assured Dan. He looked him over. "No uniform?"

"Unofficial call," Dan said.

"I see. Well, I hope there won't be any problems until we do."

"No problems," Dan replied.

The man turned to Reggie. "Make sure you give Xavier full access whenever he needs it. Any time of day — or night."

"Yeah, sure — can do."

"And keep your eye on the kids he brings in here. All those street hustlers will rip you off nowadays. I don't want them walking away with a camera or lighting equipment." The big man turned to look at Dan again. "Did he tell you what we do here?"

"No. I didn't ask."

"Well, I'll tell you. We make pornographic videos. Ever want to be a porn star?"

Dan shook his head. "Not my thing."

"Too bad. You've got the right look for it." He turned and headed up the stairs.

Reggie nodded Dan toward his apartment. Once they were inside, he closed the door behind them.

"I told you all this crazy shit goes on here. I could help you with your work. We'd be great together. I see things, you know. I'd make a great detective." He giggled. "Crazy guy, huh? No fuckin' discretion, eh?"

"Discretion is not the word that comes to mind," Dan admitted. "Who was that?"

"That's my boss. His name is Zoltan Mirovic."

TWENTY-FOUR

Chill

THE BODY HAD BEEN IN the harbour for a week or more. Dan first heard about it through a personal call from the chief of police, asking him to bring his clients to the morgue for identification as soon as possible.

"How certain are you?"

"Not certain at all, but the body fits the description."

Dan wondered how many tearful relatives the chief had informed over the years that their hopes had led to a dead end, literally and metaphorically. People who trusted him to bring home their wayward children or make brothers, sisters, and spouses see reason and return to their abandoned lives, only to hear him pronounce those chilling words: *the body fits the description.*

"Okay, thanks for that."

"And thanks for your work on those DVDs. I've passed your observations along to the sergeant in charge. I'll let you know what I hear."

Now would be the time to mention that I met Zoltan Mirovic, Dan thought. But officially he'd been told to keep out of it. The moment passed.

"Good luck with your clients," the chief said. "I hope it isn't the brother, but chances are …"

Chances were.

Dan was thankful to get Amir on the line rather than Mustafa, but the call wasn't any easier to make.

"I have news that may not be good," he began. "I want to caution you that it might not be Nabil, but a body was retrieved from the harbour early this morning."

There was a silence.

"I've been asked by the police to bring you to the city morgue to see if you can identify him. I can pick you up in my car, if you like, or I can meet you there."

Amir's response was terse. "Mustafa and I will meet you there."

Dan called Prabin next. He wasn't sure why, only a gut feeling that told him waiting wasn't going to make much of a difference to the story's ending. Prabin's voice went from cheerful to sad as Dan explained the reason for his call.

"Do you think it's him?"

"From what the chief said, I suspect it will turn out to be Nabil."

There was a long sigh on the other end.

"We tried our best, Prabin. It was like looking for a needle in a haystack, going out and trying to figure out who might have kidnapped and murdered these men."

"I could have been out there more. I could have gone each night."

"You could have done that and still not come across the killer," Dan argued. "Or you could have ended up murdered yourself. Keep that in mind."

The brothers were waiting outside the morgue. It was the first time Dan had seen either of them since Mustafa's disruption of the prayer group meeting. For once, Mustafa was the talkative one. He spoke almost non-stop about Nabil and their childhood together, an explosion of memories made more difficult for being expressed in English rather than Arabic, for Dan's benefit.

They were met by two police officers and escorted down the hall. Told they had the option of identifying their brother's body through photographs or in person, they chose the latter.

In the elevator, silence collected like a lingering odour. Dan was no stranger to the morgue, but the brothers were clearly bewildered by the byzantine surroundings: the crime labs, the storage rooms for bodies awaiting autopsies or identification, and the long, sanitary corridors. They were met by a man in a white smock, with an ironic demeanour and long cheekbones that were a cadaverous grey. He introduced himself as Stuart Morgan, chief pathologist, checked something off on a clipboard then led them to a gurney where a small mound lay covered over with a sheet.

When the brothers were asked if they were ready, it was Mustafa who agreed. Stuart nodded to an attendant who pulled the sheet partway down to expose the man lying there. Dan had never seen Nabil in person, but he knew instantly that it was him. Or what was left of him.

Both brothers cried, Amir silently and Mustafa loudly. Dan watched Mustafa to see if he could determine whether they were tears of grief or guilt. It was impossible to tell. The body was covered again, a sad final chapter to a young man's life.

There were official forms to be filled out, arrangements made for the body on completion of the autopsy. Cause of death had not yet been determined, the pathologist informed them. Nor was time of death, as the cool harbour water had kept Nabil's body from deteriorating to any great degree.

Thanking the brothers for their co-operation, and with condolences for their loss, the pathologist left them. Dan led the pair back upstairs and outside, where it seemed easier to breathe. Cold air hit them in the face, a snap back to reality.

"I'm very sorry," Dan said. "I hoped I could find Nabil alive."

Mustafa said something to Amir in Arabic. Amir turned to Dan. "We must accept his death. It is as God wills."

A cruel god then, Dan thought, but kept it to himself.

They stood together at the corner, watching the world go by.

"I will follow up on everything," Dan told them. "You don't have to do anything more at this point except to arrange for your brother's burial. If you need help with that, let me know and I can point you in the right direction."

They nodded their understanding. But even as he made the offer Dan knew that he, a non-Muslim, would not be asked to help with a Muslim funeral. He felt as though he'd done nothing, had redeemed no one.

Leaving them there on the corner, he went home and ate an early supper with Ked, then turned off his phone and fell into a sleep that was like oblivion.

It wasn't until he woke the following morning that he discovered the trail of messages from Reggie. He'd missed their date. The superintendent's voice went from hopeful through bewildered to angry over the course of several hours, as he waited for Dan to show up at their appointed rendezvous.

Dan found Reggie's card and called back.

Reggie's voice was cold. "I knew I couldn't trust you."

"I'm sorry, Reggie. I got caught up in something." Dan hesitated, wondering whether to tell him about the discovery of Nabil's body, but decided against it. Reggie didn't need to know his business. Nor did he need to make excuses. "We can do it another time. I'll have to check my schedule and let you know."

"Don't bother."

The line went dead.

Dan sighed. If the super was that temperamental it wouldn't be worth trying to explain.

He thought he'd heard the last from him, so he was surprised the following day to find a follow-up message from the rejected superintendent of the Viking. Despite his disappointment in Dan, he'd been pursuing a private investigation of his own. It had yielded some surprising results that "will be of great interest to you," he claimed. There was no indication of what he'd found. The message ended.

"Hi, Reggie — this is Dan Sharp."

"I know who it is."

Clearly there was still some soothing needed. "I'd like to apologize again for missing our date the other night. It was work-related. I'm afraid I had no choice."

"You could've phoned."

"If I'd remembered I would have, but something came up suddenly and I lost track of everything else."

"They found that body in the harbour. That's why you didn't show up."

"Yes, that's right," Dan said slowly. "How did you know?"

"I saw it on the news. When they said he'd gone missing from the gay community I knew it was the guy you were looking for."

"Good guess."

"It wasn't a guess. It was a deduction."

"Smart deduction, then."

"You see — I can help you."

"I believe you. What was it you found that might interest me?"

Reggie's voice was smug. "Not *might* interest — *will* interest. Guaranteed."

"You've got my full attention."

"It's about the lockers."

"In the basement?"

"Yes, those lockers."

"You're right — I am definitely interested." This was met with another silence. Talking with Reggie was like pulling teeth. "Are you going to tell me or should I guess?"

"You need to come over here to see."

Dan looked at his watch. "I'm in the middle of something —"

"Okay, forget it then," Reggie said with a tone of finality.

"Wait!"

Clearly, Reggie had the makings of a martinet. With his unremarkable station in life and a boss who terrified him, it was no wonder he nurtured whatever scraps of power he could wield over others.

The silence hummed on the line.

"Well …? Are you interested?"

"I'll come over when I'm done. Five o'clock?"

"Five o'clock. Don't screw up again."

At five minutes to five, Dan parked outside the Viking. Reggie answered his knock with a superior look. The cat savouring its cream.

"I knew you'd come," he said. "I figured out you didn't stand me up on purpose, so I gave you another chance."

"Thank you for that," Dan said. "You're right — I didn't mean to stand you up the last time."

Reggie held up a warning finger. "But this isn't a date — you still owe me."

"We'll arrange something. I'm curious to know what you found."

"Right this way."

Reggie grabbed his flashlight and keys. Dan followed him to the basement and down the indented stairs once again. The atmosphere felt fraught, as though they'd come for a secret tryst. Dan hoped Reggie hadn't made up an excuse just to get him alone. He brushed the thought aside as if brushing a cobweb from his mind.

They soon came to the blue door. Everything looked the same inside. The Star-X locker was intact. Reggie nudged Dan and pointed to the right, where a padlock had been cut.

"I remembered the tenant moved out and never came back, so I took a hacksaw and broke in."

The door swung open. The space was empty.

Dan turned to Reggie. "What am I looking at?"

Reggie smiled. "Watch."

He stepped inside and went to the adjoining wall, removing three boards, one after the other, until there was a space large enough to slip through into Star-X's locker. He gestured for Dan to follow.

"Come on."

Dan slid into the darkened space, lit up haphazardly by Reggie's flashlight. He could make out a low-lying cot with a chair set beside it. As with the arrangement of the chair and couch in Sam's apartment, it felt monastic, as though someone had sat a vigil there.

It reminded him of an abandoned Jesuit lodge he'd discovered one summer when he and three friends stayed at a family cottage. Days they'd spent in the water, holding their breath and competing to see who could stay under the longest. Dan had always turned out to be the winner. He'd thought his record was three and a half minutes until one day he emerged to find scared looks on the faces of the others. *Four minutes,* they declared. *How did you do it? Willpower,* he said, though in truth he didn't know. *You start to feel like you could stay down there forever,* he told them. *After that it's easy.* One afternoon, tiring of this game, they canoed to the end of the lake. There they spied a cabin with the words *Villa de moi-seule* hand-painted on the lintel. They'd heard the rumours that monks practised self-flagellation, and approached the cabin nervously, thinking of the horrors they might find. When they'd looked in, however, all it contained was a cot with a thin blanket and a single chair set at one end.

"And there's this," Reggie said in a whisper, pointing the light to a cape hanging on the back of the door.

Dan fingered the garment. High-quality leather, hand stitched by a talented craftsman.

"Check the inside pocket," the super said excitedly, holding the light high. "But be careful not to touch it with your fingers."

Dan felt a lump. He pulled the fabric aside and peered in. A small wooden box lay nestled at the bottom.

Reggie held out a handkerchief. "Take it out with this," he said. The amateur sleuth.

Dan retrieved the box. The lid gave way with a gentle tug, emitting an odour of something long dead. Inside lay the last thing he might have expected to find there: a set of dentures. But not just any dentures. He held them up to Reggie's light. It was a full set of teeth with glittering canines extending into a pair of fangs stained dark red.

"It's blood," Reggie said.

"It looks like it," Dan agreed.

"It *is* blood. Look how it's dried and flaking around the edges."

"I think you're right."

"I *am* right."

Dan set the teeth back in the box, closed the lid, and slid it back into the pocket of the cape.

"There's more," Reggie said excitedly. "Under the bed."

Dan gave him a curious look then knelt and peered

beneath the cot. A knife blade glinted in the flashlight beam. He pulled it out; it too was stained red.

"And this," Reggie said, pointing his light to the floor where an uneven spot on the concrete showed a similar discolouration. "I think something bad happened here. What do you think?"

"Good sleuthing is what I think."

Dan sat on the chair. He took Reggie's flashlight and shone it around the space. Apart from the cot and the cape, there was little else to see.

Reggie nodded eagerly. "You see? I told you we'd be good to work together."

"You're right. Now let's put everything back the way it was and get out of here."

They stepped back through the opening into the next locker. Dan watched as Reggie replaced the boards, closing the gap with careful gravity, wondering if he'd done all this just to impress him.

The super turned to him. "So what do you think?"

"I think it looks like a film set."

"Sure, they make videos down here. But it's creepy, eh?"

"It certainly is that," Dan agreed, thinking of Edie Foxe's repulsive achievement.

"So what do we do now?"

"We need to let the police know what you found —"

"No way!" Reggie looked startled by Dan's suggestion. "You can't tell anyone. I'd lose my job if they found out about this."

"It doesn't have to come from you," Dan said. "Remember — I'm the furnace inspector. You can tell your boss I paid an unexpected visit."

"But still, he'd know I let you in."

"Reggie, someone has to tell them."

He shook his head. "No. I found it. It's my discovery. You can't tell anyone. If I thought you would blab about this I'd never have shown you."

"Then what do you propose to do?"

"I'll think of something. Leave it with me."

"Okay. For now, at least." Dan looked at his watch. "I've got to go."

A chill had seeped into the passageway. The furnace chugged on as they passed it, obliterating the silence. Dan saw the orange glow around the door. He didn't like the look of it then any more than he had the first time.

"Wanna come back to my place?" Reggie asked as they climbed the stairs and locked the door behind them. "We could chill, smoke some dope."

Reggie waited hopefully as Dan shook his head.

"I'm sorry. I can't do that, Reggie."

"Okay, but you still owe me that date."

"I won't forget this time."

Reggie smirked. "Yeah, right. Famous last words, eh?"

TWENTY-FIVE

That Sinking Feeling

THE CORONER'S OFFICE CALLED THE next morning. Dan made an appointment for two o'clock that afternoon. Then he called Woody and asked to meet for coffee in the same café they'd met at previously. It would be a difficult interview, Dan knew, but one he felt was necessary.

Woody's expression was jovial when he arrived, but Dan's sombre mien brought a worried look to his face. Again, the owner fussed, but even he seemed to sense the gravity of the situation, his greetings less effusive than on the previous visit.

Dan waited till the coffee was set in front of them before speaking.

"How are you, Woody?" he asked at last.

"I'm okay, but I have this awful feeling you're going to give me bad news about something."

Dan nodded. "You're right. Nabil Ahmad's body was pulled out of the harbour two days ago."

Woody looked away. Dan saw something register privately in his eyes before his gaze returned to Dan's.

"I'm real sorry to hear that."

Dan took out his cellphone and held up the nude photo of Nabil. Woody took the phone without a word. He studied it a moment, as though to verify its authenticity, then handed the phone back to Dan.

"It's mine. I took it."

"Why did you lie to me about knowing him?"

Woody spread his palms across the table. For a moment, he didn't speak. Dan waited.

"I was afraid," Woody said at last. "When you said he was missing, I just thought it was better to stay out of it entirely."

"But you knew I was looking for him."

"I couldn't have told you anything, Dan. I didn't know where he'd gone. I didn't even know he was missing until you told me. It was just … I made a stupid decision."

"Were you lovers?"

"I … yeah. I just didn't know what good it would do to tell you." His face wore a twisted expression. "I mean, it wouldn't have helped find him sooner, would it?"

"I hate to think so, but it might have."

"But how?" Woody was nonplussed. "I mean, what we had was so long ago."

Dan looked sharply at him. "How long ago?"

"Maybe a year or more ago."

"Not more recently?"

Woody shook his head. "No. Not at all. He was seeing someone else."

"Who?"

"I don't know. He never told me except to say it could never work out between them. Said they were worlds apart in their thinking."

"How did you meet?"

"At the Y. He wasn't out to anyone. I paid him attention, flattered his ego by asking to take his photograph, and the next thing you know we ended up in bed together."

"Just one of many," Dan said.

"You know me, Dan. I never stick around. That's just who I am. No hard feelings, right?"

"No, of course not. No hard feelings." He waited. "Did you know about the websites he operated?"

"Not at first. That came after I was with him. When I knew him he was too naive and closeted to do anything like that. It was like I gave him permission to be himself. He was doing security guard work when we met. He barely made enough to live on. I told him he had a beautiful body and people would pay to see it online. I didn't think he'd actually follow my suggestion. But he did."

"How'd you find out about them?"

"Nabil was angry with me for a long time. Really angry. He said I lured him out of the closet and left him high and dry. When he showed up at Spearhead, I suspected it was a trap. Like he wanted to get revenge or something. He told me what he was doing. Said he was making a lot of money, lots of guys wanted him. I think I was supposed to feel jealous or something." He shrugged. "So when you said he disappeared, I wondered if it had something to do with the sites."

"You got worried you might be blamed."

"Something like that." He nodded and looked away. The coffee was getting cold on the table between them. "I never said my standards were high. I offer good times, a whirl on the Ferris Wheel, and then I'm gone again. I always feel I let everyone down eventually, myself included. I just never wanted to see anyone to get hurt by it."

Dan picked up his cup and drained it, then set it down again. "Okay, well, thanks for being honest now."

Woody looked worried again. "So, where will you take this?"

"Nabil mentioned you in his diary entries. If it goes to court, I'll have to drag you into it."

Woody stared at him for a long time. "Really? You'd do that to me?"

"I would. No hard feelings, though."

When Dan arrived at the morgue, the pathologist from the previous afternoon was outside finishing a cigarette, the hollows of his cheeks sunk deep in a death's mask with each inhalation. He looked Dan over as though sizing him up for a body bag, then ground the butt beneath his shoe and waved him over.

Dan extended a hand. "Hello, again. Dan Sharp."

"Good afternoon. Stuart Morgan."

"Thanks for seeing me. I hope you don't mind the interruption."

"Not at all," Stuart replied, though his smile said otherwise. "I have to say I'm impressed. You've got friends in high places. The chief called personally to ask me to give you my report. Preliminary findings only, of course. The full report will take a few days longer."

"Understood," Dan said.

Inside, Stuart indicated a vending station at the far end of the hall. "Would you like coffee? Something to eat, perhaps?"

"I'm good," Dan said.

"Yes, some prefer not," he said. "Well then, come with me."

Dan followed him down the hall and into the elevator. They waited in silence as the doors slowly closed on the light of day then reopened in the basement. In the same cold room they'd been in previously, Stuart pulled out a drawer containing a body bag as casually as if he'd been opening a bureau for old linen.

"People often ask if we ever make mistakes. In fact, it does happen. Historically, the point of keeping bodies in storage was to give them time to revive in case they weren't actually dead." He patted the bag. "I'm sure it would be extremely uncomfortable to wake up in one of these, but better than not waking up at all. There was a recent case in Europe where a woman was declared dead then woke up two days later. I gather her doctor lost some credibility."

His nicotine-stained fingers struggled with the bag's zipper. It held for a moment then gave suddenly, revealing Nabil looking much as he had the last time.

"Have you determined how long he was in the water?" Dan asked.

"An excellent question. The answer is 'not precisely.' I can, however, make an educated guess. No less than one week, but more likely closer to two."

Dan calculated back: according to his brothers, Nabil had vanished a little over two weeks ago.

Stuart continued. "Drowning results in a condition known as hypoxia, or a lack of oxygen supplied to heart and brain. Sometimes cold water can slow this effect. There are cases on record of people being revived with little or no mental impairment after being in the water for an hour or more. Rare, of course, and in your friend's current state not likely to happen."

He unzipped the bag the rest of the way, leaving Nabil fully exposed.

"In the case of someone recovered from water, it becomes essential to look for clues telling us the decompositional rate. Determining the post-mortem interval is often a challenge. Water temperature is the determining factor. To put it simply, bodies decompose more slowly in cold water. At first there will be indications such as the wrinkling of skin or the loosening of hair and nails. But by the second week, there will be a detachment of the skin itself, particularly in the digits."

He held Nabil's left hand, palm up, turning it from side to side as though giving Dan an ironic wave.

"Our skin is made up of both dead and living tissue. When immersed in water, dead tissues absorb water like a sponge and start to swell, putting downward pressure on the deeper layers, resulting in irregular patterns known as wrinkles. This is what causes the ridges on your fingers when you get out of a particularly long, hot bath."

He lay the hand gently back at Nabil's side.

"People think we perform magic here. In fact, it is a form of magic, looking at a corpse and asking it to tell us how it got here. The necromancer's art of making the dead speak. It was once commonly believed that the last thing a dying person saw was trapped as an image on the retinas. Therefore, if you were murdered, your murderer's image would presumably be imprinted there. Not true, of course. Similarly, others believed that the last thoughts a person had could be made known by touching the body. Also untrue, in my experience. On touching a dead body I've often thought of nothing other than what I would be having for lunch in an hour or two."

"And what was the cause of death in this case?" Dan asked.

"Another excellent question. And one for which I can give you a precise answer."

Light shone through a frosted window at street level. Movement caught Dan's eye, the interplay of light and shadow, the footfalls of everyday people heading to work assignations, business lunches or romantic trysts, ticking off life's comforting ebb and flow while it lasted.

"Sometimes," Stuart continued, "the answer to how a person died is obvious, as when we get the body of someone who hanged himself or who was pulled from a car wreck. Other times, we're fortunate to have eyewitness accounts. Barring these, however, we look for outward signs. Age can be a clue. For instance, the highest number of heart attacks occur in the fifty to sixty age bracket. Obesity and a history of smoking are also telling. We eat, drink, and make merry, while inside the worm gnaws silently away at the bud, the canker eating us away from inside."

He gave Dan a hard look. "Are you a smoker?"

"No."

"Heavy drinker?"

"Not currently."

"Hmmm," he intoned mysteriously. "And by the looks of you, you're in top physical shape and still under fifty.

Nevertheless, it frequently happens to men in their forties."

"I'll keep that in mind," Dan said.

Stuart yawned and gave Dan a guilty look. "Perhaps I'm the one who should have had coffee," he said.

"I can wait if you like."

"No reason to."

A Y-incision extended from Nabil's pelvis to his sternum. Stuart slipped on a pair of latex gloves, raising the edges of skin as gently as if he were lifting a veil from a bride's face. A mishmash of colours and shapes revealed themselves, the red lozenges of the lungs set alongside ropy, yellow ribbons of fat and the purple, sausage-like string of intestines. Death casually revealed as if in the window of a butcher shop.

Dan was thankful he hadn't had that cup of coffee.

"Where the difficulty for a pathologist comes in trying to determine a precise cause of death is when the antecedent factors are not known and there are no eyewitness accounts or obvious signs of trauma."

He closed the skin flap with a sigh, as though disappointed by its reluctance to share its secrets.

"We already know your friend, Mr. Ahmad, was in the water, so we don't really need evidence of that. We do, however, need to remember that not all bodies pulled from the water died by drowning. First we have to ask why they are in the water. Sometimes people have too much alcohol in their systems and we may conclude that they simply fell in. In your friend's case, however, there was no alcohol in his system."

"He was Muslim," Dan interjected, "so he probably didn't drink. Though I don't think he was a particularly devout Muslim. He was also an athlete, which may have been why he abstained from alcohol."

"Yes, I noticed the excellent condition of his muscles immediately. He took care of himself." Stuart nodded sadly. "In case you're wondering, we were also able to rule out suicide. Drownings attributed to suicide are not actually common, though it does happen. Drownings attributed to homicide, however, are far more common. In such cases, we look for signs of struggle such as skin abrasions, even finger marks to show how and where the victim was held down."

"Did you find any indication of that?"

"Sadly, no." Stuart looked off for a moment, as though collecting his thoughts. "The fact is, you don't have to sink very far to drown. Technically, you could drown in your bath — ergo the infamous bride-in-the-bath murders in England in the last century. Deep-water immersion is more common, insofar as the victim falls into deep water. Bodies submerged at great depths often show fewer signs of trauma because it's much colder, and also the likelihood of having your body swayed by current is lower, resulting in less rubbing against rocks and coral and such."

Dan wondered when he would get to his point, but Stuart seemed to be enjoying his captive audience of one.

"In the case of the Toronto Harbour, it's mostly sand instead of rocks. But for the sake of argument, we'll say he went all the way down. The body gets waterlogged and it sinks. It's what I call 'that sinking feeling.' In this case, some-times the marks we see are the result of disturbances caused by marine animals — usually fish nibbling away. This, for instance." He pointed to a notched groove on Nabil's left ear. "But they can also be the result of being chopped by a propeller blade, which may make it look as though the body has been attacked." He looked at Dan and smiled, a teacher patiently explaining his lesson to a slow pupil. "In the absence of any and all of these, however, we look for other determining factors. On opening your friend's lungs, for instance, we found none of the obvious signs to provide evidence of drowning. Pulmonary edema, for instance, which is a fancy term for fluid in the lungs."

"In other words …?"

"In other words, what we found in Mr. Ahmad's lungs showed something entirely different from what we would expect to find when a body is recovered from the water."

"Meaning?"

"Meaning he had no water in his lungs. He did, however, die due to a lack of oxygen to the heart and brain. The foam in the lungs and throat, for instance, is in fact similar to that of drowning victims. This is caused by the mixing of mucus and air in the trachea as the victim struggles to breathe. But one of the giveaways — if you will look closely at the skin — is cyanosis of the skin."

Dan noted the blue discolouration, which he'd attributed simply to death.

"However, the telltale symptom," Stuart continued, pulling back Nabil's eyelids, like a magician pulling a dove from a hat, "is when the whites of the eyes turn bright red, like this."

He clicked on a mini-mag and held it directly up to Nabil's face. In the bone-white gleam, Dan could make out tiny pinpricks of blood. Demon eyes. Nabil had the look of a man possessed. As though he might suddenly sit up and start speaking in tongues.

"Bloodshot eyes — also known as subconjunctival hemorrhaging — are a result of capillaries bursting in the eyes when pressure builds up in the head due to lack of oxygen."

"So you're saying — ?"

"I'm saying that although your friend was fished out of the harbour, he did not drown." Stuart folded his arms across his chest. "He was placed there by person or persons unknown after being suffocated."

TWENTY-SIX

Meet Your Local Pornographer

DAN LEFT THE MORTUARY AND returned to his office, thinking about his next move. After some serious deliberation, he got Prabin on the phone.

Prabin's voice was grave. "So now we know it's murder."

"I'm afraid so. But before you start beating yourself up again, I think you should know that Nabil has probably been dead for a while. Maybe even before we started going to the bars."

"Why did they find him and not the others?"

"Impossible to say at this point. My best guess is that for some reason the killer got nervous and realized he had to dispose of the body fast, whereas with the others he had more time to hide them."

Dan looked out the window over the river, the landscape frozen and grey. With the rapid freeze setting in, the ground would have been too hard to shovel without a lot of effort. That increased the possibility someone might be seen in a ravine digging a hole that was considerably larger than a dog's grave.

"As sad as it is, we can now lay this to rest and let the police do their business —" Dan began.

"I'm going back out."

"To the bars? That won't bring Nabil back."

"No, but it might prevent someone else from disappearing."

Dan could hear the conviction in his voice. "I might have a better idea," he said.

"What's that?"

Prabin listened attentively as Dan laid out his plan.

"Huh," he said when Dan had finished.

"If you still want to do this, then that's the best way I can think of doing it. It's a little risky, but it won't be dangerous."

"Not with a personal bodyguard on the premises."

"Exactly."

"I trust you, Dan. I know you want to make this right as much as I do. Especially now that we know Nabil was deliberately killed."

"I will be there in the building the entire time," he concluded. "Nothing can possibly happen to you with me there."

"Let's do this."

Dan retrieved Sasha's card from his wallet and read off the number. "Call and ask for an audition then let me know the time. When I show up for an unscheduled visit from the furnace inspector, I can make sure you don't run into any trouble."

†

An hour later, Prabin called to say he'd set up a date for the following afternoon at three. At noon the next day, Dan called Reggie. In his most winning tone, he asked the super whether he'd be willing to help him with his investigation. As he'd suspected, the super jumped at the chance.

"Here's what I need," he said, giving him an address in the west end. "There's a coffee shop on the corner right across the street. Get there early and try to get a window seat. That way you won't be seen. I need to know if a white van with a Nova Scotia licence plate shows up between two and four this afternoon."

"That's it?" Reggie, said, sounding disappointed.

"Don't worry, I'll pay you for your time."

"What's this about?"

"I can't tell you yet, but it could be extremely important to the case."

"Okay," Reggie said, brightening. "I'll be there."

Dan left his office and headed to a costume rental outlet. He went through the racks that held everything from priests' cassocks, bakers' hats, and undertaker suits, through to uniforms for sailors and soldiers. Once, presumably, they'd been the property of living people. Now, however, they'd fallen into the murky realm of the public domain, where just about anyone with a little cash could slip out of one identity and into another.

He chose a brown zip-up jacket with a yellow logo that could have designated anything from a plumber to a department-store deliveryman, then tossed in a pair of brown brogues to match: Mr. General Serviceman.

Back home, he thought of Domingo's admonition as he put on the outfit: *This man is a master of disguise.* Just before leaving, he slipped a gold band on his ring finger and looked at himself in the mirror. He was getting pretty good with disguises himself.

He drove to the Second Cup and waited. Ten minutes later Prabin came through the door, took one look at Dan's uniform, and laughed.

"Convincing," he said. "And we all love a man in uniform."

Prabin had dressed in his gym sweats, with a nylon jacket over top. The ta'wiz glinted above the neck of his T-shirt. Not bad for a would-be porn star. As he swung a chair around, Dan saw several of the customers throw him admiring glances.

"You're popular," Dan said.

"Yeah, but I figure I'm a wannabe, so it doesn't really matter how I dress so long as I show off my muscles."

"Good choice. Make sure you tell them you work for cash only. That'll make you even more attractive to them. And find a way to let slip that your visa has expired."

By the time Dan parked a block away from the Viking, Prabin had broken into a sweat. He gave Dan a grim smile.

"Okay, so I'm a bit nervous," he said in a plausible-sounding Middle Eastern accent.

"That's good. You're auditioning. You're supposed to be nervous."

"And this is my Uncle Hamid's accent, in case you're wondering."

"Sounds authentic to me."

"Me, too. Let's hope I can keep it up."

Dan grabbed a tool box from the backseat. They parted at the corner. Prabin walked on ahead. Dan stopped down the street and waited till his cellphone rang. He answered without speaking and heard the apartment buzzer sound. A voice replied telling Prabin to wait.

He headed for the building. Ten seconds later, he heard the door click open. "You Jameel?"

"Yeah, that's me," Dan heard Prabin say right before his cell clicked off.

"Hold on!" Dan called out, dashing up the walkway behind him. The ferrety director turned as Dan flashed a card. "Furnace inspection. The super here?"

Egeli scowled. "No, he went out."

"That's okay, he doesn't need to be here. I just need to get downstairs."

"I don't have time for this."

Dan gave him a stern look. "Sir, I've been asked by the city to make sure the furnace is in compliance with regulations. Who's in charge of the building?"

Egeli sighed and made a call on his cell. "Furnace inspector wants access to the basement," he said into the phone. He ended the call and turned to Prabin. "You can go upstairs. Third floor. Just wait in the hall till someone calls you."

"Thanks," Prabin said, giving Dan a last look before he went up the stairs.

Egeli turned back to Dan. "Hang on. Someone's coming with the keys."

A voice called from the floor above as unseen hands tossed the director a set of keys. He caught them and headed for the basement door. "I'll leave it unlocked. Just let me know when you're done. We're upstairs in 303. Make sure you knock first."

"Okay. Thanks."

At the bottom of the stairs, Dan looked around. The furnace was chugging hard, threatening to tear itself free from its base. No doubt it was on its last legs. It would need more than an inspector when the time came.

He found the cold-air return and stuck his head in the opening, listening for sounds. One of the tenants was a jazz fan. That was all he heard apart from the opening and closing of a door somewhere above. If Prabin yelled for help, he wouldn't hear it over the hum of the furnace and other ambient sounds old buildings made.

He waited a few minutes then crept slowly upstairs, but it was impossible to move noiselessly. Each step had its own particular creak and groan.

He'd just reached the third-floor landing — 303 was on the left — when he heard footsteps from inside. There was nowhere to hide. Running would give him away instantly.

The apartment door opened and Zoltan Mirovic peered out. Recognition showed in his eyes. "Ah, you were here the other day," he said.

"I was sent back." Dan checked his notebook. "Something to do with a clogged cold-air return."

"I thought maybe you changed your mind and came to audition for us. I like your uniform. Maybe I could write a furnace repairman into the script. Have you ever been in an adult film?"

"Not my thing, thanks."

Zoltan laughed loudly. "Too bad. I pay very well. I mean, how much can you make doing furnace inspection?"

"I do okay," Dan said. "Besides, my wife might not like it." He flashed his wedding band.

"If she's anything like you, I'd be happy to include her. You straight or gay?"

"Wife." Dan held up his hand again. "Straight."

Zoltan's smile faded. He nodded to the far end of the hallway. "The cold-air return is down there."

The door closed. Dan brought out his screwdriver and unfastened the vent cover. He poked around with his fingers then reached into his shirt pocket for a small flashlight. Something actually was clogging the vent where it narrowed just out of reach of the light. He leaned closer. Whatever it was felt soft, furry. Instinct made him yank his hand back, cutting his thumb in the process. He reached into his tool kit for a rag to wipe the blood from his fingers.

He took out his cellphone and screwed it onto a stick, then checked the flash and set the timer. With his good hand he pushed the shutter and dipped it back down into the vent until he heard a satisfied click. Then he withdrew it.

At first it was hard to make out. Then suddenly it came together: a small skull, its teeth bared in a grimace. The rest of it was clad in what looked like a miniature fur coat too large for its desiccated frame. He shivered, thankful its biting days were over.

He retrieved a plastic container from the tool box, bent a wire, and hooked the carcass out, dropping it into the bin. It was too bad he wasn't getting paid for this furnace inspection gig.

The door of 303 opened and closed. Prabin emerged and headed down the stairs. Dan checked his watch: he'd been in there a little more than twenty minutes. He waited a beat, then picked up his prize and headed over. Voices carried through the door.

"I like this one. He looks good on camera."

"I'm not sure he's into it," Xavier said. "I don't want more trouble like last time."

Mirovic made a dismissive sound. "There are ways of getting him to do what we want."

"He doesn't do drugs. He already told us."

There was a silence. Then, "He doesn't have to know."

"No way. We'll end up with another overdose on our hands. It's easier just getting someone who does what we say. There are lots of hungry whores out there."

"You can't always do it the easy way." There was anger in Mirovic's voice. "Or we offer to give him his papers, like we said. It's what they all want."

"I'm getting nervous about these papers."

The voices died down, but the talking continued.

Footsteps headed toward the door. Dan stepped back a few feet then looked up with a surprised expression when Mirovic appeared.

His glance was ominous. "What do you want now?"

Dan smiled. "Looks like I solved your problem. You won't believe what I found in that vent."

He held up the container. Zoltan peered at the dead rat with disgust.

"Your tenants ever complain of lingering odours?" Dan asked.

Zoltan looked at him dismissively. "No. Whatever it is, just get rid of it."

"Okay."

Dan headed back down the stairs.

"Wait one second."

Dan froze. He turned and looked back at the big man. "What is our deadline for replacing the furnace?"

Dan pulled out a notepad and flipped through the pages. He shook his head. "It's in my other book," he said.

"And where is that?"

"It's in my van. I can go get it, if you need to know right now."

The suggestion hung in the air. Finally Zoltan shook his head. "Never mind. I'm sure Reggie can tell me."

"All right," Dan said, and headed back down the stairs.

Prabin was waiting in the car when Dan got in. He sat rigid, looking straight ahead. "Let's go," he said.

Dan started the engine. "You okay?" He turned to look at Prabin, who appeared shaken.

"I'm okay. Just … let's go."

Dan put the car in gear and drove off.

Prabin sighed heavily. "That was really humiliating," he said, then shook his head. "At first they were quite nice. It was all from the shoulders up. They told me I looked great on camera, complimented my physique. When I said I only worked for cash, it seemed to make them happy. They reassured me they always paid cash, with no records and nothing to trace. I'm thinking, okay, this is not so hard."

He looked out the window at the traffic, people walking about on sidewalks, ordinary things.

"Then they told me to strip. Not a big deal. I was expecting that. I pretended to be nervous, which wasn't hard because I really was. When I was finally undressed they brought out a pair of handcuffs and told me to put them on ... behind my back. I knew I was stupid to do it, but I didn't want to piss them off. So I put them on. Again, no big deal, right? I mean, I've tried weird sex before. Not my thing, but whatever. So far everything's jokey, even though I'm cuffed to the bed. Then, just as I started to relax, they asked how I felt about violence. I didn't want them to send me packing, so I said I'd be fine with it so long as it wasn't real. The director gave me this eerie smile and asked if I'd let them draw blood. Just a slice here and there, he said. Nothing that would show. Even though I knew you were in the building, it unnerved me. I started to think about Nabil. I mean, they could have killed me right then and there, you know? They talked about how much money I would get if I did whatever they asked. When I didn't reply, they said they could help me get my papers to work in the country. I said I'd think about it. The whole time I'm sitting there handcuffed to the bed and they're filming me. I asked if they would uncuff me, because I was starting to feel really vulnerable. They said, 'Not yet,' and kept filming. It freaked me out. I've never felt so helpless. It was as if they were trying to break me psychologically."

"I think that was the point." Dan nosed the car around a corner. "They wanted to see if you were the sort of material they could exploit. If you're desperate, you'll do whatever they want."

Prabin turned to stare out the window. "Well, that's it then. I don't want my fifteen minutes of fame as a porn star. That was completely degrading, and it was just an audition!"

"I'm sorry," Dan said.

Prabin shook his head forcefully. "You don't have to be sorry. I was the one who wanted to do this."

"Did they tell you they wanted to use you?"

"That's the funny thing — after telling me how great I was they got very cool and businesslike at the end and said they'd let me know."

"They want to keep you guessing. My guess is you'll get a call in a day or two with an offer. But this has to be the end of it. You can't go through with it for real."

"Don't worry, I won't. That was really creepy," Prabin said. "But what are you going to do?"

"I'll have a talk with the chief and tell him what happened in there."

"If it were up to me I'd lock them both up right now."

Dan dropped Prabin off down the street from the condo to avoid running into Donny. *One more lie,* he thought, *this time to a best friend. Where do they end?*

He turned the car around just as a text came through from Reggie: *No white van,* it said. *Let me know if you need any other help.*

TWENTY-SEVEN

Venus in Polythene

THE CHIEF WATCHED AS THE server set a plate with a large slice of pie in front of Dan, then looked down at his own plate of hash browns and fried eggs. Either it was Mandy's day off or else she'd finally been arrested.

The chief didn't look pleased. Nor did he sound it. "I did tell you not to get *too* involved in this stuff."

Dan tried to smile reassuringly, but it was a bit early in the morning to be faking it. "Officially, yes. You said officially."

The chief sighed. "Do you have to be so literal? There's officially 'looking into' something and then there's under-cover infiltration, which is essentially what you were doing."

"Admittedly."

The chief raised his eyes from his coffee cup, weariness written all over his face. No resolution at home, was Dan's guess. "Couldn't you have just looked into things from a distance?"

"What would I learn from that? Besides, you said you like it when I don't do what I'm told."

"True enough." The chief shrugged. "At least your friend wasn't hurt. He must be brave."

"And determined."

"So they're auditioning for dirty vids, your friend says they got a little heavy with him, but nothing coercive. There's nothing illegal there so far as I can see. I'm not sure where that leaves us."

"Me either, but the whole scene is a little disturbing."

"Disturbing? You haven't seen disturbing," the chief said.

Oh, yes I have. Dan thought of the forty dollars he'd laid on the sill of the ticket window the previous evening, after dropping Prabin off at home following his audition.

"Forty dollars is a lot for a sex show," he'd told the man — or maybe woman, he wasn't sure which — who sold him his ticket. His or her lipstick had been put on crookedly. Someone who wasn't sure themselves what they were.

"It's not a sex show," came the gravelly response. "It's a demonstration of the psycho-sexual aspects of sado-masochism."

"So then it's a sex show with a Ph.D.," Dan joked. The ticket seller's expression didn't change.

"Go in there," the seller said, pointing off to the right.

Dan grabbed his ticket with the words *Sex Wrap* embossed on it. He headed for the entrance and nearly stumbled trying to find a seat in the dark. It took a while before he became accustomed to the gloom. The room was an antechamber, with maybe forty people at best. The lights rose as the performers entered, a display of physical beauty in all shapes and sizes, including a muscular dwarf barely four feet tall. His stature may have been short, but his sexual aura extended well out into the audience. A century earlier and he'd have ended up in a carnival sideshow. Now, he was box-office draw.

"There was also the drugging they discussed when I was outside the door," Dan said now.

The chief shook his head. "No proof. And if I tell you how many overdose cases arrive at the local hospital every day, you'd understand why I can't be bothered to check on it without at least a name or a date."

"We've still got an autopsy report that shows Nabil Ahmad was asphyxiated before being dumped in the water. We've also got the photograph showing he was in Sam's apartment at some point. That could tie him in with Star-X."

The chief paused, fork halfway to his mouth. "You said some of his pictures disappeared between the time you first saw the computer and the next time the brothers let you in for a look?"

Dan nodded.

"That in itself bothers me. We might call it destroying evidence. But there's still no proof he was involved with the porn operation," the chief grunted. "Besides, it could be coincidental that he visited a guy who lived in the same building." He took a bite of sausage and made a face.

"No good cop would believe that," Dan said.

"Don't tell me what I believe," the chief growled. "I've now done a thorough search of the names you gave me: Sam Bashir and the other two. Adam Carnivale and Saleem Mansouri. Bashir came over from Iran on a student visa and attended theatre school for a while. Apparently he was a puppeteer." The chief shrugged. "Do they still have puppeteers? Anyway, his visa expired last year, but we have no record of his leaving the country. The obvious conclusion is that he chose to stay illegally. Saleem Mansouri's a permanent resident. He was a dentist back home in Turkey, but couldn't use his credentials here. Adam Carnivale's real name was Farid Malek. He came here a few years ago from Bosnia as a temporary visitor. Again, I can't find anyone by those names leaving the country." He looked at Dan. "But you were right — they're all Muslim. You get big points on that. However, when I asked for a trace on any other relevant missing persons who fit the same profile, guess what? I found eleven, including your four. It's impossible to keep tabs on them all."

"I don't know about the others," Dan said, "but we know Sam Bashir still keeps his apartment here."

"Not illegal, even if you're not a citizen."

"Is it possible he changed his name?"

The chief shrugged impatiently. "Changed his name, changed his sex. It's hard enough tracking down killers when we know what they look like, but these days the kids are all swapping identities. We took forever to find one guy, a dealer with thirteen aliases and a Facebook page for each one. It was a frigging nightmare trying to figure out who to charge!"

When Dan had asked Domingo the day before, she'd told him she didn't know whether Edie Foxe had another name.

"She came from Sarajevo as a temporary resident," Domingo had said. "Her papers expired and she ended up on the streets. But she was determined to stay in Canada.

She started off as a prostitute to support herself then she discovered there were people with real money who would pay her to put the fear of god into them."

But she refused to talk to him, Domingo said. Even after she explained what Dan was after.

"I'm surprised. What kind of performer doesn't want to talk about her art?" Dan asked.

"A scared one is my guess. Anyway, she said no dice." There'd been a silence over the line. "She has a performance tonight at Lola's Cabaret. You didn't hear it from me."

"Thanks."

The chief pushed his plate aside and concentrated on the coffee. "If these people need money, the sex trade's one of the easiest ways to get it." He looked down at Dan's pie then back to his own unfinished plate. "Should have got that, I guess." He sighed. "The whole Middle East is set to explode. Could happen any day … Syria, Libya. People jumping ship everywhere. Every day someone shows up claiming refugee status. Some are legit, some are not. And getting fake papers is not that hard. I read a report from CSIS the other day — there could be up to a hundred terrorists in the country. Half their budget is spent on counter-terrorism, if that tells you anything. Our border's porous, illegals cross over from the U.S. all the time. To them, we're a haven. But that's not my problem. What *is* my problem is when they end up here in the city, where it's easier for them to blend in. It gives me ulcers just thinking about it. Take my word for it, your guy is one of those, whether his name is Sam or Mahmoud. Anyway, we now know what became of Nabil Ahmad. I'm sorry for your clients. How are they holding up?"

"As well as can be expected," Dan said.

The chief nodded. "If your suspicions are correct then we'll probably come across the bodies of the others at some point. Maybe not until the spring thaw."

"Why *did* we find Nabil's body, but not the other two? Change of MO?"

He thought of the bluish colour beneath Nabil Ahmad's skin. The cyanosis that Stuart had pointed out. Edie's show had included a discussion of *agalmatophilia*, a doll fetish named for a killer who bleached his victim's bodies to resemble wax mannequins. And that, the coroner on the case concluded, was when he fucked them.

The chief nodded. "A change of tactics is quite possible, yes. You never know, though. They could be right outside the docks at Queen's Quay just waiting to surface. The water's unpredictable that way."

The server refilled their coffee cups and asked about their meals. The chief looked down at his plate where the egg yolk had seeped into the toast. Half of it was unfinished.

"Yeah, good," he said. "I'm done."

The server picked up the plate and headed back to the kitchen.

The chief continued. "All these guys left a pretty thin trail behind them. There's just not enough to go on. Somehow they've vanished into thin air, as the saying goes."

"That's why our killer chooses them," Dan said. "He knows they won't be missed. Nabil was the exception. Maybe the killer didn't know about the brothers when he chose him for his next victim."

"Possibly. On the other hand, if your theory is correct and it really is Muslims killing Muslims, then maybe one or both of the brothers is behind it."

"I thought of that."

The lights had come up higher as Edie walked on stage draped in fur and carrying a purse. Without her street drag she looked completely feminine, her curves accentuated beneath the pelts. Between the Mr. Leatherman contests and the sex shows, Dan thought, the animal mortality rate in the gay community must have been pretty high. Not to mention her costume budget.

Two women came over and began to caress Edie's feet. The goddess adored. The dwarf wheeled in an arm-chair and Edie sat. She reached into her purse to retrieve a tube of lipstick, cardinal red, and began applying it to her lips. The women grew more passionate, kissing her ankles and calves then reaching upward until she slapped their hands away.

"Naughty, naughty!" she'd cried to the audience's titters.

"As for your pornographer, Xavier Egeli, I did a little bit of digging. He was also involved in the fighting in Sarajevo." The chief eyed Dan. "Ethnic cleansing. Muslims. Like his boss, Zoltan Mirovic, he was cleared in a postwar investigation. So now you see why I didn't want to declare the men publicly as having been kidnapped or killed by other Muslims."

"And Mirovic? Did you find anything new on him?"

"Mirovic always stays one step ahead of the law. He's a slippery customer. He gets away with what he does because he's smart. He makes sure anything illegal is at arm's length."

"So he's a crime boss."

"Pretty much. As I said before, these are not nice men. I'm advising you to leave them to us. So this is official: don't try to get back in that group."

"Okay."

The show had ramped up. Edie kept up a steady patter in a demonstration of *forniphilia*. Human furniture. Dan wished he'd brought Donny along for the running commentary as a faux living room was assembled using bodies as footstools, chairs, and settees. A young man perched on his haunches opened his mouth whenever someone stepped on his foot. Dan squirmed as a lit cigarette was doused on his tongue. The human ashtray.

Edie stood and clapped her hands. "Let's have the slave, please."

The others cleared off as a young woman walked on stage, naked, and stood meekly at its centre. Edie looked her over and turned to the audience. "Very nice, yes?"

There was applause. Next, two assistants came out grasping a roll of polythene. Heading across the stage in careful choreography, they bound the slave while Edie watched. When the woman's body was totally encased in transparent wrap, the assistants rolled out a large St. Andrew's cross and positioned it behind her, gagging and securing her to the arms. She hung there limply, like a puppet. One of her legs twitched.

"This exercise must be done carefully," Edie advised. "Otherwise you could end up with a corpse on your hands. A real one."

She caressed the woman's face and kissed her on both cheeks. She removed a plastic bag from her purse and held it up. The slave looked frightened and began to moan. Edie placed the bag over the woman's head and secured it behind her neck.

Dan looked at his watch.

"When breathing is restricted, it can cause bleeding around the eyes," Edie informed them. "You will find this on people who have been strangled and asphyxiated."

In his mind, Dan was back at the morgue listening to Stuart Morgan talk about bleeding under the conjunctiva. Nabil's bloodshot eyes.

The slave thrashed. Edie sat and applied her bronzer, continuing her commentary. All eyes were on the bag as it began to fog over.

Dan checked his watch again. One minute and forty-five seconds.

"You need signals so you don't go too far," Edie told them. "Something for your slave to let you know when he or she has reached a sexual threshold."

"Then you'll investigate the basement?" Dan asked the chief. "There might be other things to find."

A look of concern crossed the chief's face. "I'm going to have a hard time getting a search warrant. I can't just go on your say-so that you found a set of dentures with bloody incisors. That brings up a whole raft of problems. It would also implicate your superintendent."

"What about a complaint from a performer that she'd been drugged and abused by them?"

The chief nodded and sipped his coffee. "That might do it. Especially if she pointed out the basement as the place where she was drugged and abused."

"It would have to be anonymous," Dan said. "She's terrified they'll kill her."

A chill had set over the audience. Edie turned away from the cross. "Bodies aren't easy to dispose of, so make sure your slave doesn't kick it. This is not something you should attempt when using drugs or alcohol."

Dan's watch read four minutes and thirty seconds — it surpassed anything he'd managed as a teenager. The entire room was holding its breath. The slave thrashed a final time and went still. The bag was entirely opaque. Dan thought of a tramp he'd discovered on the sidewalk outside his warehouse early one morning. Pale, unmoving. Shortly after he'd called 911, however, the tramp revived. He'd glanced up at Dan standing over him with a look of concern. "Fuck off," he snarled just as the first ambulance arrived.

Five minutes and fifteen seconds.

Edie walked over to the suspended figure, slowly unfastened the clasp then whipped the bag off. The slave's head hung down on her chest. Edie stepped into the light and bowed. The audience clapped half-heartedly, too stunned to know what was real and what fake. When Edie indicated the slave with her hand, the woman suddenly perked up and broke into a grin. The applause grew as the other performers filed back on stage.

More bows. The show was over.

"It's enough to make me start smoking again," the chief told him.

Dan had been waiting in the dressing room when the door opened and Edie entered, still dressed in her furs. *At least they're real*, Dan thought.

"Good show."

"Friend of Domingo's, right?"

She sat at the mirror, ran her fingers through her hair then picked up a cotton ball and began to remove her makeup. She seemed ordinary once again, the adolescent boy peeking through, Dan thought. It was as though he were looking at someone who'd just been exorcised of a demon.

"She said you didn't want to talk to me. I thought I'd try to convince you."

"What is this about?"

"Murder. You could be implicated."

She laughed out loud. "For my show? Not likely. You saw that girl walk off stage of her own volition."

"I was referring to your association with Star-X Productions."

Her eyes caught his in the mirror. "Those guys are sons of bitches. Somebody needs to tell them BDSM isn't for real."

"There's the pot calling the kettle black," Dan said.

She whirled to face him. "Nobody gets hurt in my show."

"Not even your human ashtray?"

She sneered. "His tongue is coated. All he would feel is a little heat. Nothing lasting."

"And the polythene wrap girl?"

"Elena is a trained athlete. She can hold her breath for up to six minutes. Do you think I want fucking bodies littering the theatre? I hate being upstaged."

"So it was all faked?"

She turned back to the mirror. "It's the psychology of fear and submission I'm teaching. People need that. It's a release from their own fear of sexuality."

"Have you ever gone too far?"

She met his eyes in the mirror again. "You mean have I ever killed anyone? No. There are signals. If someone can't stand it, they say, 'Ow, that really hurts, Edie,' and I stop whatever I'm doing."

"And the gagged girl. How does she say 'ow'?"

"She wriggles her toes. That's my cue to remove the hood. None of it's real."

"Yes, I saw your shoddy little rope video."

Her eyes narrowed. "My shoddy little video?"

"Yes, the one with the burn marks. How did you fake those?"

She stood and glared at him for a moment. Then slowly she turned her back, letting the fur slide to the floor. "Does that look fake to you?"

The chief shook his head. "I deal with this shit all the time. Most of it doesn't even make it into the news. 'Cause frankly, it's not all that newsworthy. Weird yes, but not newsworthy."

"A little public pressure might help your cause," Dan suggested.

"The public is unpredictable. You have to be careful how you unleash it. Sometimes it works with you, other times against. It's hard to gauge. But once you get the public involved you have to ride the ride where it takes you. They don't soon forget when you disappoint them."

Edie had sat facing the mirror again, the fur lying on the floor between them.

"You live in a free country. You have no idea what it's like in a place where you have no rights at all, knowing someone can walk into your home at any moment and rape or kill you. You would do anything to escape. When I met these guys they asked if I minded a little pain. I said no, as long as I got my papers. I was stupid. I should have asked what they were talking about. I don't even remember the end of the video." She wiped lipstick off on a Kleenex, the

269

red smearing across the white tissue. "They drugged me. The next day, when I woke up, there were burn marks all over my body. About half went away in a few weeks. The doctors say the rest will never heal completely. Some days it takes me an hour to make myself up so it doesn't show on stage. I still don't have the fucking papers."

"Did you try to do anything about it?"

"You mean legally? No, I couldn't. I signed a release in case anything went wrong. 'Nothing to worry about,' Mirovic said. 'We're careful.' Yeah, very careful when it comes to covering his ass."

"The complaint could be anonymous. He wouldn't have to know it was you."

She shook her head. "I'm sorry about your friend, but I can't make a complaint. I know Zoltan. He'd kill me. I have no doubt of that."

"A man was murdered," Dan said. "Maybe more than one."

"I doubt he's the first. And he won't be the last."

Dan put his coffee cup down and stood up. "She needs papers," he said, letting a twenty fall onto the tabletop. "Real papers. Anything you could do about that?"

The chief looked up. His eyes looked sad and old. "I could try. No guarantees, though."

"I'll get your complaint. Finish your breakfast. I've gotta go."

Two days later, Dan heard back from the chief. The judge had consented to conditions of anonymity and granted a search warrant on the basis of Edie's complaints. They

270

had done a thorough search of the basement, but turned up little.

"Videos for all tastes and fetishes," the chief told him. "Nothing new there, but we found your vampire film. It's called *Bite Me*. We analyzed the blood we found on the props and in the locker. It was from pigs. Somebody's butcher must have done them a favour. Now I've got a new problem. Mirovic is fighting back. He lodged a complaint, saying I violated his rights to go about his business in a fair and open manner. Like he's some sort of missionary for the sexually advanced or some such."

"Is he going to get anywhere with it?"

"I suspect he's trying to kick up a smokescreen while he covers his tracks. We'll have to wait and see. In the meantime, it occurs to me he might be looking for revenge. You should keep an eye on your source."

"We kept her anonymous. Apparently there were enough others with similar complaints that he won't know for sure that it came from her."

"Still, there might be repercussions. Don't underestimate these men. Better safe than sorry, is my call."

TWENTY-EIGHT

Buzzed

It was 2:58 a.m. The phone was on the second ring when Dan rolled over and picked up the receiver.

"Sharp."

"I told you not to go to the police."

The voice was male, accusatory, stinging. It sounded familiar. Then he placed it.

"I had to, Reggie. You can't withhold evidence of a potential crime."

"Right. In the meantime, you nearly got me killed."

Dan's mind went on the alert. Too late, he recalled the chief's warning. "What happened?"

"Xavier. He cleared out his stuff earlier. I thought he was gone, but he came back. He knocked on my door. A guy named Sasha was with him. He works at Zipperz. He's the tough guy."

"I know who Sasha is. Did you let them in?"

"I wasn't going to, but they made so much noise I was afraid they'd wake up the whole building."

"What did they do?"

"They beat me up." There was a pounding in the background. "Oh, shit. They're back!"

"Okay, try to calm down. Did you call the police?"

"No."

"I'll call them for you."

"No! I don't want their help! This is your fault for telling them about what I showed you in the basement!"

"Do you want me to come over?"

The pounding continued in the background.

"Are you all right?"

"I'm freaking out. I have no one else to call."

"Tell them you're calling 911. You don't have to call, but let them think you're going to if they don't leave."

Dan heard Reggie call out over the noise. "Xavier, if you guys don't leave I'm going to call 911."

The pounding let up.

"What do you hear?" Dan asked.

"Footsteps. I think they're leaving." Reggie waited. "Now what? I'm afraid they're going to come back."

"Give me fifteen minutes. I'll get dressed and come right over. If they show up again, call 911 for real."

When Dan got to the Viking, there was no sign of Xavier or Sasha. He buzzed. Once, twice, three times. He was about to go bang on Reggie's window when the lock clicked open. Reggie stuck his head out into the hallway and glanced warily around.

"Did they come back?"

"No."

Dan looked him over. He had a welt on the side of his face. Apart from that, he looked more unsettled than injured. Dan followed him into his apartment. Reggie sat at the kitchen table. He slipped a joint from his pocket and lit up.

"Tell me what happened," Dan said.

Reggie's hands trembled as he reached for the ashtray. He took a toke, exhaled, and sighed.

"Around ten o'clock Xavier came with some guys and took his things from the studio apartment upstairs. Sasha was with them. I heard them, but I didn't come out. Then they left. Later, Xavier came back and pounded on my door. He said he needed to get something from his locker. I asked him did he know what time it was and he said yeah, he knew, but so what? When I let him in, Sasha was with him. He took a swing at me. Xavier started screaming that I called the cops on him. I said it wasn't me, but he didn't believe it." He slumped against the wall and cradled his head. "I knew this would happen."

"I'm sorry. I didn't think they'd connect you with the search."

Reggie glared. "I told you we could've solved this together. We didn't need the cops. Why couldn't you just leave it alone?"

"Because time was running out. When I was here the other day —"

"Zoltan told me you came by. The furnace inspector. You didn't tell me about that either." Reggie sounded stung. "There was no fucking white van. You made that up."

He took another toke and flicked the ash in the tray.

"I'm sorry," Dan said. "I didn't want to involve you. And it gave you a perfect excuse not to be here so they wouldn't suspect you. I brought along a friend to help me find out what was going on."

"Yeah, they showed me his tape." Reggie giggled. "I thought maybe it was you, but it was only that Jameel dude. They asked me if I knew who it was. I said I never saw him before. Then they asked about you."

"What did you tell them?"

"Just that you showed up one day and said you were there to inspect the furnace. How was I to know you were a fake inspector? 'How come you didn't notice he wasn't wearing a uniform?' they asked. I said I didn't think about it. There were problems with the furnace and we were supposed to replace it, so it made sense when you came to the door. How could I know?"

"Good thinking."

"Yeah, but I still got this." He pointed to the welt on his face. He looked morose. "And now I'm gonna lose my job. And probably my apartment."

"If you do, I'll help get you a recommendation to get you another one."

Reggie looked exasperated. "You don't understand — I like living here! I don't want to move."

"We'll cross that bridge when we come to it. The chief of police is putting the squeeze on your boss's operations. That's probably why Egeli moved his things. You may never see either of them again."

"That would be a big improvement." He ground out the joint in the ashtray and shoved it aside.

"What do you know about these guys?" Dan asked.

"Nothing. Zoltan hired me to look after the building and maintain the premises if anyone had problems with their heat or anything like that. He's not the owner, though. That's some company overseas. Zoltan just runs the place for them. He and Xavier make the films together. I just stay out of their way."

"Reggie, these men are criminals."

"Yeah, no shit."

"When I was here the other day I overheard them talking about drugging one of the performers. Do you know if there was an overdose while they were filming?"

Reggie nodded. He was looking a little buzzed. "Yeah, a couple months ago. Something happened and they took a girl out in a cab so they could drop her at the hospital instead of calling the ambulance to come here."

"Did she die?"

"I didn't ask. Are you crazy? I know these guys are dangerous! I just do what they tell me to do."

"The reason the police were able to get a search warrant was because one of the performers who worked for them put in a complaint that they'd been physically abusive. The police were looking for evidence to back that up."

Reggie stared at him. "Did they find anything?"

"Nothing that would implicate them."

"Well, they should've looked harder. Cops aren't very smart."

"Were you here when they came?"

"Sure. I let them in and showed them which locker was Xavier's. I had to call Zoltan to tell him what was going on. That's when he freaked out and started asking about you.

Where was I when the furnace inspector called? I couldn't tell him I was out looking for a white van that didn't even exist. That's how I figured it came from you. I'll be lucky if all I lose is my job." He watched Dan. "Now what's going to happen? Will they go to jail?"

"I don't know. The blood on the teeth and the knife turned out to be pig's blood."

Reggie made a face. "Pig's blood?"

"The whole thing was faked. So as far as the police could ascertain, no one was hurt during the filming process."

He sneered. "I still say they didn't look hard enough."

"Maybe, but they did what they could." Dan checked his watch. It was nearly four. "I've got to go. Will you be okay? Is there someplace you can go for a night or two?"

Reggie looked disgusted. "I'm the super. I'm supposed to be here."

"Not if you're worried about your safety. Do you want me to call someone for you?"

Reggie shook his head and looked at Dan. "You could stay the night."

"Sorry, I have to go. My son's alone at home."

Disbelief came over Reggie's face. "You have a son?"

"Yes."

"Are you straight?"

"No, I told you. I'm gay."

Reggie nodded. "Accidents happen, eh?"

"You could put it that way."

Dan stood and headed for the door.

"When will I see you again?" Reggie asked.

Dan turned. "We'll have that date one of these days."

"You're always too busy."

"I'll make time," Dan said. "Call me if those guys show up again. You sure you don't want me to contact the police for you?"

Reggie glowered. "Forget it. The police are fucking idiots."

"Don't answer the phone or buzz them in if they come back."

"I'm not stupid," Reggie said. "It won't happen again."

TWENTY-NINE

Disappearance

THE FOLLOWING AFTERNOON, DAN sat in his office looking at the skyline across the Don River. Winter had arrived for real. Temperatures plummeted. The snow fell heavily all day, transforming the city into a wonderland of fantastical white castles.

Ked called to say he and Elizabeth were going to catch an early movie. "You're on your own, Dad," he said.

"No worries. I'll manage."

Five o'clock came. The sky was already midnight-dark. Dan shut his office and locked everything down. The city glittered with pre-Christmas lights and decorations. Instead of going home, he found himself walking the snow-covered streets, trekking up Parliament Street and across Wellesley to the University of Toronto.

The Soldiers' Tower was lit up with floodlights, all the dearly departed war dead eulogized in script on its walls, their names remembered by few among the living, time's wearying tide rolling on without them. The windows of Hart

House threw a cheerful glow onto the whitened grounds. Inside, students shrugged into overcoats, shouldering knapsacks full of books, preparing to defy the cold that threatened to seep into their bones.

Ked had been conceived not far from where Dan stood, after a drunken night out with Kendra. She had already suspected Dan was gay, but was not above having a good time with her brother's dormitory mate. It turned out to be one of the most decisive dates Dan ever had. No doubt about it, Fate was inscrutable.

He stood under the pink aureole of the street lamps, reviving old memories. Then, feeling the cold, he turned and headed back across Yonge Street and on to Church Street. Instead of heading south toward home, however, he went north, dodging the Christmas shoppers and office workers released from their daily conscript.

Without quite knowing why, he turned on Gloucester and stopped in front of the Viking's funereal facade. He'd felt it drawing him from a distance, dogging his footsteps and pulling him onward. With the slant of the street lights and the falling snow, it appeared isolated from its fellow buildings, a solitary ghost ship manned by an invisible crew afloat on a sea of white.

From down the long alleyway between the buildings, a glow lit up the final window. Sam's window.

Dan's heart pounded as he tromped through the snow past Reggie's window, dark as the grave, and all the way down to Sam's. When he got there, however, he saw it was only a light from the building opposite reflected in the glass, making it look as though it was lit from within. Phantom glimmers. A shadow play of appearance versus reality.

He stood there, listening to the wind, thinking of men who disappeared without a trace.

Ked was still out when he got home. Ralph was asleep on his bed in the kitchen. Dan left the lights off downstairs and went up to his office. He turned Nabil's computer on and reread everything in his diary. *S* had referred to Nabil as his *toy*, his *plaything*. Nabil had called him his *string-puller*. *S* was in fact his master. A puppet master tugging on the strings of destiny from within the realm of shadow.

The killer is cruel and arrogant, Domingo had said. He'd met plenty of men like that in the past month, with Zoltan Mirovic topping the list. But he could certainly see similar traits in Xavier Egeli, his thug Sasha, and even Hanani Sheikh.

Men who thought they were smarter than others. Men who believed they were beyond the law and could get away with what they did because of it. The accounts of history were full of men like that, the ledgers of the ones who took always outweighing the ones who gave.

He put his head down on the desk, exhaustion taking over. The days had been long and the news cheerless. The weight of Nabil's death had stayed with him. He was letting it get to him.

When he looked up, it was an hour later. His cell showed three missed calls from Prabin. A text followed. Dan felt a chill as he read the words: *I've got a date with* S. *Will keep you posted.*

His call went straight to voicemail. *Where are you?* he texted, praying Prabin would text back with details, saying everything was all right. After fifteen minutes, when there was still no response, he called Donny.

"Is Prabin with you?"

"No. He's at the gym."

Dan took a breath. "He's not at the gym. I'm coming over."

Dan got in his car and headed to Jarvis Street, cursing the slow-changing lights and the cars overly cautious of slipping on the snow-covered pavement.

He was at the condo by 10:30. It had been a little over an hour since Prabin's text. Dan sat at the table while Donny stared him down.

"Are you saying you asked him to play Muslim For A Day to help find this killer? No, wait!" He held up a hand. "He asked *you* to help *him*. Am I right?"

"He didn't ask. He said he was going to do it with or without me. I always went with him before. This time he went without telling me."

"That doesn't absolve you."

"I know."

Donny looked off to the skyline view from his balcony, the night hard and clear, the cold just a thin windowpane away.

"What happens when even your friends turn out to be your enemies?" he asked Dan's reflection. Dan said nothing. Donny turned back to him. "I'll tell you what happens. You think you've found just a little bit of happiness, but when you sit back for a minute it's gone."

"He's not gone. Not yet. I can find him."

"Then bring him back!" Donny's voice was a near scream. He crumpled into a chair. "Every couple of months, and sometimes more often, I hear about bodies being retrieved from the flowerbeds below my balcony. Why? Because gay men get lonely at night. Because we get tired of the drugs and the discos and the boys and we realize we've ended up alone. But I was stupid enough to believe I'd escaped all that." He sat forward. "So you get out there and *bring him back*!" He slumped in his chair again, exhausted. His voice was sad and quiet now. "Do that for me and I might forgive you."

Dan pulled out his cell and checked the time: 11:32 p.m. It was late, but he called anyway. At this point he needed all the help and reassurance he could get. What was the worst that could happen?

Adele answered.

"Hello, Adele. It's Dan Sharp. I'm sorry for calling so late. It's important, otherwise I wouldn't have called. Can I speak to Domingo?"

"No. You can't."

The answer was abrupt. Dan was about to apologize again for having called when Adele continued.

"Oh, Dan! She's not here. She's in the hospital."

"What happened?"

"She collapsed this afternoon. I don't know for sure." Her voice was shaky. "She was having pains in her back. I just got back from the hospital. I haven't had time to call anyone." There was a long pause. "I think it might be the cancer come back."

"I'm sorry. Is there anything I can do?"

"Not at the moment, but thank you. We just have to wait and see."

"Okay. Please let her know I'm thinking of her. Whatever she needs ..."

The call clicked off. He felt a stab of cold white fear — for Domingo and Adele, for Donny and Prabin — for himself. It was a long time since he'd felt like this. Not since he was a young father trying to raise a son largely on his own. His head throbbed.

It seemed ages since Prabin's text appeared, but in fact it had been just over two hours. Two hours in which anything might have happened.

Outside, the snow beat against the window, clinging for a second before melting and running down the glass. Tears for the dead.

THIRTY

Tableau

W̲H̲E̲N̲ ̲H̲E̲ ̲H̲A̲D̲N̲'̲T̲ ̲H̲E̲A̲R̲D̲ ̲F̲R̲O̲M̲ Prabin by midnight, Dan ground some coffee beans and sat over a steaming espresso. He took out his phone and flipped through his messages to Terence's text. Sam's face smiled out at him. A sweet-looking guy whose visa was about to expire. Nabil had known about Hanani Sheikh's sideline and offered to help. But Hanani claimed he hadn't given Nabil any papers, despite his urgent request.

In his calendar Nabil had said Sam liked "to get rough," describing him as "quite a conceited little ass under the skin," while Reggie called him a "pretentious little twit." But Terence had said he was the ideal boyfriend, a simple man of exquisite manners. How could you be all those things to different people? He supposed it was possible. Dan was a father to his son, a friend to his friends, and a lover to his lover when he had one. But he was, for all intents and purposes, still the same man inside, not one thing in the light and another in the dark. Not just a shadow taking on the form of something as different as the dead from the living.

Donny called frantically every fifteen minutes, interrupting his thinking, till Dan ordered him to sedate himself and go to bed.

"I'm going out to look for him," Dan assured him.

"I want to come with you, wherever you're going."

"No good. I can't have you tagging along."

He closed his computer. Somehow, his gut told him, it all connected with those grinning devil dolls strung up on a wire. Why was he looking in the diary of a dead man when the answer lay in the apartment of another dead man?

He got back in his car and took the expressway, bypassing the city streets. The lanes were deserted. But in a few hours, he knew, they'd be full again. Hell on wheels. No turning right or left till you exited, cursing and vowing never to take that route again. As if that were possible. What made all those commuters so dedicated to their work? Dan wondered. Ambition? Pride? Child support payments?

Down again, a couple of turns, then up Church Street to Wellesley. Even in the cold, the hookers and drug peddlers still hawked their wares. Just a block farther to where the Viking waited for him like an old nemesis silently planning its revenge. Darkness shrouded the windows, front and sides.

He parked and waited. Icicles clung to the eaves, deadly cleavers waiting to fall on the unsuspecting. The front porch light was still out. It was one of the first things he'd noticed about the place. Maybe the tenants preferred it that way to conceal their nefarious comings and goings.

If he rang Reggie's buzzer, Dan knew, the super would join him. But he didn't want help. He just wanted to be sure he didn't rouse him and get tackled again. Then again, all reports indicated that potheads slept more soundly than the rest of the world.

A scrofulous-looking bunch headed his way, weaving and wandering along the sidewalk. Drunken partyers, long-past-midnight revellers making their way through the snow and cold. One of them stopped to light a cigarette, fumbled with the flame, struck flint again and again. He spotted Dan sitting behind the wheel, grinned and waved like they were old friends before getting back to the task of striking up. It made Dan so tense he wanted to go over and take it from him, light his cigarette and tell this drunken asshole to get the fuck out of there and join AA.

Finally, when he was sure no one was watching, he pocketed his flashlight and crept along the side of the building. The moonlight shone in Sam's window. There was nothing happening inside the apartment, but that didn't mean …

Then it struck him — the curtains were fully open.

He gripped the ledge, but his fingers slipped on the icy sill. He looked around and found a loose brick, chipping at the ice and brushing it away. He tried again. This time his grip was better, but the ledge was still too high up to see inside properly.

He found a stump by the garage and set it up directly beneath the window. His breath came out in white flags as a terrifying drum beat pounded in the back of his head: *Hurry, hurry, hurry!*

The lock was secure. The only way in was to break the window. But that would bring the police, who would keep him tied up for hours as he tried to explain that he needed to find his friend before it was too late and he, too, ended up in the harbour.

Dan retraced his tracks to the front of the building. For once, he was thankful for the burned-out bulb, even though there was no one around. The lock resisted, stiff with cold and creaking in protest, before suddenly giving way.

The wind blew the door shut behind him. He stood there, feeling naked in the hall light. The lobby's hush told him he was the only living thing moving about at that hour. The exit sign cast an eerie red glow as he crossed to the apartment on the left.

Sam's lock was not so easy to pick. The old-fashioned skeleton key had hinted at a vulnerability that wasn't the case. What with pornographers, drug dealers, and mysterious puppeteers on the premises, security was probably far more of a concern than it appeared on the surface.

Finally, just as he was about to give up and call Reggie, he heard the pins click and give way. He slipped inside the apartment, shutting the door and waiting as his eyes grew accustomed to the gloom. The moon emitted a faint glow through the windows. A radiator let out a sigh, the last gasp of the dying. He took a step. The floorboard screamed like a banshee in the tomb-like silence.

He stopped and listened, but nothing changed. He was alone in an empty apartment with no sound but the wind and the occasional slushing of a car making its way past in the darkened street.

He switched on his Maglite and palmed the lens. His hand glowed red, a demon buried inside his skin as he moved about the room, following the glow emitted through his flesh.

Dan stopped dead. Something had been placed on the tabletop. It seemed out of place in his memory. Throwing caution aside, he pointed the beam at it, causing an explosion of yellow in the darkness. A bouquet of fresh chrysanthemums. He calculated back: it was two weeks since his first visit. Cut flowers didn't last that long, so make it more recent than that. He picked up the card. Hearts and flowers, with a script in a flowing hand: *To Sam, my puppet master — Nabil.*

How ...?

Dan turned and looked at the dumb-show of faces, those miniature envoys of evil. They seemed to dance in the air, each one dressed with precision and expert attention to detail. Some grinned, while others were mawkish, still others sad. All eyes were on him, as though they knew something. A secret, a sad truth.

He reached out and plucked one off its hook, shining his flashlight on it as though he were interrogating it. "What do you know?" he asked. The puppet grinned back.

Dan hung it back on its wire, shining his light on the others. A lady in a blue velvet robe wore a death mask, lifting her skirts in oblivious abandon to life's sad waltz, time's purposeful march to the edge. Next to her, a tuxedoed gentleman grinned his grim approval.

He continued down the line. The third puppet in wore a ta'wiz. A crescent moon with five stars inscribed inside its arms.

He held the light closer to be sure, but there was no doubt. It was Nabil's. The one Dan had given Prabin to catch a killer. There were other makeshift souvenirs: rings, a necklace, a tooth on a thin chain. Then a small, white bone. From a finger.

Sam was not as far off as he appeared. What had Reggie said? *In the city you can just disappear.* In fact, Sam had been here all the time, coming and going invisibly. A grim killer reaping his trophies. All along, the puppets had been mocking him, offering their clues like trinkets in a box of deadly secrets.

Dan stepped back. Something crunched beneath his foot. A tiny, puppet-sized arm. He shone his light over the floor. Pieces of puppet bodies lay strewn across the wood. As though God had run amok in his own kingdom.

On an antique tabletop a marionette theatre had been smashed to pieces, but there was no time to think what it meant. Footsteps announced themselves in the hallway. Dan switched off his light and held his breath as a hand turned the handle, first one way then the other.

He cast around for a weapon. His eyes turned to the fireplace: a poker. Not a bad choice, he thought, but again the floorboards betrayed him, screaming out his presence. He hefted the iron, imagining the sound it would make on a skull. He might have a split second to decide whether to hit with intent to wound or to kill and leave no second chances. Neither choice appealed to him.

He pulled his cell from his pocket and pressed 911, ready to hit SEND the moment anything happened.

Seconds passed. The footsteps turned and moved off.

Dan waited, but they didn't return. A late-night booty call? A misdirected fellow tenant stumbling home drunk and showing up at the wrong door?

Maybe, but not likely.

He looked at his phone's glowing screen, thankful he hadn't dialed after all. What would he have told the dispatcher? *I broke into an apartment and the owner came back unexpectedly. I need help.*

He listened for sounds from the hallway; all he heard was the soft chugging of the monster furnace turning on in the basement.

Still clutching the poker, he crept over and pressed his ear to the door. Silence. He got down on his knees. Light seeped through, but the gap was too narrow to see if anyone stood just on the other side.

Time slipped past. He could stay there all night or he could chance getting out to continue his search for Prabin. *Tick-tick-tick.* Maybe he should rouse Reggie and ask him to help, taking him on as the sleuth he longed to be.

He turned the lock and opened the door. The hallway was deserted. The exit sign glowed red, like a demon eye. He should just make his getaway.

He stepped out. Nothing happened. By all rights, it wasn't supposed to be this easy. The killer would be waiting just outside the front door with an ironic smile, gun barrel raised to catch him in his sights. A single bullet would take him out. He'd be found rigid in the snow by an early-morning passerby. His son would wonder where his father was when he got up, but he wouldn't think it unusual. Ked would head off to class, then, later that afternoon, Kendra would notify the school and he'd be called to the principal's office. Or, worse, he might not find out until after he got home, cooked himself a meal, and settled on the couch to watch the evening news.

Dan closed the apartment door behind him, using his shirttail to wipe the knob free of prints.

Then he turned and saw the basement door ajar.

THIRTY-ONE

Out from the Shadows

DAN TENSED AS HE REACHED for the railing. Silence met his ears, but what else would there be at — he glanced at his watch — 3:28 in the morning? He put his foot on the top stair and started down, one step at a time. Like the road to sobriety. Not quite where he was going, but it was still reassuring.

Something glistened on a step partway down. A dark patch, small but shiny enough to reflect the faint light behind him. He bent and touched it, bringing his finger to his face. It looked black, but thinned to red when he rubbed it with his thumb. Someone had passed this way, bleeding as they went. The blood skipped a couple of steps before continuing at the bottom, a curious trail leading him to who knew where. Wasn't it a trail of breadcrumbs that got Hansel and Gretel in all that trouble?

Keeping the poker raised, he inched his way into the room where the tentacles of the giant furnace reached up through the ceiling. The grate was open, an orange glow throwing shadows on the walls. A small shovel sat upright against the furnace's bulk, as though to feed it when it got hungry.

From some long-ago literature course, he remembered Dante's vision of hell. It was highly ordered, every sin having its allotted space within nine concentric circles at the centre of the earth. The version of hell Dan found himself facing wasn't orderly, just dusty and dirty. Boxes had been piled up with their forgotten contents. Off in a corner, a broken lamp stood like a forsaken scarecrow.

There was another glimmer on the floor ahead. Whoever was bleeding had come this way. And would no doubt have to come back out again. From far off came the sound of a truck passing in the street.

Still keeping the poker raised, he made his way into the next room. He barely heard the shadowy figure approaching him from behind.

His first thought was that he was paralyzed. Nothing moved, nothing worked. Something warm oozed down the back of his neck where he felt a stabbing pain. It was a ten out of ten he would say, if anyone asked.

He raised his head and tried to focus. Little halos surrounded everything: the pipes in the ceiling, the boxes piled against the wall. He was back in the other room. Someone had … he couldn't remember. His thoughts splintered.

He tried to move. His feet were free but his arms were pinned behind him. He heard the furnace right behind him. Its heat warmed his fingers.

He closed his eyes.

When he opened them again the figure standing over him seemed to be an angel. An angel of darkness come to inquire about his troubles. The look on the angel's face said it felt his pain and understood his sorrows, both spoken and unspoken, for now and for all time to come.

"Brother," it said. "Are you ready for paradise?"

The angel leaned down. A half-familiar face, like something from a dream. Boyish. Half child and half adult. Forgiving and gentle.

The face changed. It was suddenly judgemental, wrathful. The angel pointed a retributive finger at him.

"All I wanted was one date."

Dan blinked. "Help me," he croaked out.

The angel looked pityingly at the ropes binding Dan to the chair. "Now you want my help."

Dan strained briefly against his restraints, but there was no give.

"Don't struggle. It's not manly."

Reggie stepped into the light. His shirttail was out and his forehead shone with sweat. There was a deep scratch on his jaw. He looked as though he'd been in a fight.

"What have you done with Prabin?"

"You mean Jameel? The one in the video? I recognized him in the bar tonight. I asked him if he wanted to meet Sam. Of course he came with me. They're all so stupid, aren't they? Every one of them." He smirked. "Just like you."

"You better not have hurt him," Dan said.

"He fought me. He was stronger than I expected. Ironic, isn't it? You tried to use him as bait to catch me. Then I used him as bait to catch you." He shrugged. "It wasn't the first time I met him. I danced with him at Zipperz. You were there. Only you didn't recognize me. Nobody ever does."

Dan wanted to kick himself. He'd been so worried Xavier was after Prabin that he barely noticed the boy he'd been dancing with.

"Where is Sam?"

"With the others." Reggie shook his head, as though saddened by a child slow at learning his lessons. "Were you hoping for a date with Sam? Is that why you broke into his apartment?" He paused. "Everyone wants to sleep with Sam. No one wants Reggie. He's just the superintendent of a small apartment building. A loser, in other words." He cocked his head. "I think Nabil liked me for me."

Dan saw it now. "He sent you flowers."

"Well, yes, but not *those* flowers. You know that." He shrugged. "Did you like the card? I thought that was a nice touch. You probably think it's pathetic that I kept it." He sneered. "I warned him. The Quran's teachings are clear. We must keep clean — both physically and spiritually."

"Is that why you killed those men? Because they were unclean?"

"I was helping them. I made them confess before sending them to paradise. Even the police were stupid. They stood right here asking me questions and didn't once look in the right direction." He glanced over at the furnace, its orange glow lighting up the grate. "It takes a long time to get rid of a body. You have no idea how hard it is."

"Why did you destroy the puppets?"

Anger lit Reggie's face. "Zoltan did that after the police came. He broke in and smashed them to pieces. Your fault again." All of a sudden he looked as though he might cry. "I was going to take them with me."

"Where?"

He shrugged. "Somewhere far from here. Somewhere warm. I can't stand the cold. I've always hated this country."

He turned and looked around then bent and picked something up. Dan tried not to panic as Reggie held up a plastic bag.

"Don't do this," Dan said.

"You should have been nicer to me," Reggie said. "I might've kept you around longer."

He fished in his pocket and brought out a roll of electrical tape, then slipped the bag over Dan's head, sealing it around his neck.

Four minutes!

As Reggie stepped back, Dan rocked back and forth. The knife edge of panic grew as he thought of all he would miss, starting with his son and extending on from there. Donny, Prabin, Domingo, his cousin Leyla who always called on his birthday.

Reggie pulled up a chair and sat close to watch. "You're holding your breath," he said. "It never helps. Not for long, anyway."

All the minutiae of life came into focus, like the plastic brushing against his cheeks, the weight of his chest as he clung to his breath, the heat from the furnace gnawing at his hands, the pain where the rope bit his flesh. If he inhaled quickly he might be able to grip the bag with his teeth and tear a hole in it, but he still needed his hands free.

Three minutes!

The plastic was beginning to fog over. Sweat rolled down into his eyes. In his mind, he was back on the lake that summer as his friends declared him the winner of the underwater breath-holding contest. *You start to feel like you could stay down there forever*, he had told them. *After that it's easy.* But he had never gone past that point.

Reggie was just two feet away from him. If he kicked out he might just manage to ... but something blurred the edge of his vision, a black smudge against the light. A figure lurched out of the shadows, arms extended like a sideshow zombie. *I'm hallucinating,* Dan thought. *My brain's deprived of oxygen.*

But the creature came closer, hissing and gasping.

Reggie's voice was panicked. "Zoltan!"

The super shrank back, casting around for something to defend himself with. Dan inched his chair closer to the furnace, his palm searing against the door. He bit down to keep from crying out, scraping the rope against the door where it burned hottest, scorching his wrists and making him want to scream.

One minute!

He rubbed harder, trying to keep his eyes on Reggie, blinking away the sweat blurring his vision.

The zombie-like figure tried to speak, but it came out in a gurgle of rage and agony. "You ...! Far-gher ...!"

Reggie leapt aside, landing in the dirt, crawling backward like a shipwrecked crab as Zoltan lurched and fell on top of him. Dan's hands were on fire, the smell of burning nylon mingling with the smell of burning flesh, until the ropes gave way with a sudden tug. He reached up, clawing at the bag and pulling it aside to take in that first, sweet, cool breath.

He watched as Reggie grasped a brick and brought it down on his boss's head. Zoltan shuddered. Reggie hit him again, the brick biting into his skull. Dan thought of the inmates of the prison camp forced to kill one another with hammers.

Reggie sat limply in the chair, arms bound behind him. Zoltan lay in a heap on the floor, his head twisted at an obscene angle to his body. There was blood everywhere: on the floor, on the walls, even on the ceiling.

Dan called 911 first. Then he called Donny.

"He's alive," he said, worriedly watching the unconscious Prabin lying on the cot in the Star-X locker. "I can't say more than that right now."

Finally, he called the chief.

"What a way to start my morning," the chief said.

"One day you'll thank me," Dan said.

EPILOGUE

A Killer's Return

IN FACT, IT WAS JUST the next day when the chief called. Mirovic was dead. Egeli and his sidekick Sasha had disappeared, but he was inclined to be gloomy on the matter. In all likelihood, he told Dan, they would just start up again in another city far from Toronto after a period of inactivity. There was no stopping people like that, he said.

He'd done some digging into Reggie's background and found out a great deal more about him. He'd come from Iran, arriving with his family as an adolescent named Rashid Khan. After being shunted around for nearly a decade, the family was finally deported when his father proved to have been involved with terrorist activity back home. By then, however, Rashid had developed a taste for North America. Rather than return with the family, he disappeared, re-emerging under the name Reggie Kane. Still a non-person without papers, he lay low until he killed Sam Bashir and took over his identity.

"That's why he pressed Nabil for help with his visa," Dan said. "And probably why he let him live as long as he did."

"I suspect so, yes."

As for Nabil's brothers, Mustafa and Amir, the chief had turned up nothing to indicate inappropriate activities, although erasing Nabil's photos had seemed a red flag at the time.

"Family pride," the chief told Dan. "It's the twenty-first century, but your sort still isn't welcome everywhere. Have you been to the States lately?"

"That will change," Dan said.

"You're optimistic."

"Not overly, but I've already seen the wave overturn things in my lifetime. There'll be more. What about that video I told you about? The one that looks like a snuff film?"

"The snuff part is dubious, but the abuse looks real. Now that the circus has skipped town, we may never know," the chief said. "Meanwhile, the world's getting nuttier every day. One more reason you should come and work for me. If nothing else, you'd be a hell of a lot safer."

"Maybe." Dan grinned, thinking he was going to miss those early-morning greasy-spoon get-togethers. "But the day I need a gun to defend myself is the day I hang up my gloves."

The chief groaned. "Now I know you're insane. I mean that in the nicest possible way, of course."

"Of course."

"Now your turn. While I was looking into all this I came across another name. I think it was you who told me he designed websites for Nabil Ahmad. Sheikh Something, I think. Anything else you can tell me about him?"

"Hanani Sheikh. Nah, he checked out. He's clean," Dan said, hoping it would be the last lie he told the chief.

"Okay, I'll take your word for it." He was about to hang up when he said, "Oh, I almost forgot to tell you. Your source might hear some good news about her immigration papers very soon. But you didn't hear it from me."

Coincidence? Dan thought. With the chief you never knew, but it was probably the only good news he was going to get that day. As for Randy Melchior, the news media had gone quiet, the press no longer interested in the story. The trial was still a long way off. Justice was a long, lonely road.

The party was set to happen at four. Dan arrived early to have a word with the guest of honour, though he was well aware the honours were far from what they should have been on a day like this.

Domingo greeted him in a tie-dyed robe exploding with swirls of colour. "Come in," she said, shivering as she closed the door.

He'd last seen her a week previously. Her face looked a little less sunken.

"How are you feeling?"

"Terrible, but I'll fake it if you will." She managed a smile.

"I'll do my best."

They went into the living room.

"Where's Adele?" Dan asked.

"Out buying flowers. She thinks it will put me in a healing mood."

"Can't hurt."

She shrugged and smiled again. "We'll see. No promises. What will you have to drink?"

"Water's good."

"No, it isn't. Have something fun at least. Even if it's just a spritzer."

"All right. I'll take whatever you give me."

"That's probably the first time anybody's heard those words coming from your lips."

She headed for the kitchen while Dan sat and looked around. He'd always liked her place, though he seldom paid much attention to it. He was suddenly aware how fraught with meaning everything became when threatened with change.

On the mantel over the fire, a photograph showed a teenage Domingo with her mother and an older sister. No brother.

"So," she said, returning with two tall, brightly coloured glasses.

They clinked.

"Here's to your recovery," Dan said, eyeing her directly.

"Thank you."

"I want you to know I will do whatever I can, whatever you need. Drives to the hospital, chemo waiting-room visitations … anything."

She nodded. "Thank you for that offer and for all your years of friendship. I'm not sure I'll need the help, however. I've been down this road before. Which is to say, there may not be any chemo sessions."

Dan studied her face. "Your choice or the doctor's advice?"

"My choice."

"You have to fight this."

"Do I?"

Dan had no answer. If it had been him, he might have felt the same. But for Ked. His anchor. His life.

"What do your visions say?"

"That there's a light at the end of the tunnel."

He was perplexed. "Then that's good. Isn't it?"

"I think the tunnel is death."

"Then how can there be …?"

"A light? Good news? There just is."

He nodded. "I see."

"Do you?"

"Maybe not."

If the bullet has your name on it …

He'd sat in that chair with a bag over his head, listening to Reggie and expecting to be killed and have his body fed into the flames. It was almost a shock to have come out of the ordeal alive. If you dodged the bullet, Domingo had said, then someone else had to take your place.

She sat back. "So you've had quite the adventure."

"You can call it that, yes."

She put a hand on his arm. "I wish you'd heeded my warning, but you were never very good about that sort of thing."

"I wasn't worried about myself," he said, wondering if it were true. "But I was worried about Prabin. You're right, though. I'm no good at listening to advice. Reggie'd killed at least five people, maybe more. And he was exactly what you said — cruel and arrogant, as well as a master of disguise."

"No one ever sees the puppet master. But you did at last."

"It's frightening to think how close things came. I just hope …"

Domingo looked at him. "You hope what?"

"I hope Donny forgives me."

Domingo nodded. "He's stayed angry a lot longer than usual — at least for him. But I can say this — you both know each other profoundly to the core without having to explain how or why. That's friendship. If you met him a thousand years from now you'd still be friends, not strangers. He's not going to give that up."

"Do you think so?"

"I know it."

"I hope you're right."

"What happened wasn't your fault," Domingo said. "After Randy, Prabin would have done anything to resolve his guilty feelings. It was something he needed to do."

"Yes, I know."

Dan turned to the window. The sun was already setting over a wintry landscape, the trees barren of leaves, the clouds thin and cheerless.

"Shortest day of the year," he said.

"It all begins again."

Silence enveloped the room like a warm blanket.

"Have you told your family?" Dan asked, glancing at the photograph on the mantel.

"Some," Domingo said, catching his gaze. "The ones I know I can count on."

"But not your brother?"

"No," she said. "Not Rodney."

Dan thought she wasn't going to talk about it. Whatever *it* was. But at least now the brother had a name. That was enough. He knew about the messes families left you with, the ghostly feelings they bequeathed to you to sort out. A spiritual legacy of sorts.

"When I was fourteen," she began, "I told Rodney I liked women. He said he'd always known. He put his hand on my shoulder. I felt pleased. At eighteen, my sister was already a religious nut, so I knew I couldn't tell her about it. Or my mother." She took a deep breath and looked off. "The next day, I took a shortcut on my way home from school. I was walking through the brush when Rodney appeared. 'What's up?' I asked. 'I'm going to help you, sis,' he said. Four other boys came out of the bushes behind him. They held me down for an hour. All five of them, even Rodney."

Dan took her hand. He brought it to his face and pressed it against his cheek. "I'm so sorry," he said.

"So am I," she said. "Even though it was a long time ago."

They sat there unspeaking for a full minute.

"Enough gloom for now," Domingo said at last. "It's my birthday, remember?" She smiled. "What of your romance calendar? I haven't been much good at filling it lately. Shall I get out my Ouija board and try again?"

Dan laughed and thought of the charming but distant Terence. "Despite your best intentions I don't think I'm going to turn out to be the marrying kind."

She shook her head. "You are the marrying kind, Dan — you just haven't met your match."

"Is that what your visions say?" he asked.

She squeezed his hand and released it. "It's what I say. There will be someone for you at the end of the day, though it won't be easy. God help him, whoever he is, you will not make it easy for him."

"Now that's a prediction even I could have made."

"Then I hope you remember me when it comes true."

Dan held up a finger. "Enough gloom, remember?"

Footsteps sounded outside. The front door opened.

"Here come the troops," she said, getting unsteadily to her feet.

From the hallway, Dan could hear the combined voices of Donny, Prabin, and Adele arriving at the same time.

They entered the room and stopped, looking in at Domingo and Dan sitting there together.

"Happy birthday!" they cried.

ACKNOWLEDGEMENTS

THANKS TO STEVE CUMYN AND Geordie Johnson for inspiration on the perils of dating an actor, Sheetal Nanda for her expert advice on immigration issues, Kayla Kent for her under-praised archival work, and to the City of Toronto for being a very cool place to live. Once again I extend my immense gratitude to my editor, Jess Shulman, who always makes me dig deeper, deeper, deeper, and to the good folks at Dundurn, who contribute at every turn. Laura Boyle, your covers rock! Thanks also to David and Joe for being my sounding boards. My description of the nude photo of the character Nabil Ahmad was inspired by a portrait of mountaineer George Mallory taken by Duncan Grant in 1911. It can be found online. Musical vibes on this one are courtesy of the Beatles, who gave us love, light, and expanded consciousness, and New Order, who gave us darkness.

Mystery and Crime Fiction from Dundurn Press

Birder Murder Mysteries
by Steve Burrows
(BIRDING, BRITISH COASTAL TOWN
MYSTERIES)
A Siege of Bitterns
A Pitying of Doves
A Cast of Falcons
A Shimmer of Hummingbirds
A Tiding of Magpies

Amanda Doucette Mysteries
by Barbara Fradkin
(PTSD, CROSS-CANADA TOUR)
Fire in the Stars
The Trickster's Lullaby
Prisoners of Hope

B.C. Blues Crime Novels
by R.M. Greenaway
(BRITISH COLUMBIA, POLICE
PROCEDURAL)
Cold Girl
Undertow
Creep

Stonechild & Rouleau Mysteries
by Brenda Chapman
(FIRST NATIONS, KINGSTON,
POLICE PROCEDURAL)
Cold Mourning
Butterfly Kills
Tumbled Graves
Shallow End
Bleeding Darkness

Jenny Willson Mysteries
by Dave Butler
(NATIONAL PARKS,
ANIMAL PROTECTTION)
Full Curl
No Place for Wolverines

Falls Mysteries
by Jayne Barnard
(RURAL ALBERTA, FEMALE SLEUTH)
When the Flood Falls

Foreign Affairs Mysteries
by Nick Wilkshire
(GLOBAL CRIME FICTION, HUMOUR)
Escape to Havana
The Moscow Code
Remember Tokyo

Dan Sharp Mysteries
by Jeffrey Round
(LGBTQ, TORONTO)
Lake on the Mountain
Pumpkin Eater
The Jade Butterfly
After the Horses
The God Game

Max O'Brien Mysteries
by Mario Bolduc
(TRANSLATION, POLITICAL THRILLER,
CON MAN)
The Kashmir Trap
The Roma Plot

Cullen and Cobb Mysteries
by David A. Poulsen
(CALGARY, PRIVATE INVESTIGATORS,
ORGANIZED CRIME)
Serpents Rising
Dead Air
Last Song Sung

Strange Things Done
by Elle Wild
(YUKON, DARK THRILLER)

Salvage
by Stephen Maher
(NOVA SCOTIA, FAST-PACED THRILLER)

Crang Mysteries
by Jack Batten
(HUMOUR, TORONTO)
Crang Plays the Ace
Straight No Chaser
Riviera Blues
Blood Count